Can't Fight Love

KC Luck

This book is a work of fiction. Names, characters, places, and incidents are products of the author's imagination and/or are used fictitiously. Any resemblance to actual events, locales or persons either living or dead is entirely coincidental.

Copyright © 2022 KC Luck Media

All rights reserved, including the right to reproduce this book or portions thereof in any form whatsoever.

Chapter One

Shifting left and right on the balls of her feet, Kara Roberts waited with her blue eyes fixed on the blank, white wall twenty-five feet in front of her. Her right hand held the leather wrapped handle of the short racquet. Firm but not too tight. She was ready to spring in any direction, trusting her instincts to move her body the right way before there was even time to calculate trajectories. "Fourteen-fourteen," Kara's best friend, Annette, said a moment before she bounced the rubber racquetball and smacked it with her racquet. The blue sphere shot toward the front wall and then ricocheted back. It was a good serve, but not great, and Kara pounced on the ball as soon as it bounced. A swift backhand sent the thing flying at an angle to hit the sidewall first, then the front wall, before dropping to the ground. Annette ran to make a volley but came up short and Kara pumped her fist.

"My serve," she said as Annette picked up the rolling ball and tossed it to her. While tucking the loose end of a pesky light brown curl back into her ponytail, Kara took her place in the server's zone.

"You always get me with that same damn shot," Annette said, taking up a position where Kara stood a moment before.

Kara grinned. "Stop serving to my backhand," she said, bouncing the ball once in front of her. "We go over this every time."

"I thought you were distracted today because of the new job," Annette replied. "And maybe I could sneak it by you."

Holding the ball against the strings of her racquet, Kara shook her head. "Nice try," she said. "Yes, I'm thinking about the production assistant gig, but beating you comes first."

"Sometimes you are too competitive, but let's see what you've got," Annette said, and Kara forced herself to focus. Her best friend was right. Her mind was on the new job she picked up for a few months. Nothing permanent because the last thing she wanted was to be a bottom rung production assistant for long, but the work would pay her rent with a little extra money to spare. Money she very much needed to keep her documentary film project afloat.

Taking a deep breath, she let it out slowly and concentrated on her next shot. *Keep the ball down and to her left*, she thought a moment before she served. Annette wasn't fooled and returned the shot, but softer than she should have, leaving Kara time to set up her swing. With a perfect stroke, the ball flew true and struck the front wall less than an inch above the floor. Even though Annette raced forward, the rubber skipped twice. Game point. Match over.

Annette groaned. "Nice shot," she said, taking off her goggles as she led the way off the court. "You're ruthless today. I give up."

"Giving up doesn't mean you aren't buying dinner,"

Kara said, picking up her towel from the bench and wiping her sweaty face. "Where do you want to go?"

Swallowing a gulp of water from her bottle, Annette shrugged. "The Arena?" she asked, and Kara rolled her eyes.

"Can we not do a sports bar tonight?" she said. "I think I'll be getting enough time with jocks starting tomorrow."

"True," her best friend said with a laugh. "But nobody said you had to sign on with ESPN. There were other PA jobs." Annette was right. Kara picked the position from a list of a half dozen others the hiring agency offered her.

There was one clear difference with the one she decided on. "It's the only PA spot working on documentaries," she said. "Sure, they are about athletes and coaches, but still make for good practice. Even more importantly, it looks good on my resume." *And I need to keep building that up*, she thought while putting her racquet away in the sleeve and zipping it. *If I ever want to get help with funding stuff of my own.*

Alexa Knight loved the purr of the sports car beneath her while she waited at the stoplight on Sunset Boulevard. It was a turbocharged, midnight-black Camaro that went from zero to sixty in five point four seconds. Of course, the car was only one of her four vehicles, but overall, her favorite. Alexa liked speed and the power that generated it. The temptation to floor the accelerator the moment the light switched to green made her fingers tighten on the steering wheel. *But I'm going to resist this time*, she thought with a glance at her passenger—a sexy blonde woman in a very short, white dress. *There's no sense scaring the shit out of her and besides, I don't need the publicity of another speeding ticket.*

When the light changed, Alexa behaved and eased the car off the line to roll with the flow of light traffic around her. "I love your car," the blonde gushed, as she had been since Alexa picked her up from her condo ten minutes ago. "I mean it's so cool. And fits you, you know?"

Alexa raised her dark eyebrows over her vivid green eyes. "Fits me?"

"Yes," the woman said, touching Alexa's shoulder. "You're a little mysterious and so..." She bit her lip. "So dangerous." Forcing herself to refrain from rolling her eyes at the obvious come on, Alexa cruised the Camaro around a slower moving, brown UPS van. *Why did I agree to this blind date?* she wondered. *I can't believe they talked me into this.* She sighed, frustrated at the entire situation, but not sure why. The blonde was both attractive and a popular television actress. When Alexa's manager suggested the date, Alexa reluctantly agreed. *Go out. Be seen with a beautiful woman. Show the world there's more to me than fighting.* She clenched her jaw. There seemed no point. She was, in fact, Alexa Knight: mixed martial arts star, and UFC bantamweight champion.

"Thank you," Alexa finally replied. "But I'm not that dangerous. Only when I must be."

The woman's hand lingered on Alexa's sleeve. "And when that happens, you're so exciting," she said. "I find it very sexy."

"I see," Alexa said, once again wondering what could possibly be sexy about MMA fighting. Strangely, she received the compliment a lot, from men and women. Alexa understood the excitement part, the thrill of two fighters face to face in a ring trying to outmatch their opponent through strength, skill, or both. There was something electrifying about the pairing of wills, the standing up to a challenger, and seeing who wanted victory more. Sexy, however, made little sense to her. Understandably there were women who asked Alexa to dominate them and take part in varying degrees of BDSM, but she always politely declined. Often that met with confusion as if delivering a spinning backfist into an opponent's face somehow translated to pleasure in spanking another woman. Something about the way the blonde was eyeing her gave Alexa the impression tonight would be another one of those nights.

Putting all that out of her mind for the moment, she focused on the fact they were less than four blocks away from the restaurant where Alexa most enjoyed eating. A bit off the main drag, few tourists ever found it so she could have a nice dinner without interruptions for autographs. Not to mention the chef made the best lasagna in the city. She had been craving some for weeks.

Yet, as she made the turn to take them away from Sunset Boulevard, Alexa suddenly had second thoughts. She rarely took anyone to her little hideaway and as the blonde beside her continued to babble about life as a television celebrity, Alexa didn't want to take her there. *No*, she thought. *No pasta tonight*. As they started to pass in front of her favorite restaurant, Alexa looked at her date. "I've changed my mind about what I want to eat tonight," she said. "What are you in the mood—"

"Hey!" she suddenly heard a woman yell a beat before noticing two people were in the street. She slammed on the brakes a split second before hitting anyone. "What in the hell is wrong with you?" the woman in the street said, slapping the hood of Alexa's car. Blinking with surprise, Alexa looked through the windshield into the angry blue eyes of a woman with a racquetball bag slung over her shoulder.

One minute Kara walked with Annette toward a restaurant she wanted to try and then in the next a black sports car came roaring at them. Throwing out an arm to stop Annette from taking another step into the path, Kara hoped the driver would pay attention in time. *Or the son of a bitch is going to hit me,* she thought in the same second she instinctively yelled "Hey" to get the person's attention. Thankfully, the car came to a screeching halt less than an inch from her leg. With fear and anger pumping through her veins, she slapped her hand on the hood of the expensive vehicle. "What in the hell is wrong with you?" Her eyes met the sharp green ones of the driver. A woman with shoulder-length, black hair sat behind the wheel staring at her. For a second, she looked shocked but that was quickly replaced with a stare that Kara couldn't read. *Like she's about to apologize?* she wondered. *Or is mad I slapped her a car?*

Suddenly, the passenger side window went down. "Are you stupid?" yelled a blonde woman who Kara hadn't even noticed yet. "You can't walk out into traffic and then be pissed when you almost get run over."

Oh no she did not call me stupid, Kara thought moving toward the passenger side. Still high on adrenaline, she wasn't about to back down. "What did you say to me?"

Annette grabbed her by the arm before she could get into the blonde's face. "Kara, wait," she said. "Let's leave it and go to dinner, okay? Nobody got hurt." Her friend's warning did no good when the blonde opened the passenger door and stepped out in five inch heels and a white dress that barely covered her ass. After a beat, Kara noticed the driver's side door opening too. That was fine with her because the reckless driver was the one she was mad at, not the stripper in the white dress.

Still, the blonde stomped in her direction. "I asked if you were stupid," she said, but Kara dismissed her with a wave as a waste of time. She knew a B-list Hollywood actress when she saw one. Instead, she focused on the black-haired woman slowly walking toward her. Unlike the clumsy movement of the irritating passenger, the driver moved with a certain graceful confidence as she came around the hood. Her green eyes, framed with long, black eyelashes, met Kara's again and held them for a moment. The stare was intense, and like before, completely unreadable. For a moment Kara wondered if she made a mistake not walking away, but then the stranger's eyes flicked in the direction of the blonde.

"Get back in the car, please," the driver said in a quiet tone that left no room for argument. "I don't want a scene." The blonde opened her mouth as if to talk back, but then closed it before retreating to her car door.

"I'm sorry," she mumbled as she slipped back into the passenger seat.

The driver returned her attention Kara. "I apologize for that," she said. "But you should be more careful where you walk."

Kara's eyes widened. "I should be more careful?" she asked. "How about you should watch where you are driving your fancy sports car?"

The driver shrugged a shoulder. "Maybe," she said starting to walk away. "At least I didn't fly off the handle." She opened the driver's side door and paused before slipping behind the wheel. She met Kara's eyes again. "And slap your car like a child."

Stunned by the insult, Kara couldn't think of a cutting response before the woman was in her car and driving away. The last thing she saw was the bimbo blonde giving her a little wave as they drove past and then the black Camaro turned the corner to roll out of sight.

Chapter Two

Waiting at yet another stoplight, Alexa drummed her fingers on the steering wheel. Her earlier pleasure sitting in the Camaro was gone. The altercation irritated her, but not nearly as much as the tirade from her date.

"Can you believe that woman's nerve?" the blonde in the passenger seat said with a huff while pulling the car visor down to look in the small mirror. Running her fingers through her hair as she turned her head left and right, she kept up her rant. "I mean, she hit your car. Who does that?" She closed the visor as the light changed to green, but clearly wasn't done. "I don't know why you let her get away with it."

Alexa took a deep breath to relax but it wasn't enough to keep the sarcasm out of her voice. "Did you expect me to grab her in a rear naked choke?"

There was a pause, making Alexa glance over. "Maybe," the blonde said, her eyes narrowed. "I expected you to at least do something. You let her get away with assault on your property." She was turned in her seat to face Alexa. Clearly, she intended for the conversation to go on, which was the last thing Alexa wanted tonight. *Or any night,* she thought beginning to wonder if there was a way to end the date early.

"I didn't see what she did as assault and frankly, the whole thing wasn't worth starting trouble over," Alexa said refocusing on the street ahead. "Before long someone would have come out of the restaurant and started filming us with their phone." She shook her head. "My manager would shoot me."

"Fine," the blonde said, making Alexa hope the conversation was over. No such luck. "At least we should go back and get her name."

Alexa pursed her lips. "Why would I need that?"

"So, you can consider pressing charges."

Alexa blinked. First her date said they were assaulted and then suddenly brought up pressing charges. *What is going on?* she wondered, becoming more and more uncomfortable. *Is she one of those celebrities trying to go viral on Twitter? After all, she did jump out of the car and start making a scene.* Alexa nodded. The time had come to cut bait and go home.

Slowing the car to whip a U-turn in the street, Alexa already looked forward to a quiet night in her home gym. "I'm not feeling well," she said before her date could ask what she was doing. "I'm afraid I need to take you home."

"What? You can't be serious."

Alexa nodded. "I am quite serious," she said, speeding up as the idea of ditching the blonde became even more appetizing. "I'd hate for you to catch what I am coming down with."

"There is no way I am going home," the blonde

surprised Alexa by saying. "I didn't dress like this to ride around in your car." Suddenly, Alexa felt the woman's finger running down her sleeve again. "I'm not afraid of getting sick." Her irritated tone had dropped to a coo. "And I'm happy to go home with you." Alexa sensed her leaning closer but stayed focused on where they were going. "And help you feel better."

Unable to help herself, Alexa laughed, thinking it was unlikely her date would offer to make chicken soup. "That's very kind of you," she replied. "But I think it's best I be alone."

She heard her date slump back in her seat. "Whatever," she said. "Take me to the Viper Room. It's too early to go home." Normally, Alexa would argue against leaving her date without a ride, but she had enough for the night.

She sensed her date was well versed in taking care of herself. "My pleasure," she said and drove a little faster.

Kara mimicked her adversary's last words "Like a child." She and Annette were settled in a booth at a table covered with plates of steaming Italian food. A variety of pastas in red and white sauces plus garlic bread and a bottle of burgundy wine would normally have Kara licking her lips. Unfortunately, her irritation at what happened distracted her. "She came within an inch of hitting us."

Annette speared her fork into a pile of noodles and started to twist it to gather a bite. "Who exactly are you so pissed at? The blonde or the brunette?" she asked before putting the food in her mouth only to roll her eyes while she ate. "Oh my God, you need to let it go and try this. Tastes fabulous."

Reluctantly, Kara grabbed a piece of the bread from the

wicker basket and thought about her friend's question. *Who am I really mad at? The blonde who wanted to get in my face or the driver who insulted me before driving away?* For some reason, it was the insult that rankled her the most. "The brunette," she said holding the food poised in the air. "I mean, did you hear with she said to me?" She took a bite and felt the mixture of garlic, butter, and some other herb she couldn't identify burst across her tongue. Her friend was right, the food was terrific.

Annette pointed her fork in Kara's direction. "See?" she said with a smile. "Aren't you glad we finally tried here?" With her mouth full of delicious flavor all Kara could do was nod. For a month they walked past the trattoria three times a week after racquetball but never stopped. Digging into her lasagna, from the smell alone, she already wished they had come sooner. Chewing, the delicious meal was almost enough to make her forget about the woman driving the black Camaro. But not quite. Aside from anger over the insult, there was something in the woman's entire aura that Kara found unnerving. Picturing the stranger in her mind, she remembered how she walked around the car toward her. The way her green eyes held hers in a stare that hinted of something powerful behind them. As if daring Kara to challenge her. Then a word came to her—arrogant. *Yes, that's it. She moved like she was absolutely fearless,* she thought. *As if having no doubt things would go her way.* Staring out the window, Kara picked up her wine to take a sip. *What would it be like to have confidence like that?*

"Hello, Earth to Kara," her best friend said. "You're not hearing a word I'm saying, are you?"

Kara returned her focus to her dinner. "Sorry," she said. "I promise to stop stewing over what happened. I didn't exactly get her license plate number."

"Correct, so let's talk about something else," Annette said. "Like how we are going to get Brady to propose to me."

Unable to keep from smiling at the familiar topic, Kara nodded. "You're right," she said preparing to take another bite of the pasta. "Your hints aren't working at all?"

Her mouth full, Annette raised her napkin to hide her lips as she spoke around the food. "Everything but writing it in lipstick on the bathroom mirror."

Chewing, Kara held in a laugh. Brady was either incredibly dense, which was what she thought was the case, or he never intended to marry Annette. The latter would be a shame because the two were perfect for each other. Whenever she hung out with the pair, their chemistry filled the room. Although she loved her best friend entirely, there were times, every once in a while, she was a tad jealous at their connection. So far, Kara hadn't even come close to meeting someone special.

A bead of sweat slipped down Alexa's back to drip onto the mat beneath her. Her entire body glistened as she flowed from one pose to the next. Set at an exact one hundred and five degrees, the special studio she had built in her home was sweltering. The quiet room was one of her favorite places. Total peace where she could block out everything else in her world but for holding the next position. Measuring her breath while her muscles tightened, Alexa focused on nothing but maintaining her toehold. One foot supported her entire bodyweight requiring a perfect blend of strength and balance. Slowly exhaling, she counted down from sixty. Controlling her breathing was as important to her as the physical challenge. She strived for complete mastery of every part of her body.

Reaching zero, Alexa unwound her leg before lowering onto her back flat on the mat. Strangely, the next pose was one of her hardest—dead body. Mastering the skill of holding absolutely still in such a vulnerable position for sixty-seconds challenged her. She was a creature of motion, even when that motion was nothing more than slowly squeezing the body of her opponent until she tapped in surrender.

Thankfully, the minute passed, and Alexa glided through the remaining positions to finish the Bikram flow. As she lifted herself from the floor, she heard a tap on the steam-covered glass door. With a smile, she took a blue microfiber towel from the hook on the wall and wiped her face. She had hoped she would have a visitor tonight. "Come in," Alexa said, rubbing the sweat from her neck. "But I warn you, it's hot in here."

The door swung open, but her visitor didn't step inside. "I don't see why you do yoga in a sauna," said the slender man in very tight, very expensive black jeans and a black, perfectly-fitted long-sleeved t-shirt. His dark hair cascaded to his shoulders, offsetting the pale skin of his thin face. To Alexa, he was the handsomest man in the world, and she loved him with all her heart. He held up a tumbler of ice water. "Actually, I don't understand yoga at all, but I brought you this."

"Thank you," Alexa said as she crossed the polished wood floor to take the offering. "And I don't understand why you insist on dressing like a vampire."

The man laughed as he leaned against the doorjamb. "Because today, I am one," he said. "They gave me a few pints of blood to top me off." Alexa frowned. She hated when he joked about his treatments, but she knew it was one of the ways he chose to deal with his leukemia.

Taking a long drink of the cold water, she chose to ignore his joke and change the subject. "You know you shouldn't barge in here," she said. "I had a date tonight. I could have been in the middle of something."

Her visitor shrugged. "I did text first, but you weren't answering," he replied. "So, I stopped in. If I heard screams of ecstasy coming through the door, I'd have left."

Alexa swatted him with the towel. "Don't make me start hanging a sock on the front doorhandle," she said. "If I don't text, it's because I'm busy."

With an innocent smile, the man's green eyes twinkled. "Oh, dear sister of mine, you're never too busy for your twin, are you?" he asked, and Alexa shook her head. Her twin brother was right, and they both knew it. She would do anything for Anthony. Born first by six minutes, Alexa was the older sister after all.

"Go make me a protein shake for a nightcap while I take a shower," she said. "Then you can tell me why you are here."

"Okay, you can tell me all about your fabulous date that ended up with you doing yoga until you're a sweaty mess," Anthony said, straightening to go. "I'm sure she was memorable."

Alexa snorted a laugh. "Not so much," she said. "Although there was one interesting encounter tonight." For a second, her mind went back to the face of the angry woman who slapped her car.

"Oh, yeah?" her brother asked. "You going to see her again?"

Rubbing the back of her neck with the towel, she shook her head. "No," she answered. "Which is probably best anyway."

Anthony raised an eyebrow. "Why?"

Alexa started to walk away to go to the shower. "Because I almost hit her with my car," she said. "And needless to say, she was really pissed. So, no, I won't see her again."

Chapter Three

The gentle feel of a little cat's paw on her cheek brought Kara from a deep sleep. One she only fell into a few hours before. After tossing and turning all night over her decision to work as a lowly production assistant for ESPN, her exhaustion finally won out. Unfortunately, it left her groggy and disoriented as she fumbled for her phone on the nightstand. "What time is it, Oliver?" she mumbled to her gray and brown tabby companion. "God, I feel like I've been hit by a truck."

Bringing the phone to her face, it took a moment for her eyes to focus on the small numbers on the screen. Seven-twenty-seven a.m. She blinked. *What the hell?* was her first thought. *Why is it so late?* Bolting upright in bed, causing Oliver to have to dance out of the way with a disgruntled meow, Kara looked at the time again, praying she was wrong. The alarm should have gone off an hour ago. *Shit.* Tossing the phone aside, Kara rushed out of the bed of twisted sheets making a beeline for her bathroom. She would have to forgo her normal morning routine of meditation and freewriting. She was expected at her new job in exactly thirty-three-minutes.

Jumping in the shower before the water was barely warm enough to endure, she let out a growl. *This is all karma,* she thought with a shiver. *I should never have broken down and taken this corporate gig.* Still, money was money and at the moment she had next to zero. Only a small loan from her parents last month kept her tiny one bedroom apartment's landlord from knocking on her door. She didn't want to have to keep going back to them, even though both reassured her they would always be there for her. At thirty-years-old, Kara believed she was long past when she should be relying on her parents to help pay her bills.

After breaking a speed record soaping and rinsing her body, she turned off the water. Unfortunately, there wasn't time to get her hair wet even though that meant it would be a curly brown mess all day. *I'll have to tie it back,* she thought, knowing the casual look wasn't how she wanted to make a first impression, but there wasn't time to style her hair. *It's not like they are hiring me to be a fashion model.* Still, only a miracle would keep her from being late as it was, and Kara hated to be late, new job or otherwise. While she quickly dried with a towel, Oliver sauntered in and jumped on the back of the toilet to watch her with his wide, yellow eyes. "Thank you for waking me up, big guy," Kara said. "Who knows how late I would have slept without you? Then I would really be screwed." She shook her head and looked in the mirror at her reflection. Her natural curls were everywhere, and a hint of dark circles lay under her eyes. "Oh, great. I look like some wild woman off the streets. They are going to take one look at me and tell me to take a hike."

Luckily, she had already interviewed with the HR rep

and apparently made a decent first impression. The man had hired her for the three-month assignment, so she must have done something right. The last thing she wanted was to make him regret the decision on the first day of work. Just then her phone chimed on the bed, and she grabbed the thing to look at who sent a text while on her way to grab some underwear and a bra. "You ready to kick some ass today?" her friend Annette's text read. "Can't wait to hear about it."

After jumping into a pair of jeans, pulling on a cream blouse, and slipping on her shoes, Kara shot off her reply. "Overslept. Not even there yet."

A wide-eyed emoji came back. "Oh wow."

"Exactly. I'll text you later," Kara replied as she grabbed her keys and headed for the door without even time for a cup of coffee. It was going to be a bitch of a day.

Sipping her coffee, Alexa tried not to grimace at the weak, bitter flavor. She had no problem with admitting she was a coffee snob but decided asking for something different wouldn't amount in anything better. It would make her look difficult, which normally wasn't a problem, but today she wasn't in the mood. Instead, she set the mug emblazoned with the ESPN logo on the conference table and sat back in the soft leather chair to wait. "It's truly horrible, isn't it," Alexa's manager said from where she sat beside her. "You would think a network of this size could at least spend a few extra pennies on a decent blend."

Alexa chuckled. "I'm glad I'm not the only one who thinks so," she said. "I hate to always be the diva."

At that, her manager and long-time friend, smiled.

"You're still the diva," she said. "It's part of your brand. But we won't make a scene today."

"Thank you for the reminder, Jess," Alexa said but with a smile. "I'd hate for anyone to think I'm a nice person."

Jess touched her forearm. "You are a very nice person," she said. "I know that, and you know that. But the rest of the world? Not so much. You are the arrogant, ruthless, and often difficult Alexa Knight." With a sigh, Alexa nodded. From the beginning of her MMA career, she and Jess had masterminded the perfect persona. Fans and foes alike were drawn in by her mysterious and seemingly complex demeanor, while behind the scenes, Alexa kept her personal life private. *But all the charades will be behind me soon,* she thought as the door to the conference room opened. *I can't wait.*

The program director Jess told her about bustled in. Dressed in kakis and a white polo shirt with the ESPN logo embroidered above the pocket, he looked exactly like she described, and Alexa wondered if he always dressed that way. From her experience, they were very gung-ho in corporations like Disney and ESPN. Being someone who struggled with conforming to even the most basic norms, she didn't quite understand the attraction. "Sorry for the delay. A mix up with the PAs," he said, taking a seat at the head of the table.

"Thank you for being willing to do this with us, Ms. Knight. We here at ESPN know your upcoming fight, being your last, is special. Letting us have an insider's view on how you will prepare is an honor."

Alexa nodded. "Your network has been good to me," she said. "Before I retire, I want to pay that back."

The media, but ESPN in particular, had taken a liking to Alexa's bold personality from the start. The fact she could back up any trash talk with superior fighting only made her more attractive. Her decision to do a short docuseries with the network leading up to her final bout, was an easy one and had been in the works for weeks. Training camp started in less than three days and the last little details were being ironed out. For the most part, Alexa left all the decisions to Jess, but today she would be meeting the small film crew. Part of the arrangement was for her to have final say on who would be allowed in to watch her prepare. If she felt a bad vibe from someone, it could be disruptive and derail her preparation. Going into a fight to defend her title was as much an exercise in mental focus as the physical training.

The program director rubbed his hands together. "I've assembled the best possible crew for you," he said. "Lots of experience shooting documentary film here at the network. Shall we meet them?"

Trying to compose herself, Kara swallowed what may have been the most disgusting sip of coffee in her life. The only redeeming factor was there was caffeine involved and she desperately needed some of that.

Ever since she arrived at ESPN's West Coast Headquarters building in Los Angeles things were thrown at her nonstop. Walking in the door at exactly eight o'clock didn't help and especially frustrated her because, normally, she would have been at least a half an hour early and had time to get the lay of the land. In fact, she almost felt like the universe was punishing her for taking the job. The minute she had stepped off the elevator on the sixth floor to join new hire orientation, some guy rushing by pointed his finger at her to call her out.

"Are you the new PA?" he had asked, sounding none too happy.

Too late to sneak back to the elevator, she had wanted to fall into a black hole on the spot. Not until later did Kara understand the program director wasn't upset because of her, but rather upset at someone else calling in sick at the last minute.

Kara had nodded. "Yes, sir," she said. "I'd have been here sooner—"

The man waved a hand to stop her midsentence. "Just get in the staff room," he said. "Wait with the others and someone can explain later."

Blinking with confusion, Kara looked around. "Um, which way is the staff room?"

"Jesus, what a disaster," he growled, running a hand through the little bit of gray hair still on his head, and already turning to go take on another task. "End of the hall, last door on the left." Then, he was gone in the other direction leaving Kara to stand alone and wonder what the hell happened. *I guess I better find the staff room*, she thought, heading toward where she hoped he meant. *At least let there be coffee in there.* There was coffee, as well as three other people.

When she had walked in, all eyes stared at her. "Who the hell are you?" asked the man leaning against the wall at the back. He was tall, lanky, and clearly not in a great mood from the frown on his face. "And where is Maggie?"

Not thrilled with the welcome but wanting to fit in as quickly as she could, Kara shook her head. "I'm not sure who Maggie is, but I'm Kara. The new PA."

"New PA?" asked another man seated at one of the round tables. Unlike his coworker, he looked shorter and stubbier. The image of the classic comedy team Laurel and

Hardy came to mind, except neither of the men seemed especially funny at the moment. Instead, they looked irritated.

Kara pointed at the coffee station. "Do you mind if I have some coffee? My brain will function better and maybe we can clear this up."

"Help yourself," the third person in the room said—a woman with a spikey blonde haircut colored with pinks and blues and what looked to be coke-bottle-thick eyeglasses. "And it's nice to meet you, Kara. But seriously, why are you here?"

After pouring herself a mug of the much needed java, Kara turned to the group. "I have no idea," she said. "I walked in the door and some guy in kakis and a white shirt told me to come in here. He looked a little..." She cocked her head to think of the word. "Panicked?"

Just then, the lanky man's cellphone buzzed in his pocket. As soon as he glanced at the screen, he started to swear.

"What?" the chubby man asked, at the same time his own phone on the table buzzed.

Before the chubby man could look at it, the lanky man dropped his phone back in his pocket. "Maggie's out of commission with appendicitis. She's not going to be here."

All eyes turned to Kara again and all she could do was shrug. "I guess I'm your new PA."

Chapter Four

The program director buzzed someone from the phone on the conference room table and a few moments later, a small group of people trooped in. *This is an interesting assortment,* Alexa thought without letting any hint of an expression other than a frown show on her face. She was back to Alexa the Difficult mode and only her green eyes moved as she took in the new arrivals. A tall guy, a heavy guy, a woman with cool hair and glasses, and someone she couldn't quite see in the back. *Like she's hiding behind the rest of them.* Before she could look closer, the program director made introductions. "Ms. Knight, this is your docuseries crew," he said, pointing at the tall guy first. "Greg Wilson is your cinematographer." Greg nodded, but nothing else. Alexa didn't get a sense he disliked the assignment but rather he let his camera do the talking. She respected that and focused on the next person.

"This is Eric Phillips," the program director said, and the heavyset guy gave her a wide smile. "He's your primary camera man."

From the look on his face, Alexa guessed Eric was

clearly happy to be on the gig and an MMA supporter. "Ms. Knight, I am grateful to be on your crew for this," he said, confirming her prediction. "I'm a huge fan and have followed your career since your first pro fight against Rose Toledo."

"That was a long time ago," Alexa said with a straight face. Although meeting a fan was generally welcome, and she would sign autographs and pose for selfies when it was unavoidable, she often gave them a cold shoulder. Everyone expected no less.

When she said nothing else after a beat, the program director looked a little concerned but moved on to the spiky-haired woman in glasses. "Bobby Simon," he said. "She will act as your director."

Alexa raised an eyebrow. "My director?"

The program director shook his head, but before he could respond Bobby spoke up. "Not like you're thinking," she said. "I'm on the crew to determine what shots to take and when to take them." A smile played over her lips. "Basically, I tell the rest of them what to do."

"But never Alexa," Alexa's manager, Jess, said, and it wasn't a question.

Bobby gave a slow nod, no longer smiling. "I would never make that mistake."

Considering her answer for a moment, Alexa decided she liked her and believed what she said regarding the directing. "Good." Letting her eyes drift to the final person in the quartet, she paused. The last person was another woman, only with curly, brown hair that looked like she was trying to contain it with a hair tie without much luck. She was staring straight at the table and not meeting anyone's eye. What was most interesting, though, was how familiar she looked. Alexa squinted her eyes. *Have I met her some-*

where? At a fight? Or a club? she thought, unable to make a connection. "Who is this?"

At the question, the woman looked at her at the same time the program director cleared his throat. "This is, uh..." he hesitated. "So, she's your temporary production assistant. There is another—"

Suddenly, Alexa recognized the woman and almost laughed at the irony. "I know you," she said. "You slapped my car."

"After you almost ran me over," the woman shot back with irritation in her voice. The already quiet room went dead silent. If Alexa didn't know better, she would guess everyone else was holding their breath.

Finally, Jess cleared her throat from beside her. "You two know each other?" she asked, and Alexa, tilting her head, waited for the answer.

As if suddenly realizing where she was and what she did, the woman bit her lip. "Not really," she finally said. "And I didn't know it was her."

Alexa loved the answer and fought to keep from smiling. "Would that have made any difference?"

Again, silence in the room while the woman met her eye. "Nope."

After a short coughing fit, the program director pointed at Kara. "I think you just set a record," he growled, glaring at Kara like he was ready to strangle her. "For being fired in the shortest amount of time at ESPN." Kara sighed, knowing her actions warranted his words, but she hadn't been able to help herself. Alexa irritated her, and so she told the truth. *Not the wisest thing in the world,* she thought. *But I didn't really want this job anyway.* About to tell the program director exactly that, she opened her mouth only to be interrupted.

"Wait," Alexa said. "Not yet."

The program director waved his hands as if wanting to erase the entire situation. "Really, Ms. Knight, I apologize. She started this morning and—"

Kara watched Alexa pin him with her bright green eyes. "Do you even know her name?"

Not sure what was happening, Kara watched the exchange like a spectator. *There's no way he knows it,* she thought, and he immediately proved her right. "No," he answered. "And now I don't—"

"Who are you?" Alexa interrupted as her laser stare turned to Kara.

"Yes," the woman in the business suit sitting beside Alexa said. "Who are you?"

Kara raised her chin. "I'm Kara Roberts, an independent filmmaker." She heard the spiky-haired blonde beside her groan, but Kara figured she was on her way out the door anyway. "I make documentaries." She hesitated, but then could not help but add, "on serious topics."

She watched Alexa lean back in her chair, holding the stare. Kara found it impossible to read anything in them. *She could be pissed. She could be amused. Hell, she could even be turned on,* she thought, not quite sure what to do, but unwilling to apologize for anything, she crossed her arms and stared right back. *This woman doesn't scare me although apparently, she should according to Eric.* Back in the staff room, Eric the camera man had given her a sixty-second run down. They were the team assigned to follow MMA bantamweight champion Alexa Knight's every move for nine weeks while she trained for her fight against her greatest adversary, Rachel Rhodes. Kara didn't have the heart to tell them she was pretty clueless on who those people were and why they were fighting. Regardless, she would lean on her strength of figuring everything out on the fly.

"Do you like MMA, Kara Roberts?" Alexa asked, still not dropping her eyes.

Not sure how to answer, Kara took a deep breath as she stalled for time. She was on the edge of losing her job, so it might be time to start playing it safe, but that was never her style. *Oh screw it*, she thought. *I've dug myself this deep, so I won't stop digging now.* "I honestly don't see the point," she answered and heard Eric snicker.

"You have got to be kidding me," the program director burst out, making Kara jump. "Not only are you fired, but so is whoever hired you. Get out. Now."

Thankful for the excuse to look somewhere other than at Alexa, Kara started for the door. Enough was enough.

"Stop," Alexa ordered in a voice that left no room for disagreement. "Are you a good PA, Kara Roberts?"

At that, Kara looked hard at the program director, making sure she had his complete attention. "Actually, I'm excellent. I worked my way up from there." If he was at all impressed, his red face didn't show it. "And I know what it takes to run a shoot."

Alexa kept going. "Bobby, you're the director. Does it matter if Kara knows MMA? Or even..." She paused long enough for Kara to glance at her. "...doesn't like it?" For a second, Kara was certain she saw a hint of a smile twitch on the fighter's lips.

"Well," Bobby said, drawing out the word while she clearly processed the question. "No, not if she knows her job otherwise. And the more that I think about it, her inexperience with the sport might work in our favor." Bobby had

Kara's full attention as the woman tapped her forefinger against her chin. "A fresh set of eyes could help us capture a unique perspective."

The docuseries director said exactly what Alexa hoped. Based on what she had heard so far, she had come to the same conclusion. A novice to the world of professional fighting on the team would make life more interesting, thus make the docuseries more so too. Not that she expected to have Kara on film, but her questions would generate different perspectives the rest of them might not consider. "I agree," Alexa said, watching Kara to see her reaction. There was a possibility she would refuse on principle. *After all, she had documentaries to make on serious topics,* Alexa thought, continuing to respect the woman even more. *She's brave, that's for sure.*

"Well, Kara, what do you say?" Alexa asked. "Still want the job?" Kara bit her lip again, and Alexa wondered if she even knew she had that habit. There was something a little sexy about it.

As if reading her mind and picking up on the sexy aspect, her manager turned to Alexa. "Are you sure you don't want to think about this?" she asked, waiting for Alexa to look at her as if she wanted to make sure she had her full attention. "Training camp is serious business, and a new perspective might be a... distraction."

Jess's innuendo was so obvious to Alexa it was all she could do not to laugh. Her manager made a good point, but Alexa wasn't worried. Although Kara was attractive in a girl-next-door sort of way, it was clear the woman seriously disliked her. Even saving her job wouldn't erase the distaste Alexa saw in her eyes.

"There won't be a problem," Alexa said refocusing on Kara. "Well?"

That time, the woman didn't hesitate as if realizing the opportunity might be fading. *She must need this job pretty badly*, she thought, guessing independent documentary film making didn't pay very well. "I'll do it," she said. "And I won't get in the way."

The program director clapped his hands together, a wide smile on his face. "Then it's settled," he said as if the entire fifteen minutes of tension never happened. "We start filming tomorrow. First, some day-in-the-life footage before we move on to training camp." Completely back to business, he looked at Alexa. "Are you satisfied with the crew?" She nodded and he turned his attention back to the others. "All good? Bobby, do you four want to stay in here and start laying out ideas of what you want to shoot over the next few days?"

"Absolutely," Bobby said, and Alexa took that as her cue for them to go. As she and Jess stood, Alexa couldn't help but notice Kara was watching her from near the exit.

Curious, she stepped away from Jess to pause beside the PA. *Maybe she doesn't hate me as much as I thought?* she wondered. "Did you have something you wanted to say?" she asked when they were face to face and watched as Kara squared her shoulders. *Or maybe not a thank you after all.* After years of stare-downs, she knew a defiant look when she saw one.

Kara took a deep breath. "I appreciate you stepping in on my behalf," she said. "But I want to be clear. I can fight my own battles, so don't think I owe you anything."

Alexa narrowed her eyes. Kara proved to be even more fearless than she thought, feeling more intrigued by the second. Then, she stomped the attraction down. *And I cannot let her be a distraction,* she thought, knowing Jess was one hundred percent correct in her advice. *Not at this point in my career.* Without even a hint of a reaction on her face, Alexa turned to go. "I never thought otherwise," she said over her shoulder. "See you tomorrow."

Chapter Five

"Well, that was certainly interesting," Bobby said as soon as everyone including the program director left the room. "You have got some real balls, Kara Roberts."

Shaking his head, Greg slipped his long body into one of the chairs around the table. "Honestly, I can't believe she kept you."

Eric joined him at the table, looking equally surprised. "Especially since you don't know MMA."

"All right, guys," Bobby interrupted as she walked to the front of the room to stand near a large whiteboard. "Give her a break. I think we can make the most of this at least until Maggie comes back. Then we'll see where we're at."

Frowning, Kara wasn't thrilled with the insinuation she was only temporary. "I'm a good PA," she said. "I've been doing this stuff since I was sixteen."

Greg shook his head. "Hey, I'm sure you're fine, but we worked as a team for five years. We are a well-oiled machine. You have some big shoes to fill."

Kara swallowed hard. She could get where he was

coming from. When she could work on her documentary, there were a few go-tos she relied on. "Just give me a chance," she said. "That's all I ask."

"Fine," Bobby said as she picked up a marker and pulled off the cap. "Your first assignment is to go get us some decent coffee. What's your cell number, and we will all text you our orders."

"I'm on it," Kara said, rattling off her number right before she all but ran to the elevator, while at the same time googling the closest coffee shop. Luckily, there was one close enough she could walk there, and in less than three minutes she saw the sign. As she neared, she recognized the black Camaro sitting out front. *Oh, great*, she thought. *This will be awkward.* Realizing she'd been a bit harsh toward Alexa when they separated back in the conference room, Kara decided she owed her an apology. Squaring her shoulders, she walked into the shop and immediately met eyes with Alexa. Determined, Kara marched across the room while the woman's eyes followed her every step.

Before she could say a word, someone stepped in her path. He held out his phone toward Alexa. "I'm a huge fan," he said. "Can we take a selfie?"

Alexa's eyes flicked past him for a second, catching Kara's again for a beat and then she refocused on her fan. "Sure," she murmured, and as soon as the man got close enough, Alexa lifted her fists in a fighting pose as he took the picture. *She looks like she's done this a million times*, Kara thought, and watched as a group converged around Alexa. *What would it be like to be so famous that you couldn't even go into a coffee shop?* Suddenly, she felt someone beside her and looked to see the woman who had been sitting next to Alexa during the meeting.

She held out her hand. "Hi, I'm Jess," woman said. "Alexa's manager. Can I ask you question?"

Kara raised an eyebrow. "Yes."

"Do you really know your stuff?"

Kara tried not to take offense, but she was getting tired of being challenged today. "Yes," she said. "I will not be a liability and I will not get in the way."

"Good," Jess said. "This is an important fight for Alexa."

"I get the sense that it is," Kara said, and Jess shook her head.

"You really don't know anything about the sport, do you?"

Kara shrugged. "Honestly," she said. "I couldn't have picked Alexa out of a lineup if my life depended on it."

Jess stared. "Incredible. Well then, I suggest you spend some time this evening doing a little research on the internet." Without another word, Jess picked up the two coffees waiting on the counter and waded into the crowd to stand beside Alexa. "That's enough photos," she said to the others. "We have an appointment."

With that, Kara watched as the two women left while fans continued to snap pictures. Jess was right. She needed to do some homework.

With people still taking pictures even as she climbed into her Camaro and drove away, Alexa could never quite comprehend how someone could become such a fan of a person they didn't truly know. *They have no idea what I am really like*, she thought. *But I guess they are the ones who buy my brand, so I should be grateful.*

"What are you thinking about?" Jess asked from the

passenger seat. "Please tell me it is not the production assistant."

Alexa glanced over with a raised eyebrow. "Actually, I'm not. And why would I be thinking about the production assistant?" she asked, and Jess snorted a laugh.

"Don't act like I don't know you," she said. "You couldn't keep your eyes off her during the meeting."

Holding back a smile, Alexa navigated through traffic on the way to West Hollywood. "Maybe that is because I'm not used to people standing up to me," Alexa replied. "It has nothing to do with her looks or any other attraction."

"Really?" Jess said. "You always love a challenge."

Alexa shook her head. "Not when it comes to women," she said. "Unless she's stupid enough to step into the ring."

When Jess didn't answer immediately, Alexa looked again. Her friend's eyes were narrowed. "Well, don't lose concentration. We have one more fight."

"I'm very aware of that, manager," Alexa said with a small smile. "I promise I will be one hundred percent dedicated to nothing but this fight."

"Good," Jess said, and Alexa heard her relax back into her seat. "Because we need to beat Rachel Rhodes." Alexa nodded. She felt the same. *I never thought it would ever come to this*, she thought. Rhodes was her old sparring partner from when she started her career. They were even lovers one crazy weekend in Vegas right after Alexa turned pro. Although the sexual relationship went no further, the chemistry between them rolled over into the ring, which was why Rachel was the best possible sparring partner—until she got jealous of Alexa's fame and wanted a career of her own. Alexa sighed. *And we could never get past it.*

Although she was a few years behind on the MMA pro circuit, Rhodes quickly made a name for herself by trash talking Alexa. The paparazzi could not get enough of the drama, but Alexa ignored most of it. Rhodes was a decent fighter, but not of Alexa's caliber, yet that didn't stop her from constantly calling Alexa out to fight. In the end, Alexa decided she would let Rhodes be her final challenger and give her a shot at the bantamweight belt. She had no intention of losing.

"Remind me about what's going on this weekend," Alexa said, changing the subject. Discussion about the evil Rachel Rhodes could go on for hours. The only person who disliked the woman more than Alexa was Jess. She had been forced to watch the way Rachel tried to manipulate her, to take advantage, and they were never friends.

Out of the corner of her eye, Alexa saw Jess flip through her tablet. "All right, I can see you would rather not talk about the production assistant or your fight," she said. "So, let's recount what is going to happen between now and when you start training camp on Monday. Tomorrow, you have your MMA video game premier. Since you're on the cover, they want you there. Saturday is the presentation and photoshoot for your LGBTQ+ Equality Visibility Award. Did you look over the speech?"

"No, but I will tonight," Alexa answered, doing her best to not get overwhelmed. She wasn't a fan of being paraded around, although the award was a true honor. "Please tell me you were able to keep Sunday clear." It would be the last time she could be alone until the fight was over.

Jess closed the cover of her tablet with a clap. "Yes, Sunday is yours. I expect you to stay home, watch Netflix, and keep out of the public eye so you're fresh and ready to go on Monday.

"Yes, ma'am," Alexa said, as they pulled up in front of Jess's condo. "I will be ready."

Jess put her hand on Alexa's forearm. "You know I love you, right?" she asked, and Alexa nodded.

"I do. And everything will work out. I promise."

As Kara reclined on her best friend's sofa, Annette's boyfriend Brady paced the room. She had never seen the normally soft-spoken man so animated. "So, let me get this straight," he said, stopping in front of her. "You are on the team filming Alexa Knight as she prepares for the ultimate fight against Rachel Rhodes?"

"Yes," Kara said. "I'm glad you're so excited."

Brady grabbed his short, blond hair. "How can you not be excited? It's almost sacrilege that you're on this job knowing so little."

"Which is exactly why I'm here," Kara said as she picked up her glass of wine from the coffee table. "So you can tell me all about her."

Annette walked into the room from the kitchen carrying an open bottle of wine and a can of beer. "Pizza will be here in twenty minutes," she said, holding up the beverages. "Do you want more to drink?"

Kara looked at her nearly empty glass and nodded. "If I'm going to have to sit through watching two women needlessly punching each other, I'm going to need a lot of wine."

"Hey, this is the ultimate sport," Brady said, and Annette rolled her eyes.

"Would you like another beer, darling?"

"Yes, please, babe," Brady said, picking up the remote. "Let's start at the beginning."

Annette shook her head as she placed the can and bottle on the coffee table. "You guys can start at the beginning," she said. "I'm going to go study. Yell when the pizza is here."

Brady crossed to Annette and kissed her gently on the lips. "I promise to help you with flashcards later tonight," he said. "You're going to make the world's greatest high school English teacher."

"Thank you, dear," Annette said and with a little wave went into the bedroom.

"Okay, where were we?" Brady asked, moving back to stand beside the TV as if giving a rehearsed presentation.

Kara smiled. *At least he is making this fun,* she thought. "I do believe starting at the beginning," Kara said. Brady pressed a button and a picture of Alexa, albeit much younger looking, filled the giant TV screen. The green eyes stared back at her with an intensity she was learning too well. *I would be afraid to fight her from that look alone.* She cocked her head, trying to decide what she could see in the woman's face. *Determination for sure. So fearless...* "How old is she here?"

"Twenty-two. Right before her first pro fight against Rose Toledo."

"And now?"

"Thirty-four," Brady answered. "And eighteen-and-oh in professional fights. No one can beat her." He grinned. "Here's the fight." Brady pushed play on the remote and Kara watched as the camera panned to an octagon-shaped ring. She recognized Alexa. Dressed in green and black shorts and bra, her hair in cornrows, she stood perfectly still and trained her laser focus stare on her opponent who paced the fence like an animal.

"They look ready to kill each other," Kara murmured sinking lower into the couch cushions.

Brady pushed pause. "They kind of are," Brady said. "Keep in mind, the fighting world expected Alexa to lose this fight against a veteran who clearly outmatched her.

Vegas odds were crazy in Toledo's favor." He shook his head as if still amazed at the upset. "Now, don't blink." He pushed play and Kara watched as the minute the referee dropped his hand, Alexa stormed across the ring. Her opponent looked surprised at the sudden aggressive attack, sliding to her right to avoid the bullrush. As if expecting Toledo to do exactly that, Alexa shifted her weight to pivot on her left foot and delivered a wicked spinning heel kick to her opponent's temple. Kara covered her mouth with both hands as Rose Toledo dropped like a stone to the canvas. Only the speed of the referee kept Alexa from jumping on the unconscious woman, apparently with every intent of doing more damage.

Kara stared as Alexa strutted around the octagon celebrating her dominate win. "Wow," was all Kara could think to say, not sure if she should be impressed or horrified.

"Seven seconds," Brady said, pausing the screen again. "I can show you fight after fight where she knocks out her opponent with vicious strikes and kicks." Picking up his beer, he plopped on the couch beside her and cracked open the can. "But she's not a one trick pony. She grapples well too. Three wins by submission. Want to see one?"

Kara didn't know what submission meant precisely, but she got the idea. "I think I'm good," she answered as she focused on the paused image of Alexa Knight, triumphant fists raised in the air. To her, there wasn't anything more she needed to know.

Chapter Six

Using her Japanese chef's knife with deft precision, Alexa diced the onions before dumping the mix in with the vegetables already frying in the wok. Although the media was not aware of it, she was an excellent cook. Her mother made learning how to use everything in the kitchen an essential part of her upbringing. Although Alexa's heritage was Italian and there were a lot of pasta dishes, that didn't mean her mother wasn't open-minded to other cuisines. Some of Alexa's fondest memories were with her mom in the kitchen and she enjoyed the downtime to make something from scratch for her and Anthony's lunch.

Her twin sat at the counter on a stool and watched her as she stirred the mixture. "That smells fantastic," Anthony said. "You're making my stomach growl."

"When was the last time you ate?" Alexa asked him, knowing he rarely had an appetite and stir-fry was his favorite. He needed strong flavors to keep his interest, so she added a dash of chili sauce a moment before grabbing the bowl full of chopped chicken breast she had grilled earlier.

Anthony averted his eyes. "I had breakfast," he mumbled.

"Anthony," Alexa said. "What was breakfast?"

He coughed. "That might've been a couple of donuts and a double expresso venti cup of coffee."

Alexa shook her head but didn't give him grief. He could eat whatever made him happy, in her opinion, as long as he consumed calories. *At least there's veggies and protein in this,* she thought plating their lunch. Walking around the counter, she set down the plates and sat on the stool beside him.

Anthony took a bite and closed his eyes with a moan. "This is fantastic. As always."

"Thank you," Alexa said, picking up her chopsticks to try the food.

Anthony swallowed. "So, are you ready for your big video game debut tonight?"

"As ready as I'm going to be I guess," Alexa said with a sigh. "The new film crew will be there too, so I have to get all dressed up and make a real show. Strut my badass champion self around." The whole idea of the event that night made her frustrated, but celebrity appearances were part of her job.

Anthony gave her an understanding look. "I know you're sick of it," he said, touching her shoulder. "Not much longer."

Nodding, Alexa couldn't wait. "I may shave my head and never wear makeup again." Anthony squinted his eyes as if trying to imagine what she would look like bald. Then Alexa realized what she said. There were times in Anthony's life when he didn't have hair because of chemotherapy.

Before she could apologize for the dumb statement, he grinned. "I think you'd look a lot like me," Anthony said.

"And I know what you're thinking. So, stop. It's all good fun. Now, about this game. Have you ever even played a video game?"

Alexa shrugged. "No," she said. "I've never had time. And I'm not entirely sure why some people sit in front of a television for hours when you can be doing the real thing."

"Well, it's a fighting game," Anthony said with a grin. "Unlike you, not everybody can do the real thing." He laughed. "You better hope they don't make you do a demonstration."

Setting down her chopsticks, Alexa dabbed at her mouth with a napkin. She hadn't thought about that scenario. *What if they do expect me to do a demonstration?* she wondered. *I'm not even sure how to turn the thing on.* "Just what would I do if I had to?" she asked feeling an unusual sense of panic.

Anthony stared hard into her eyes, totally serious. "All you have to do is press the hell out of the A-button," he said. Alexa raised an eyebrow, not sure what to make of his advice and then he burst out in giggles. "And know that I'm in the crowd laughing my ass off."

"You're no help," Alexa said, punching him gently in the shoulder. "Are you really going to come to the event?" She didn't like him to go to things, because if the media realized her twin was there, they would act stupid over it. So far over her long career, Anthony kept a low profile, and although he was sometimes caught on camera or asked a question, no one outside her close family knew he battled leukemia. Alexa wanted to keep it that way. Their private life was their private life.

. . .

Not having worked as a production assistant in a half dozen years, Kara had forgotten how much hard work the job really entailed. She was on the go nonstop since the crew arrived in the van to pick her up from ESPN headquarters. Having been briefed on the shooting schedule for the day, she knew the first stop was a beauty salon of all places. When Bobby mentioned it, she was surprised, not having thought through how much prep might go into getting Alexa ready for the big event later in the evening. After watching film with Brady the night before, and drinking a lot more wine than she probably should have, Kara had in her head that Alexa's footage would be of training with lots of kicking, hitting, and sweat.

"Go park the van," Bobby said to Kara once they arrived at the salon and all the gear was unloaded. "Then get your butt back here. Ms. Knight arrives in T-30."

"On it," Kara said and luckily found a spot on the street only six blocks away. Jogging back, she caught sight of the black Camaro already there. *Oh great, she's early and found a place right out front,* she thought with a frown and ran faster.

The minute she stepped in the door Greg tossed her a roll of gaffing tape. "Get the power cables secured so nobody trips," he said, and Kara got on the task. She moved along the floor from the outlet to the edge of the black reflector panel being used to help control the lighting. Because no one called it out, she knew they weren't rolling film yet, and she stepped past the panel to check in with Bobby. In her haste, she almost ran into Alexa, already in the styling chair with a cape around her neck. Her long, dark hair was wet, falling straight down the sides of her head. As Kara looked on, she couldn't help but think how much more vulnerable the fighter looked sitting there.

"They're not expecting me to actually play the video game, are they?" Alexa asked her manager as the hairstylist started to work on her hair.

"Probably. Why?" Jess asked. "You're on the cover. It's your game, Alexa." *Video games*, Kara thought as she listened. *Is that what we are getting ready for?* "I think all you need to do is stand there and look tough while glamorous."

"No problem," Alexa said with a small laugh. Kara rolled her eyes behind Alexa's back. *The arrogance of this woman*, she thought. *Selling herself to be on the cover of a videogame. But she's probably a big gamer.* She could almost imagine the woman on the couch with the controller in her hand, wearing ragged sweats while virtually beating the crap out of someone.

Sitting in the director's chair at the edge of the stage, Alexa waited patiently while people worked to get her ready to go out on stage. A woman made a few last touch-ups on her makeup, and another man clipped a microphone to her shirt collar. Jess stood beside her, giving quiet reassurance while Kara dutifully held a bottle of water for whenever Alexa signaled that she needed a sip. *And that's the only reason I have her standing there*, Alexa reminded herself. *That's the PA's job*. Still, she had to admit there was something about the woman that Alexa found intriguing. *Maybe it's because she is so not at all impressed by me.*

The popular internet host for the online gaming show walked up to Alexa. "Are we about ready here?" he asked. "We will be streaming live to millions of game boxes in about two minutes."

Alexa swallowed hard but nodded. "I'm ready," Alexa

said. *As I'll ever be,* she thought leaning toward Jess as soon as he was out of earshot. "How do you talk me into things like this?"

Jess smiled. "It's a big deal to be on the cover of a videogame," she said. "You should be honored." She paused, before giving Alexa a wink. "That and lots of dollar signs." Out of the corner of her eye, Alexa noticed Kara give a small shake of her head. Clearly, she did not appreciate the fact Alexa would be paid a lot of money simply for her likeness.

Before Alexa could make a comment, the broadcast's assistant director was at her elbow. "It's showtime, Ms. Knight." Resolving to have a conversation with Kara Roberts later on the importance of endorsements, Alexa squared her shoulders as she strode onto the stage. Cheers erupted even though when she looked into the crowd all she saw were flashing lights. There was no way to tell if Anthony was there, but she assumed that he was, and the fact gave her a little confidence. Strangely, she was more nervous walking up to the chair to sit next to the host then she was before any of her fights. They were streaming everything live on the internet with millions of people watching the debut. A major screw up would go viral in seconds.

After a short bit of chitchat with the host about her upcoming fight, he asked the question she was afraid of. "Would you like to give the game a spin?" Alexa's stomach dropped. She was about to reveal to the world that she didn't even know how to play her own game. Buying time, she forced a laugh. "Do I get to play my own character?" That elicited a chuckle from the crowd.

The host smiled. "Of course," he said. "Do you want to play me or is there someone else you have in mind?"

"I'm definitely not playing you," she said, knowing she wouldn't last a second against him.

With a wave of his hand, the host indicated the masses around them. "Take your pick."

Jess came to mind as Alexa looked around, and then her eyes landed on Kara. "I think she would be someone fun to beat," Alexa joked and took some pleasure in watching the PA pale. Kara shook her head, but Alexa nodded and waved her forward. The host joined in and after another minute, Kara was in the chair beside Alexa.

Handing them controllers as the giant screen with the game cover on it switched to the opening credits, he grinned at Kara. "Don't hold back."

As he moved away, Alexa caught Kara's glare. "You picked me because you're thinking I don't know how to do this," Kara said, and Alexa shrugged.

"I guess we're about to find out." As soon as the action began, Alexa did exactly as her brother instructed and pounded the A-button with her thumb while Kara's character did nothing but dodge. It was without a doubt the most pathetic display of gaming skills in history and the crowd started to chant "knockout, knockout, knockout."

"Do you know what you are doing?" Kara whispered, and Alexa gave a small shake of her head.

"Not a clue," she mouthed back. Kara started to laugh and thankfully stopped running her character everywhere so Alexa could repeatedly land her punch. The fight ended with Alexa still the champion and the crowd cheering. Somehow, she wrapped up her part of the show, thanked the host, and exited stage right. Kara waited with another bottle of water.

"I think that makes us even, Ms. Knight," she said, handing the drink over.

Alexa narrowed her eyes. "How so?"

Kara smiled. "You helped me keep this gig, and I let you win."

Chapter Seven

Sitting cross legged on the floor of her apartment with her eyes closed, Kara tried to focus her mind. Her hands rested on her knees with her palms upward. A candle burned nearby, releasing the gentle scents of vanilla and lavender into the room. She was even playing soft instrumental music through her earbuds, something she only did as a last resort. Even that wasn't working. As much as she tried, Kara could not keep the image of Alexa Knight from popping up in her mind. The woman's green eyes haunted her all morning. *And most of last night*, she thought with a frown. Although she couldn't remember any details, Kara was certain the fighter had been in her dreams.

Not ready to give up, Kara forced herself to imagine a calm, sunny beach. Gentle waves lapped onto the warm, golden sand and she sighed. The vision was her happy place, and she relaxed into it, almost feeling the light breeze on her face. Turning to face the turquoise sea, suddenly a figure was walking out of the water. A very fit, very sexy Alexa Knight in nothing but the barest of swimsuits. Kara's eyes popped open. "What in the hell?" she said, not even sure how to process what she envisioned. In answer to the sound of her voice, Oliver began to rub his body against her knee as he purred. With a shake of her head, she unfolded her legs and stood. "I give up, big guy." If she couldn't meditate, then she might as well make them both something to eat.

Heading to the fridge to find eggs, mushrooms, and sharp cheddar cheese to scramble into an omelet, her phone chimed on the counter. A quick peek and she saw a message from Annette. "What's happening today?"

Kara smiled, appreciating her best friend's interest. Annette was always good about checking in. Kara had yet to tell her about last night and her interaction with Alexa over the game, but she wasn't sure she was ready to share too many details. *Maybe because I don't understand the details myself?* she wondered. Alexa needed help, Kara gave it by playing the game, and then there was... *What? A spark over a video game? With a world famous MMA champion?*

After setting the omelet ingredients on the counter, Kara took a little bag of treats from the cupboard for Oliver. "Here you go," she said as she put a few bits on the floor for her feline friend. Without a word of thanks, he started to gobble them up while Kara picked up her phone to text back. "Filming Alexa at an LGBTQ+ award luncheon," she typed. "I even have to dress up a little."

"That sounds fun," Annette answered. "What are you thinking of wearing?"

Kara pursed her lips because that was a good question. "My black slacks and cream blouse. Maybe."

Annette sent back a laughing emoji. "You're go-to outfit. Make sure you don't look like the wait staff."

"Thanks," Kara replied with a smiling emoji. "Good advice." Even though she had to be practical since you never knew what a PA would have to do, she wanted to look good. She frowned. *Why?* she wondered. *Since when does that matter on a gig?* With a groan, she knew exactly why. Alexa Knight. Thoughts about her could easily become a disaster considering how much time they would be spending together, sometimes closely. Forcing herself to stop thinking about it, she changed the subject. "What are you up to today?"

"I'm not sure," Annette answered. "Going out. But Brady is being secretive."

Reading the words, Kara's eyes widened. "Do you think?" she shot back.

She could almost hear Annette squealing with excitement. "I think so!" Kara hoped so too. Brady's proposal was long overdue.

The LGBTQ+ luncheon, the speech, and everything about the day had gone smoothly so far. As Alexa left the podium to the sound of applause, she met her manager's eye and pointed at the door to the hallway exit. She needed a moment to let the adrenaline from giving the speech settle and could use the bathroom. After making her way from the special table set aside for Alexa and her team, Jess fell into step beside her as they pushed through the heavy double doors. "You were excellent," Jess said once they were alone in the long, carpeted hallway. "Great job on the embellishment around the struggle you faced in the all-male gym and the ridicule you dealt with being an out lesbian."

"Thank you," Alexa said as they walked together toward the other end where there was a sign for restrooms. Suddenly, the door to the hallway opened again, and when Alexa looked, she saw Kara appearing with a bottle of water in her hand. The PA was dressed great, or at least more so than her usual ponytail, jeans, and sneakers, and as Alexa watched her walk their way, she tried to decide which version she liked better. They were both attractive, but there was something about the slightly disheveled look of Kara's day-to-day that Alexa found most appealing.

Jess elbowed her in the side. "Stop looking at her that way," she hissed under her breath. "You're not reassuring me." Alexa blinked because her manager was right. She had been standing there thinking of Kara as more than a production assistant. *It's because of that damn game*, she thought. *When she rescued me in front of millions of internet viewers.*

Unable to deny her interest, Alexa needed to nip any sort of friendship or more in the bud immediately or things could unravel quickly. "You're right," she murmured back at Jess. "I'll take care of it." As the woman drew close, Alexa caught her eye, making sure to keep nothing but cool indifference in her look. "Can we help you?"

Kara hesitated for a beat as if not expecting the chilly response, but then joined them, holding out the water. "I thought you might need a drink after the speech," she said. "That kind of thing always makes my mouth dry."

Before Alexa could accepted the bottle and explain she was fine without help, she heard a familiar voice from down the hallway. "Hiding Alexa?" a woman said, a sneer in her tone. "How appropriate."

Alexa looked, but already guessed her unwanted visitor was her ex-sparring partner and soon to be challenger, Rachel Rhodes. To make it worse, she had her usual posse of fans in tow. Alexa knew the woman liked to fight, but she clearly relished the stardom too.

Jess growled beside her, and Kara looked confused. "Who is that?" she asked.

Alexa frowned, not in the mood for an altercation. "Rachel Rhodes," she said under her breath. Kara's eyes widened. Unfortunately, at that moment, the doors to the hallway opened yet again, only to have Eric and Bobby step into the hall with the camera.

Clearly seeing a golden opportunity, Bobby twirled her finger at Eric. "Roll film," she said quietly.

"Oh, this is perfect, isn't it?" Rhodes said once she reached them. "You're little film crew?" She crossed her arms and smirked at Kara. "And you're new girlfriend?"

Alexa noticed color rising to Kara's cheeks and before she could intercede, the PA, with her hands on her hips, stepped directly into Rachel Rhodes' line of sight. "Not that it's your business," she snapped. "But no. I am not. And you have real nerve coming into the hall to ambush Ms. Knight." With her mouth open, Rhodes simply stared for a moment and then started to laugh. Only it sounded mean and full of venom. The groupies with her, taking their cue from Rachel, did the same.

"You've got to be kidding me," Rachel snorted. "You're a little small for a bodyguard." She looked past Kara directly into Alexa's eyes. "It's funny to see you have someone fighting your battles for you. Will she be facing me in the ring too?"

Alexa narrowed her eyes, not sure who she was madder at—Rachel for being a bitch or Kara for butting in.

Even though Kara knew she was crossing all kinds of barriers professionally, she couldn't seem to stop herself from reacting. Growing more furious by the second, the sound of Rachel Rhodes' voice grated on her, but her comments were absolutely out of line. *I am certainly not*

Alexa's new girlfriend, she thought, at the same moment she felt a hand on her elbow. Whipping her head around, she saw Alexa standing close beside her. Her green eyes blazed with what could only be anger, and the sight made Kara swallow hard. Making the champion fighter mad, especially at her, was the last things she intended. *But I really should not have jumped in. Especially since as a PA, I'm supposed to be invisible working behind the scenes.*

"If you don't mind," Alexa said, a chill to her words. "I can handle this myself."

Kara felt a flush of embarrassment but also a hint of irritation at being so dismissed. "I am sure you can," she said. "I was only trying to help you." Alexa's eyes narrowed at the statement as they looked into Kara's.

A flicker of something other than anger showed for a second, but then was gone. "I don't need anyone's help," she said, and Rachel Rhodes barked out a laugh.

"Yeah," she said. "Listen to her. Alexa Knight is a one person show and will climb over anyone to get what she wants." The woman shook her head, unveiled hatred on her face. "I know from personal experience. If I were you, I'd dump her and go find someone with a heart."

Alexa's gaze jumped from Kara to Rachel. "She's not my girlfriend," Alexa snapped, before pausing. Kara watched the fighter gather herself before continuing in a calmer, but cold tone. "Ms. Roberts is nothing but a production assistant from ESPN working on the docuseries and means absolutely nothing to me." Not understanding exactly why, Kara felt the harsh words like a dagger in her chest. *Is that all I am?* she wondered. *Absolutely nothing in her eyes?* Wanting to get away from the whole scene, she took a step back from Alexa.

"Oh look," Rachel mocked. "You hurt her feelings, Alexa. How can you always be such a bitch?"

Clearly having enough of the small circus, Jess stepped into the middle of everyone. "That's it," she said while making a cut sign at Bobby. "The shows over." She glared at Rachel. "We have nothing to say to you so leave before I call security."

Rachel raised an eyebrow but started to back away. "Security? I have every right to be here," she said. "I'm queer too, remember? Although no one seems eager to give me a fancy award for it."

"Someone would have to like you for that to ever happen," Jess shot back, taking out her phone. "I'm confident the Equality League doesn't want their guests harassed."

Rachel held up her hands in surrender. "Okay, okay," she said. "We'll go." She gave them all a smile that Kara couldn't describe as anything but evil. "We can take this up again soon. In the octagon."

"I can't wait," Alexa said as Rachel and her pack walked away.

As soon as they were out of earshot, Jess turned to Kara. "And you?" she said. "What the hell was that? Give me one reason why I shouldn't fire you right now."

"Yes, what were you doing?" Bobby chimed in, sounding even more pissed than Jess. "That was ridiculous." Kara looked from one face to another. Everyone was angry and she had two choices—apologize or quit.

Focusing on Alexa, Kara squared her shoulders. "I'm sorry. I was truly only trying to defend you from her nasty attack," she said. "It won't ever happen again."

"You're right, it won't," Alexa said. "Because I don't need anyone for that. I'm definitely capable. You're fired."

Chapter Eight

Jumping the speed rope to the sound of classic eighties rock blasting through the gym's speakers, Alexa worked to loosen her muscles. At the start of every morning, she did rope drills as her warmup. After years of experience, the routine was second nature and while she skipped over the quickly moving target again and again, her mind wandered. They were four weeks into training camp and although her body felt good, mentally she wasn't as sure about her level of preparedness. Unlike previous fights, where all she would focus on was how she would maneuver and react in the ring, the upcoming bout with Rachel Rhodes felt different. *Is it because of how much I dislike her?* she wondered. *Or maybe the lack of respect I have for her as a fighter?*

Before she could unpack her feelings around the topic, she saw the film crew coming in the gym's front door. The familiar faces of Bobby, Eric, and Greg greeted her, but a new person was with them. A short, redheaded woman in a blue, Los Angeles Dodgers baseball cap and matching hoodie. Frowning, Alexa slowed her pace. *Did Jess arrange for a new sparring partner?* she wondered. That would be unusual without giving Alexa a heads up, plus the woman was too small if she was mimicking Rachel Rhodes. Then she realized the newcomer was carrying a camera case, and the connection dawned on her. *That is probably another production assistant.* A temporary one had worked with the team from time to time since the altercation at the awards' luncheon when she fired Kara. So far, ESPN hadn't permanently filled the position, but it didn't really matter to Alexa. The PAs steered well clear of her, obviously aware of how she terminated the last one.

After a quick series of double side swipes, she brought the rope to a stop, sweat running down her back, and watched Bobby lead the stranger to her. Normally, there weren't introductions, but it appeared the docuseries director was making an exception with the newest production assistant. "Good morning, Ms. Knight," Bobby said. "This is Maggie Frankel. She is the normal member of our crew and will be the PA for the rest of the shoot."

"I see," Alexa said, feeling a strange sense of disappointment. *Why?* she wondered. *It's not like I miss Kara. Right?* Still, the permanency of the new production assistant made her realize there was no chance for Kara to return. Pushing the unwanted thoughts aside, she nodded. "Good. Glad to have things settled once and for all."

Maggie held out a bottle of water, already playing her part. "Please let me apologize for being out. I'm afraid the appendectomy took a week longer to recover from than I hoped."

Alexa frowned, not sure why they were having the conversation. "I see," she said. "As long as you're up to full speed, I guess."

"Oh, I am," the new PA said. "And I also want to apologize for what happened with Kara Roberts. That was entirely unacceptable."

Tilting her head, Alexa studied the woman's face. She was entirely sincere, yet a part of what she said didn't sit right with Alexa. "I supposed you could say that. Perhaps unprofessional but under the circumstances, not completely unwarranted."

Maggie and Bobby looked at each other. "Normally the PA stays well out of the line of the camera," Bobby explained. "And certainly does not engage in the action."

Alexa pursed her lips. "I can understand that," she said. "Although unnecessary, she was only trying to defend me. Let's not forget that." *Protect me if I'm being completely honest about what happened,* she thought. Kara had stepped in front of Alexa to take on an experienced MMA fighter, seemingly without concern for her own wellbeing in the process. *Of course, she didn't know Rachel like I do or realize the crazy woman might have thrown a punch out of animosity. Especially because she thought Kara was my girlfriend.* Suddenly, Alexa wished she hadn't been so hasty to fire Kara.

Grabbing the short, white apron off the hook in the breakroom, Kara looked at the clock over the door. *Made it with a minute to spare,* she thought with a grin as she tied the strings around her red and black waitress uniform. Her life had been incredibly hectic the last month, and her part-time job working at Nostra Ristorante Italia was a key part. After being fired by Alexa, Kara threw herself back into her own project—the documentary she worked on for the last three years. Using another small loan from her ever patient parents and with tips from the side job waitressing, she pulled together the smallest crew possible to start doing interviews again.

All of which required her to get up at four a.m. to prep, spend the day filming, and then work a six-hour evening shift at the restaurant. Luckily, waitressing was how she worked her way through college, so she picked up the restaurant's routine in a day. If nothing else, carrying the huge platters of antipasti, rigatoni, and other Italian delicacies was building up her upper body strength. The only downside to working there was being reminded of Alexa every time she arrived. Out front of Nostra was where the black Camaro had almost run her down.

As angry as she was at the woman for kicking her off the project, Kara still found herself thinking of the green-eyed, dark-haired fighter. She had even taken up watching classic MMA battles on television with Brady on her day off. Although the unnecessary violence still disgusted her at times, she was learning the true skills needed to be successful. There was more to the sport than clubbing the other person. Tactical moves, reading an opponent's body language, and timing were all elements that required mastery at the championship level. *All combined with a ferocious spirit, of course,* Kara would remind herself. *It requires the fearless heart of a warrior.* In her opinion, Alexa was all those things and even though she would never see her in person again, Kara looked forward to the fight coming up. After getting to know Rachel Rhodes for only a few minutes, she wanted Alexa to kick her ass.

"Hey there, Roberto," Kara said as she stepped into the large, wonderful smelling kitchen to get the downlow of how the day was going before starting out in the dining room. "Has it been busy tonight?"

He shrugged a shoulder as he plated two servings of

delicious looking lasagna. Kara's stomach growled. Missing lunch in her rush to get everything done that day left her starving. It was going to be a long time until break when she could eat. A perk of working at Nostra was a free house meal every shift. Considering how good the food was, it was worth almost as much as the small salary.

Roberto handed her the plates. "Not too bad for a Sunday," he said. "These are for table three. Tell Sue she can take her break while you cover section A."

"You got it," Kara said, balancing the food easily as she used her hip to bump through the double swinging doors. As she moved between the many tables and booths, Sue met her. Kara held up the plates. "These are for your table, but Roberto says you can go on break." She nodded in the direction of the booth. "Anything special I should know?"

Sue shook her head. "Nothing unusual," she said. "They ordered a bottle of chianti, and I already took them their salads and bread."

"Perfect," Kara said, moving past her to get the hot food to the table. "See you in a few."

Falling to the mat after her sparring partner used a quick outside foot sweep to take her down, Alexa growled in frustration. "What the hell is wrong with you, Alexa?" her trainer shouted. "She telegraphed that move from a mile away."

Rolling to her feet, Alexa ripped at the Velcro securing her head guard. "Yeah, I realize that," she shouted back and slammed the leather mask to the ground. "I'm not feeling it today. Give me a break."

"Give you a break?" the trainer said, more surprise in his tone than frustration. "Since when do you ask for that?"

He shook his head. "Do you think Rhodes will be giving you a break if you're not feeling it?" Alexa shook her head, having heard enough. The entire training day had sucked. Her punches were slow, her kicks sloppy, and clearly her grappling was crap if she couldn't defend the world's easiest take down.

Alexa started to climb out of the ring. "That's it for today," she said, making the trainer stare at her open mouthed. "Don't look at me like that. Even I need an evening off." Without waiting for a response, she walked to the locker room. Alexa's problem wasn't physical, she could train for hours, but her mind kept wandering and she could guess her problem, but she didn't want to think about it. By the time she crossed the room to where her stuff was piled near the lockers, her cellphone was ringing. A glance at the screen made her groan. Jess. There was no way the timing was a coincidence. Tapping the connect button, she put the call on speaker while starting to pull at the white tape around her knuckles with her teeth. "Let me guess," she mumbled without even a hello. "He called you about my attitude."

"Hello, to you too, Alexa," Jess said. "Actually, he sent a text, but yes, there is concern. Talk to me." Blowing out a frustrated breath, Alexa didn't want to talk about anything with Jess, and especially not about what she felt at the moment. *She will go nuts if I tell her I am wound up over the new PA starting*, she thought. *Because it means Kara can't possibly come back.* She started to unravel the tape, not understanding her feelings. A month had passed and clearly Kara would have found a new job. *With a boss who isn't a jerk to her when she tries to help.*

Throwing the first wrap to the floor, Alexa started on the other hand. "I'm tired," she said, not completely lying.

The month of training wore her down, although that was sort of the point if she was going to be ready. "I need a night off." There was a pause on the phone, and Alexa could almost imagine the surprised look on Jess's face. Alexa never took a night off during training camp. Normally she was a completely dialed-in, laser-focused machine.

Jess cleared her throat. "Well," she started. "Then take the night off. Call Anthony and go out, blow off some steam, whatever it will take to get you back on track. Because, Alexa, you don't have time to lose focus right now."

"I know that," Alexa snapped, but liked the idea of sending a note to Anthony. They could go to dinner at her favorite restaurant, eat tons of great food, and he would bring her out of her funk. When Jess didn't respond right away, Alexa sighed. "I'm sorry. I didn't mean to talk to you like that. But you're right. I will text him."

"Good," Jess said. "Eat lots of carbs. Hell, break all the rules and have some wine. But get your focus back." There was another pause. "Is there something you're not telling me, Alexa?"

Both hands unwrapped, Alexa shrugged on her hoodie. "No," she lied. "Like I said. I'm tired. Tomorrow everything will be fine."

"Okay," Jess said. "Have a fun night. Tell Anthony hi." Then she hung up.

Picking up the phone, Alexa shot off a text to her twin. "Busy tonight?" she sent, and the reply came right back.

"Nope. You need something?"

"A break. Dinner out," she wrote, starting for the door.

"Nostra?"

She smiled. "Perfect."

Chapter Nine

Standing in front of the bathroom mirror at the end of her break, Kara wiped at the bit of marinera sauce on her shirt with a damp paper towel. Luckily, with the top being red and black, the glob's residue didn't show much. *I got a little overzealous eating that lasagna tonight,* she thought with a laugh. *But after smelling it first thing coming in, I had to have a plateful.* She would be lucky not to go into a carb coma, which wasn't good with still two hours left on her shift. The only good news was Nostra hadn't been particularly busy all night, and Roberto was even sending Sue home early. Not that Kara minded. Her coworker had kids and a husband to look after, and Kara could use the extra tips covering her tables.

Walking back into the dining room, she gave Sue a little wave. "I'm back," she said. "So, I can take over. Who's left?"

Sue pointed at tables two, five, and eight. "Just these three right now," she said. "Table two just arrived but he's waiting for someone. Four and five have their food but table five is probably ready to be cleared and offered dessert." She leaned in closer. "Table eight is a family of six and the kiddos are having a field day with the spaghetti. Sorry, but I'm leaving you with a mess to clean up."

Kara tapped the stain on her shirt. "I'm a mess already, so no worries," she said. "Have a great rest of your evening. Are you working Tuesday?"

Starting toward the break room, Sue nodded. "Yes. Are you?"

"I am. See you then," Kara answered and then focused on welcoming the new arrival to table two. Smiling as she approached, Kara saw the young, dark-haired man was looking over the menu, and he only glanced up when she arrived at the table. When his vivid, green eyes met hers, Kara nearly stopped, and only years of practice working with customers kept her smile in place. Matched with the dark hair and shape of his face, his resemblance to Alexa Knight was uncanny. *Could he somehow be related?* she wondered. *What are the odds of that?* Then, a horrible thought came to her. *Sue said he was waiting for someone... Alexa?*

Before she could say a word to him, his eyes flicked past her, and a smile lit up his face. With a mixture of dread and unexpected excitement, Kara looked over her shoulder only to see exactly who she predicted. The dangerous, sexy Alexa Knight walked straight at her. As their eyes met, Alexa slowed her steps. "What are you doing here?" she asked, sounding almost like her words were an accusation.

Kara crossed her arms. "I work here," she said. "Thanks to you actually."

A flush came to Alexa's cheeks, but she kept walking, passing by Kara to reach the table. "I see," was all she said as she sat, and it was all Kara could do to check her temper.

The last thing she needed was another outburst because of the woman and end up unemployed again.

Forcing herself to relax, she put her waitress face back in place. "Can I bring you two anything to drink?" she asked in a voice dripping with fake congeniality. "While you look over the menu?"

She watched as the man looked from Alexa to Kara and back again. "Okay," he said, drawing out the word. "Awkward, but I'll have a glass of the zinfandel."

"Make it a bottle," Alexa said, and both looked at her with surprise.

Kara frowned. "You can't do that," she said. "You're in training. I'm shocked they let you go out at all."

Alexa glared at her. "No one tells me when I can and cannot go out," she growled. "And since when do you care about my training?"

Kara opened her mouth to respond, only to realize her answer would reveal she spent time learning more about MMA training and fighting. There was no way she would let Alexa know that because of her, Kara was something of a fan. "Seemed logical," she said with a shrug. "Assuming you're even still training."

Still shaken from finding Kara at the restaurant, Alexa scowled. "Why wouldn't I be?" she asked. "Have you heard something?"

Shaking her head, Kara was already starting to walk away. "No," she answered a little too fast. "I don't follow your sport or anything." As if in a rush, she tossed a last look over her shoulder. "I'll grab that wine." Then she was gone. Alexa blinked, not sure what to make of the entire interaction.

Anthony leaned back in his seat. "Spill it," he said. "Who is that?"

"Nobody," she said, picking up the menu even though she learned the options by heart a long time ago. When she wasn't in training, Roberto at Nostra fed her often. Unfortunately, seeing Kara again had twisted her stomach and killed any appetite. The wine, however, sounded like a fantastic idea.

Clearly not ready to drop the subject, Anthony reached across the table to pull the menu away from Alexa's face. "You can try and hide behind that if you want," he said. "But I know it's bullshit. Ten bucks says you can recite it from memory." He tilted his head. "Seriously, who is she? I can't tell if you like her or hate her."

Alexa sighed, glancing around the make sure no one was close enough to hear her. "She's the production assistant I fired," she answered, and Anthony's eyes widened.

Then, he started to laugh. "That's why she looked familiar," he said. "She let you win during your pathetic game demo."

Snapping the menu shut, Alexa was about to tell her brother to stop laughing when the restaurant owner, Roberto, arrived at their table. "Alexa. Anthony," he said with a wide grin. "Where have you two been? I thought you forgot about me."

Unable to resist the man's warmth, Alexa smiled back. "Training is all," she said. "I had to dig under the fence to get to come here."

At that, Roberto gave her a belly laugh as he set the bottle of zinfandel on the table. "It will be worth the effort," he said, pulling a wine opener from his white chef's coat pocket. "The gnocchi is perfect tonight." Grabbing the bottle, he started to twist the spiral tip into the cork with a practiced hand. Alexa slid her glass in his direction, and in seconds, the wine was open. He gave her and Anthony a healthy pour. "May your life be like good wine, tasty, sharp and clear, and like good wine may it improve with time."

Alexa picked up her glass and acknowledged Roberto's blessing with a nod before taking a generous sip. "Excellent," she said, enjoying the flavor across her tongue.

Roberto slipped the corkscrew back into his pocket. "Of course," he said with another big laugh. "Now relax since it's your night off. Kara will bring you bread in a minute."

At the woman's name, Alexa drank again. Seeing Kara throughout the meal was not going to be easy. *Especially since I can feel this wine on my very empty stomach,* she thought as Roberto left the table. *I can't believe she works here.*

"What's going through your head, sister of mine?" Anthony said, lifting his own glass. "I can tell it's going a million miles an hour." Sipping, he kept his eyes on her over the rim. When she didn't answer immediately, he shook his head. "This isn't good. You're hung up on this woman, I can see it."

Shocked, Alexa leaned over the table to be closer to him. "Keep your voice down," she said. "That's the last thing I want advertised."

Anthony raised an eyebrow. "What? That you have a thing for her?"

Sighing, Alexa lifted her glass to take another much needed swallow, already thinking they might be ordering a second bottle soon. "Yes," she said. "Because I believe I do."

. . .

I'm going to walk out there with this food like I have a hundred times before, Kara thought as she picked up the order from under the warm lights. *And serve Alexa like I've never met her in my life.* Unfortunately, it would not be that easy. Taking them bread and remembering their order had been an ordeal as it was, especially while she and Alexa both seemed to be looking everywhere but at each other. Out of the corner of her eye, Kara saw the man with Alexa, clearly a relative, grinning from ear to ear. He appeared to enjoy the awkward tension between them. Finally, she fled the table with barely enough information to tell Roberto what to make. For once, Kara wished he wasn't so efficient, because Alexa and her guest's dinners were ready before she found a way to settle her nerves. *What is the big deal?* Normally, when Kara disliked someone, she took the highroad and killed them with kindness, but with Alexa it was not easy. The woman got under her skin so quickly. Just having her in the restaurant on her shift was irritating enough. *All the more reason to feed her and have her leave.*

Approaching the table, the man with the green eyes watched her. As she set down the heavy plates, he introduced himself. "It's a shame Alexa has no manners," he said. "But I'm Anthony, her twin brother."

Considering their likeness, that made perfect sense to Kara, and she smiled at him. "It's nice to meet you, Anthony," she said. "And it is a shame, I agree."

"Hey," Alexa said, irritation in her tone along with something else. "I'm sitting right here, so you two can knock it off." Kara watched the woman down the rest of her wine and reach for the bottle. When she picked it up, the thing was empty, and Kara realized why Alexa's voice sounded different. She was tipsy. "Well, that went quick." Alexa set the bottle down in front of Kara with a thunk. "We're going to need another one of these."

Unable to help herself, Kara raised an eyebrow. "You're sure that's a good idea?" she asked, not wanting to care about Alexa but for some reason couldn't help it. "Didn't you drive over here?"

Alexa's mouth dropped open. "Do you always go outside the lines of your job?" she asked with a snarl. "I mean, you're my waitress, not my mother." Taking a step back, Kara felt like she had been slapped. Every time she tried to do anything to help Alexa, it backfired. In fact, helping had the reverse effect, making the woman even more unpleasant rather than at all grateful.

Before Kara could think of a comeback, Anthony cleared his throat. "Okay, Alexa, be nice," he said and amazingly, his words took the wind out of the fighter's sails immediately.

Alexa nodded. "You're right. I'm sorry," she said to her brother before turning to Kara. Their eyes met and the fierceness Kara was used to seeing in the woman's eyes was tempered. *Not gone though*, she thought. *I wonder if it ever is. Is there any gentle side to her?* Before tonight, she would have said no, but seeing her with Anthony changed her mind a little. Everything about her radiated a caring for him. "Kara, I'm sorry to you too. And not only for tonight. I shouldn't have fired you." Alexa said, frustration on her face. "It's just..." Her words trailed off, but she didn't look away.

"Just what?" Kara asked, feeling like whatever Alexa said next could change everything between them.

"Just I can't stop thinking about you and somehow, even in the middle of all I'm trying to do, I want to get to know you better. Will you come back?"

Until that moment, Kara hadn't realized how much she felt the same. A part of her very much wanted to know Alexa better too and explore the chemistry between them. *But that doesn't matter,* she thought. *We missed our chance and now our lives are a million miles apart.* She slowly shook her head. "I'm sorry too, Alexa," she said, feeling a lump form in her throat. "But I can't. I just can't."

Chapter Ten

In the center of the sparring ring, Alexa's fists were a blur of motion. Wearing black leather gloves on her fists, they snapped outward to pound with a crack against the red and white punching mitts her trainer wore to protect his hands. As she moved around the ring following the motions of the man, Alexa slid from one stance to another with the grace of a dancer. A picture of balance, focus, and speed as leather smacked leather. When he swiped at her with a mitt as part of the sparring routine, she ducked and maneuvered out of reach, only to relentlessly start her attack again.

"Okay, that's good," the trainer said, stopping his movement. Alexa boxed on, making the man use the padded mitts to defend himself. "Hey! Ease up, Alexa."

As if superhuman, she threw punches even faster while letting out a primal scream of all the pent up emotion inside her.

"Alexa! Stop," she heard Jess yell over the sound of her roar. "You need to take a break. Now." Her chest heaving and sweat dripping from her hot skin onto the mat, Alexa stopped punching. The anger didn't subside though.

She glared at Eric where he stood beside the ring behind his camera. "Stop filming," she snapped. "I want a private conversation with my manager, if you don't mind."

"Go ahead and cut," Bobby said from nearby. "Everybody, let's stop for lunch." Alexa watched the crew leave, happy to see them go. *Good riddance*, she thought, sick of being under the scrutiny of a camera for so many weeks. They all but followed her into the showers. Bobby and Jess still begged to let them in her house for a more personal look, but Alexa said no way. Never. Her home was a sanctuary she would not give up. Just like the upcoming fight, she was eager for the filming to be over. *Both can't get here fast enough.* Retirement called to her, and although some people claimed her reaction was burnout, she was simply ready for some peace and quiet in her life.

Stepping between the ropes, Alexa climbed out of the ring to hop to the floor beside Jess. "That was quite a show," Jess said, not sounding happy or impressed. "Except you were fighting on raw emotion and that will probably get you beaten." Alexa grabbed a towel off the edge of the ring and rubbed her face to hide her reaction. She didn't need Jess to know how true the accusation was. Everything Alexa did seemed fueled by a raw intensity, but she didn't know how to stop what was happening. "I'd let it go, but you've been acting like this for over two weeks. Where is the cool and calculated warrior inside you?"

Alexa puffed out an angry breath, not in the mood for Jess's third-degree. "I am still the warrior I was always," she replied. "Everybody needs to let me handle this my way."

Jess raised an eyebrow, but otherwise looked unruffled by Alexa's tone. "Since when is your way to be a bitch to anyone who comes near you?" she asked. "Your trainers are frustrated, and you've scared the hell out of the film crew."

"Screw them," Alexa said, her heart rate slowing enough for her to try and rein in her temper. "I'm tired of having them on top of me all the time, Jess."

Crossing her arms, Jess sighed. "I know. This whole docuseries thing was a bad idea, but we made a deal with ESPN, and face it, you need to get ready for more cameras," she said. "We fly to Las Vegas in the morning to start a week on the promotional circuit."

Alexa groaned. "I know," she said. The pre-fight interviews, photo ops, and public appearances were all a part of being a champion-level fighter. All the people listed on the fight card would be a part of the show. Run-ins with Rachel Rhodes would be unavoidable, not to mention welcomed by the producers. Drama sold tickets and more Pay-Per-Views. "One last dog- and pony show." She could hardly wait.

"Thank you, Doctor Ross," Kara said after the microphone was turned off. Spending the last fifty-minutes interviewing the pediatrician, she was pleased the session went so well. "I know you're busy, so we will get out of here as quick as we can." Thomas, her cameraman, was already packing his gear. The man was a veteran of the business and her favorite to work with. With a steady hand and a great eye for lighting and angles, he served as her cinematographer, camera operator, and even editor from time to time. When a filmmaker was on a shoestring budget, having a multiskilled pro on the team made a huge difference. Plus, he was willing to work for less than union salary, so Kara could afford him.

Dr. Ross smiled. "It is my pleasure," he said, and Kara

felt the gentleness of his presence. *What an amazing bedside manner he has,* she thought. *I can't think of a more perfect person to work with the children.* He was also a great interview. All the emotion behind the job he performed day-after-day came through as he described helping his young patients. He even went so far as to include the ways he worked with the parents as they struggled to cope with their child's cancer diagnosis. "I appreciate all the hard work you are putting into this film. These are good stories to capture, and someday we will have a cure for leukemia."

"I know there will be," Kara said. "There is so much passion behind the research." She stood and held out her hand. Dr. Ross shook it in his warm one. "Thank you again."

"You're welcome," he said standing as well. "Do you need me to walk you out to the main hallway?"

Kara shook her head. "That's not necessary, Doctor," she said, having been in the pediatric wing many times over the last year interviewing medical staff, parents, and many of the children. "We know the way."

As they left the hospital a few minutes later, she heard Thomas' stomach growl. He grinned. "Sorry, but I'm starving," he said. "Want to hit up that little Greek place across the street after I stash this camera?"

Realizing she was hungry too after skipping breakfast to start the day early, Kara nodded. "I'll go grab us a table," she said, heading for the crosswalk. When she arrived, the restaurant was packed with people on lunch. Looking around for a table, she paused when her eyes landed on Bobby, Greg, Eric, and a redheaded woman she didn't know at a spot in the corner. Not sure if she wanted to say hello, Kara started to turn her back when she heard Eric call out. "Kara, hey."

With a small sigh, she looked over and smiled. "Hey, guys," she said, moving in their direction. "How're things?"

Bobby shook her head. "Oh, they're going," she said. "Thank God. One more week on the Knight shoot and we can move onto another gig."

Raising an eyebrow, Kara wasn't sure how to take Bobby's statement because she sounded very eager to be done. "Really?" she said. "That seemed to go fast."

The redhead snorted a laugh. "Not fast enough," she said, and Kara focused on her.

"Hi, I'm Kara," she said. "I don't think we've met."

"No, we haven't," the redhead said. "But I'm Maggie, the project's PA, and I think you filled in for me?"

Remembering the name, Kara nodded. "Right," she replied. "You got sick. Good to see you made it back."

"I guess," Maggie said with a shrug of one shoulder. "I think you were the lucky one to get out when you did. That Alexa is a real b—" Kara saw Bobby give Maggie a glare. "Sorry. But let's say, she's difficult to work with. Very difficult."

Sitting in her black Camaro, Alexa stared through the windshield at Nostra Ristorante Italia and tried to figure out her next move. *I should go home and take an ice bath is what I should do*, she thought, tapping the steering wheel. Never in her life had she faced such indecision as seemed to happen repeatedly with Kara Roberts. *I don't even know what I would do if I saw her*. Driving to the restaurant as if on autopilot, Alexa's only desire was to connect with the woman again. Now that she was there, she was almost paralyzed about what to do.

After Jess gave her an earful about how she was only fighting on instinct, Alexa realized the source of the emotion centered primarily around Kara. The woman's blatant rejection was a part, but only a small one. More of it stemmed from Alexa's inability to be nice to someone she felt emotions toward. Women were fun to take on casual dates, but never to let inside her walls. Yet, when Kara stood up to her that day at ESPN headquarters, there was a special spark Alexa had never felt before. Then, when Kara defended her, something about it slipped past Alexa's armor, and she could not shake the attraction. *So, what the hell do I do with it?*

While at the restaurant weeks before, asking Kara to drop everything and come back to filming the docuseries had bordered on arrogant. But like everything with the woman, she defied Alexa's thinking and did what she wanted. Unfortunately, the conversation made Alexa furious, even when Anthony tried to tease her out of it. Add in the effects of the wine, and Alexa had been downright rude. *But if I had kept myself together, I could have asked for her phone number to talk to her later,* she thought. *Then we could have at least gotten to know each other slowly.* Taking a deep breath, she knew what she had to do. March into the restaurant, apologize to Kara, and then ask where they could go from there.

Getting out of the car, she was almost in the door to the restaurant when a man and a woman came out. Stepping aside to let them pass, the man froze in front of Alexa after a few steps. "Oh wow," he said. "You're Alexa Knight, aren't you?" Alexa grit her teeth, not at all in the mood to talk to a fan. She was two seconds from brushing him off but before she could, the man held out his hand as if to make her stay in place. "Kara said you liked to come here, but I never thought I'd get this lucky. Can I go back inside and get something for you to sign?"

Feeling her heart skip, Alexa gave the fan her full attention. "Do you know Kara?" she asked, and the woman beside him nodded.

"Best friends since grade school," she said with a raised eyebrow, a knowing look in her eyes that made Alexa think Kara had talked about her at least. "Are you looking for her? Because she's off tonight." Alexa felt her hopes fall. She was leaving for Las Vegas in the morning and would have to wait to talk to Kara after she got back. Waiting for things to happen wasn't her strong suit. *Maybe I can ask her friends for her number?* she wondered. *Or is that going to sound super weird?*

Then she had an idea. "I am looking for her," Alexa said. "I wanted to invite her to be my guest at my fight in Las Vegas next weekend." She looked at the couple. "You're welcome to come as my guests too, if you'd like."

The man gasped. "You're serious?"

"Absolutely," Alexa said feeling a bit of hope her plan might work. Getting Kara to Las Vegas would be more than she could hope for. "Do you think she'd be interested?"

With a smile on her face, Kara's best friend nodded. "Oh definitely," she said. "We will all be there."

Chapter Eleven

As the plane circled the sparkling city that stood out against the browns of the desert around it, Kara wasn't precisely sure how she ended up in Las Vegas. When Annette sprang the invite on her, Kara's first reaction was "absolutely no way." Although she had to admit seeing the fight live would be exciting, being Alexa's guest didn't sit well with her. She wasn't even sure what that entailed. But Brady had begged, literally on his knees next to where Kara sat on Annette's couch.

Although his antics were in jest, there was a bit of truth to them—the man was dying to go to the fight. "Please, Kara," he said. "You have to understand the situation. This is the chance of a lifetime."

Annette sat on the couch beside her. "It would be one thing if you were her only guest," she added, using a more subtle approach. "But we will be there with you."

Kara raised an eyebrow at her best friend. "But you don't even like fighting."

"Well, no," Annette stated with a shrug. "But I love Las

Vegas. We will go for the weekend, spend some time by the pool, and see a Cirque du Soleil show too."

In the end, the double-team plea was too much for Kara to say no. Although not much of a gambler, she did like to sit at the cheapest blackjack table she could find and enjoy the free drinks. Plus, there was the opportunity to dress up a little and get swept away with the vibrancy of the city that never sleeps. So, after another few minutes, there she was getting off the plane at the international airport on the outskirts of Las Vegas. Brady and Annette were right behind her as they descended the escalator toward the main exit. "Wow, that's totally cool," she heard Brady say and Kara looked around, not sure what he was referring to among the mass of people and strategically placed slot machines.

Then her eyes landed on a man in a black suit standing at the doors holding a sign that said "Kara Roberts" on the front. "You've got to be kidding me," she murmured, suddenly putting two and two together. Jess, Alexa's manager, had surprised Kara with a phone call a couple of days before the trio left.

The woman hadn't been exactly rude on the phone, but her tone was definitely cool. "Have you decided to come to Las Vegas?" Jess had asked, and although Kara wasn't certain she was going until that moment, something about Jess's approach made her say yes.

"I'm coming for the weekend with my two other friends. Alexa invited them too," she said. "But I'm not expecting any special treatment."

"Being a guest of Alexa Knight on the weekend of her last championship fight entitles you to special treatment whether you want it or not," Jess said, her words clipped, making it clear the invitation was not to her liking. "Now, what flight are you on?" The rest of the conversation took no more than three minutes as Kara provided her details. The last thing she thought would happen was there would be a car waiting for them at the airport.

When Kara started to drag her feet, not sure she was ready to accept the generosity, Annette took charge. "We are Ms. Roberts party," she told the waiting driver who was more than helpful getting their bags into the black town car. Clearly, Annette and Brady planned to make the most of the VIP treatment.

As soon as they were underway, Kara frowned. "Do you know where we are staying?" she asked the man behind the wheel.

The driver nodded. "I have instructions to take you to the MGM Grand Hotel."

Kara blinked "Wait, what?" she said. "Where?"

"The MGM Grand," the driver repeated. "Is that not correct?"

"Oh man, this is going to be epic," Brady whispered, but Kara still wasn't following. Before she could ask for clarification, her phone rang. Looking at the screen, she saw Jess calling her.

Well, at least I can get some answers, Kara thought as she answered. "Hello," she said. "I'm assuming the driver was organized by you, but I think there's been a mistake."

"No mistakes have been made," Jess said. "Alexa has asked that you stay at the same hotel. I have made all the arrangements, including cancelling your other reservations, and booked you two suites."

Sitting under the bright lights, Alexa answered many of the same questions for the fourth time that day. "Ms. Knight, what will you do once you retire?" the pretty young woman interviewing her from some magazine Alexa couldn't remember the name of asked. The way the interviewer leaned into the questions, fixing her with a deliberate stare, made Alexa wonder if the woman was a little more into her subject than she should have been. *Any second now, she's going to lick her lips like I'm her next snack,* Alexa thought, forcing herself to keep a serious face. Laughing would be completely out of character. She was known for being cold, calculating, and dangerous. For one more circuit, she would play that part.

"Read a lot more books," she said, breaking from her usual stock answers. "And play a lot more chess." The interviewer blinked at her, clearly expecting something more imaginative and exotic. While she worked to recover herself, Alexa looked to see Jess standing at the edge of the lights waiting for her to finish. Feeling her heart beat a little faster at the prospect her manager was about to tell her Kara had arrived, Alexa decided to wrap up the interview before they were halfway into the Q & A. She had played her part dutifully all day. Enough was enough. "I'm sorry, but I'm feeling tired. As you can imagine, I don't want to overdo it, so can we wrap this up?"

"Oh," the pretty young woman said. "I guess. Yes, sure, of course."

"Thank you," Alexa said. "Was there one last question you had for me?"

The interviewer looked at the notecards on her lap before giving Alexa a smile with some heat behind it. "Yes," she said. "About your love life, if you're willing to answer."

Alexa narrowed her eyes, usually ducking any such questions, but curious. "What is it?"

"Is there any special someone in your life?"

Out of the corner of her eye, Alexa was pretty sure she saw Jess stiffen at the question. That made sense. Anything other than saying no would start a bit of a circus as the media tried to pin her down on a name. *And I don't have a name to give them,* she thought. *Not really. Just a hope that I might someday soon.* "No, and I am not looking," she said, making sure the next question out of the interviewer's mouth wasn't an invite to her room. She unclipped the microphone from her lapel and stood. "I've got to be going."

The interviewer stood too, clearly flustered from the abruptness of everything. "Okay," she said. "Well, I appreciate your time. And thank you from—"

Alexa didn't wait around to hear the rest as she approached Jess. "Is she here?" she asked, and Jess sighed.

"Yes," she said. "The driver picked them up and brought the three of them here to the resort." She shook her head. "You know how much I don't like any of this, right?"

Alexa smiled. "It is duly noted," she said. "But this is what I want."

"Well, it might all backfire anyway," Jess said, making Alexa frown.

She didn't like the sound of that. "Why?"

Jess fixed her with a look. "Because Kara is pissed at you for making all these decisions for her. If it wasn't for her friends, I imagine she would have turned around and left. I don't know what you are planning, but good luck." Jess paused as if not sure to continue or keep something to herself. Then, she shook her head. "And she had a message for you before she hung up on me."

Bracing herself, Alexa swallowed hard. "What was it?"

"She's not for sale."

. . .

Sipping the delicious blend of ice-cold cream, vodka, and Kahlua, Kara waited for her next two cards. So far, she was up a fair bit and quite pleased with her blackjack skills. The bit of a buzz from the multiple White Russians helped too. They had been enough to slow her racing thoughts over Alexa Knight. One minute Kara was angry, the next flattered, only to be irritated at herself for letting the woman pay for their hotel. Only after some well executed debate by Brady and Annette was she persuaded to stay in Las Vegas at all. At the moment though, dressed in her little black cocktail dress and winning at blackjack, she was glad they stayed. She would deal with Alexa later. *Assuming I even see her*, she thought. Although the woman arranged the driver and rooms for them, everything went through Jess. So far, the fighter hadn't reached out directly at all. *And why does that make me feel disappointed?* It was all so frustrating.

Suddenly, a new player joined the table. As he sat in the number one spot, his eyes found hers and the green of them made Kara gasp. Alexa's brother Anthony sat across from her. Clearly seeing her response, he smiled. "Hi," he said. "Nice to meet you again."

Recovering from her surprise, Kara raised an eyebrow. "Why do I think this is not an accident?" she asked. "I mean, do you really play at the cheap tables?"

He laughed and the sound was so warm and carefree it made Kara smile in response. "Fair enough," he said. "I did see you and decided to say hello. Our last interaction was, well, a little awkward."

"You mean because your sister threw a tantrum when I said I wouldn't come back to the shoot?" Kara said, watching the dealer place cards in front of everyone seated at the table. When he came to Kara, he put one card face-down only to follow it the next time around with an ace of hearts. Excited, she looked at the hole card, finding a queen of hearts. *How appropriate,* she thought and turned it over. *Blackjack.*

"Nicely done," Anthony said to Kara, peeking at his own hole card before looking at the dealer. "Hit me." While the hand played out, Kara studied the young man. His resemblance to Alexa was uncanny. Even though it was impossible for the two to be identical twins because of their different genders, they might as well have been. After Anthony busted his hand, he returned his attention to her. "Thank you for agreeing to come to Las Vegas. It means a lot to my sister."

Kara shrugged, liking the words but not ready to reveal her feelings. "I would have no way to know," she said. "I have yet to even hear a word from her, let alone see her."

"Well, I think that's about to change," Anthony said, looking in the direction of sudden sounds of excitement. Glancing over, Kara saw people swarming around the entrance. The man to Kara's left stood, bobbing up and down as if to get a better view. Only his pile of chips appeared to keep him rooted at the table.

"Is that her?" he asked no one in particular, only to have the crowd slowly part to reveal not only Alexa Knight, but also Rachel Rhodes standing face to face. Although Kara couldn't make out the words, the two women were obviously exchanging insults. *Oh shit,* Kara thought at the same time she heard Anthony say the two words out loud. In a flash, he was moving away from the table to go help his sister while Kara stood to do the same. She only hoped between the two of them they could diffuse what was certain to be a disaster.

Chapter Twelve

Waiting for Rachel Rhodes to raise her fists first, Alexa's whole body thrummed like a live wire. She came to the gaming floor because Anthony sent her a text that Kara was there playing blackjack. "And looking hot," he had added. The last thing Alexa planned was to run into her opponent for tomorrow's fight. What was supposed to be a quiet encounter with her guest had turned into a circus when Rachel and her posse descended upon her. A large group of fans, continuing to grow, surrounded them and only a few security guards kept them at a reasonable distance.

"Look at this," Rachel mocked, a wry smile on her face. "The great champion actually honors the masses with an appearance outside the ring." The woman had a point. Alexa rarely made public appearances if she wasn't required to do so. In all her years and fights in Las Vegas, she never gambled at any of the tables. In fact, wasting money on games of chance wasn't her style, period. She was only interested when true skill was involved, and the odds were equal. Like MMA fighting. When Alexa didn't answer, Rachel Rhodes snorted. "What? No comment, oh great one?"

Alexa ground her teeth. "Not to you," was all she said. She had plenty more comments in mind but knew dozens of phones were videoing her every move. "It would be a waste of my time."

Rachel bristled at the insult, only to have her eyes suddenly widen. "Oh, now I see why you've come out of your cave," she said with a dark laugh. "Your girlfriend is here."

Shit, this is a disaster, Alexa thought as she turned to see where Rachel pointed and everyone in the crowd followed her gaze. Looking furious, Kara stood at the edge of the gathering, staring straight at her. Any hopes Alexa had of making a smooth, casual approach were crushed. *The woman will never speak to me again after this. Especially since her picture is about to go viral on social media with that accusation.* Before Alexa could say a word to dispute the claim, Kara strode in their direction. Dressed in a sexy, short black dress that fit her body perfectly, her chin up and eyes still connected with Alexa's, there was no way to tell what she was about to do. *What if she slaps me?* The thought seemed very feasible. *And in a way, I guess I deserve it by basically forcing her to come here. The media will love it.* "Kara," Alexa started when the woman reached her side, hoping to find words to apologize for the mess she put them in.

"Don't talk," Kara snapped before shifting her eyes to Rachel. "And you." She waved her hand at the fighter and the groupies around her. "What are you? In high school? This is like a scene out of some lousy mean girls movie. Ridiculous."

Her mouth dropping open, Rachel stared in complete

surprise. Alexa wanted to laugh at the look on her shocked face so badly she had to cover her mouth with her hand, but that didn't stop others. A ripple of amusement went through the crowd. Nothing Kara could have said would have been more insulting. Unfortunately, after the shock, Rachel lunged at Kara and Alexa stepped forward to shield her. Only the sudden arrival of more security guards from the fight crew, led by her brother of all people, kept the two women from coming to blows.

Anthony grabbed Alexa and Kara's arms by the elbow to pull them out of the mess. "Get out of here," he whispered to the two of them, pushing them in the direction of the elevators. "And don't show your faces again until the weigh-in tomorrow." Still angry, but listening to her brother's sound advice, Alexa felt Kara take her hand and lead her further away. When they reached the bank of elevators, one was being held open by another member of the fight event's security. The button for the penthouse was lit.

In a moment, she and Kara were alone inside the car. "That was insanity," Alexa said. "I am so sorry—"

"Shut up," Kara said, her eyes snapping with fury. "And kiss me."

As crazy as her world had suddenly become, Kara was never more turned on. Her body felt alive with intense emotions—anger, passion, need. For a fleeting moment, she thought Alexa would refuse her direct request, and then their bodies were crashing together, mouths hungry for each other. Letting the stronger woman push her back until she was pressed against the side of the elevator, Kara thought she might explode with desire. Every fantasy she had been denying, every hot dream making her wake up with an ache, every time she touched herself thinking of Alexa, all threatened to engulf her.

When she felt Alexa's hands slide down her body to the hem of her dress, Kara couldn't hold back a moan. Breaking the kiss, Alexa slid her lips along Kara's chin to her neck, leaving a blaze of heat with every touch. Kara's body quivered in response and when the fighter's hand slid under her dress to touch the inside of Kara's thigh, she gasped. "Oh God," she said. "I can't believe how much I want you to touch me." Feeling a pulse of arousal between her legs, the lacy thong she wore was soaked with her desire.

"Do you want that?" Alexa murmured against the bare skin at the base of Kara's neck. "Where?"

Kara groaned, knowing the woman teased her to make the wanting more intense. "Everywhere."

When Alexa feathered her fingers across Kara's throbbing mound, she jerked from the bolt of heat that shot through her. "Here?" Alexa teased and Kara answered by pressing her hips forward against the woman's hand.

"Yes," she breathed. "More."

"Mmm," Alexa hummed, sliding a finger under the material at the center of Kara's legs. "Here?" Then, Alexa moaned. "You are so wet."

Kara believed her, melting with the touch of Alexa's fingertip sliding incredibly slowly over her throbbing clit. "Stop teasing me," she cried. "You're driving me wild."

"If I give you what you want, will you promise to still come to my room?" Alexa whispered in her ear, her hot breath making Kara squirm. All the woman could do was nod. "I want to hear you promise."

Still nodding, she would do anything to have Alexa make her come. "Yes, I promise," she said, starting to move her hips as Alexa began to stroke her with two fingers. "Please don't stop."

"I won't stop," the woman said, her own voice thick with arousal. As turned on as Kara was, she could tell Alexa's control was slipping. Finding her lips again, she let the fighter conquer her mouth with her hungry tongue while they rocked together. Thinking she would go insane if she didn't come soon, Kara cried out when Alexa slid two fingers inside her. The feeling of being filled was exquisite as the woman pushed deeper, only to slide back to her opening and tease Kara's clit with her thumb. An ache like Kara hadn't felt before started to build in her. The intensity of being in the elevator with doors that could open at any second, certain they were on a security camera somewhere, pressed against the wall by a powerful woman, feeling her drive her fingers inside her over and over... Kara started to whimper.

Moving her hips in a rhythm with every stroke, she began to shake. Intensity built in her as the orgasm threatened to rip her apart. Alexa kissed her, thrusting her fingers in and out, while holding Kara in place against the wall. Unable to control it another moment, Kara screamed against Alexa's mouth as a wave of ecstasy roared through her body making her come.

With a sigh of utter contentment, Alexa rolled over in the soft-as-a-cloud, king-sized bed to look at the digital clock on the nightstand. The numbers glowed eleven-twenty-seven p.m. A smile played across her face. That meant she and Kara were wrapped up, pleasing each other repeatedly for more than two hours. She stretched her neck from side to side, feeling a little tightness from use, but nothing she couldn't handle. The bit of temporary discomfort was well worth it, and she savored the taste of Kara still on her lips.

Looking at her partner, naked and tangled in the sheets, the woman was fast asleep, clearly spent from all the intense sex. Her curly hair was a mess and her lips rosy from all the contact, only making her look even more irresistible. Moving closer, Alexa kissed the woman lightly on the forehead before slipping silently out of the bed. Naked herself, she padded to the penthouse's lavish on-suite bathroom to find a thick, white robe with a little MGM embroidered in gold on the front before going to the living room to find her phone. Although sleep was important, she had a couple of phone calls to make. Jess, for one, who Alexa saw had called her repeatedly and sent multiple texts. Never a good sign. Rather than read them all, she dialed her manager's number.

"Where are you?" was the first thing Jess said when the call connected, not wasting time with a hello. "I've been trying to get ahold of you all night."

Not surprised by Jess's attitude, Alexa sank onto the large, brown leather sectional couch. "In my hotel room," she said. "I've been here since the mess with Rachel Rhodes downstairs took place."

There was a pause on the phone. "I'm guessing you've not been alone all this time?"

Alexa was unable to keep from smiling as she thought of how amazing the night had been so far. "No," she answered. "Kara is here."

"She's still there?" Jess asked, sounding surprisingly less irritated than Alexa thought she would be.

"Yes," she answered. "Asleep in the bedroom. I don't plan to wake her." *Unless it's to have more fabulous sex, of course,* she thought, trying to decide how much more her body could take less than forty-eight hours before such an important fight. Wearing herself out would be too easy and she had to be somewhat responsible. People counted on her. "What's going on with social media? I can hardly imagine."

Jess snorted a laugh. "Oh, it's a three ring circus for sure. Not all bad for us though," she said. "Rachel looks like a massive bitch, and Kara's zinger plays really well. The fans love her, which leads us to a real problem."

"What?" Alexa asked, bracing herself for the bad news.

"Aside from her defending you, there are a bunch of pictures of the two of you holding hands while you get on an elevator," Jess answered. "Understandably, the entire MMA world is trying to figure out who your girlfriend is about now."

Shit, Alexa thought. *I hope Kara is ready for all that publicity.* Using some of her influence, she could try to protect her somewhat, but it was too big of a story to completely squash. Then she had a horrible thought and knew Jess was about to be very upset with her. "Jess," she said. "Don't kill me, but you need to get the security footage from that elevator and make it disappear."

Another pause, much longer than before. "You're kidding me, right?" Jess asked. "You're not that stupid."

"We were... well," she said, unable to keep from smiling even more no matter how bad of a decision it might end up being. "Caught up in the moment."

Jess swore over the phone, using words Alexa hadn't heard her use often. "I'll get my hands on it," she finally calmed down enough to say. "But it might cost you a small fortune to make it go away."

"Oh, trust me," Alexa said, feeling heat run through her body as she remembered the sounds Kara made as she came. "It was worth it."

Chapter Thirteen

When Kara found Annette and Brady outside the buffet at the Tropicana waiting for her, she was met with her best friend's open arms. "Come here," Annette said. "Are you okay?" Appreciating the much needed embrace, Kara hugged her back for a moment before answering.

Letting go, she honestly wasn't sure of the answer. "I think so," she said with a bit of a laugh. "I mean, security had to sneak me out the hotel's backdoor because reporters waited at the front door."

Brady shook his head. "Wow," he said. "Just wow. You're a celebrity now."

Raising her eyebrows, Kara wasn't sure she would go that far. "Brady, come on," she said, and the man started to show her his phone screen when Annette interceded.

"Hold on with all of that," she said. "Let's get a table and find food. I'm starving."

Liking the sound of Annette's plan and not at all sure she wanted to see Brady's phone, Kara nodded. "Lead on," she said, and Brady fell into step beside her as they made their way to the check in station.

"I hear they have made-to-order omelets to die for," he said, rubbing his stomach. "And after all the rum and cokes I had last night, I need something greasy to take the edge off."

"Ew," Annette said, giving her boyfriend's arm a slap, only making him laugh as they followed the hostess to their table. In a matter of minutes, they were seated in a corner booth, each with a heaping plateful of breakfast foods. "I don't know why I always take so much food."

Examining her own half dozen random selections, Kara wasn't sure either. "Part of being in Las Vegas," she said with a shrug before picking up a fork to attack the problem. "Did you two have fun last night?"

"Not as much fun as you," Brady said around a mouthful of his eggs, ham, and cheese omelet. "So, is Alexa Knight really your girlfriend?"

"Shhh," Annette said, glancing around. "Let's not be super obvious. Kara had to sneak over here to meet us."

Brady shrugged. "Okay, you're right," he said. "People might start lining up for selfies."

With a scoff, Kara picked up her orange juice. "Let's not get carried away, Brady," she said. "I'm pretty sure no one will care I'm sitting here."

"Oh yeah?" Brady said, picking up his phone from the table. He tapped at the screen and then held it for her to see. "I think over a million views is a good start to being famous."

"Oh shit," was all Kara could think to say, letting her mouth drop open. The YouTube video was a great shot of her in the middle of the crowd that gathered last night. Whoever the amateur cameraman was, he had talent, catching her angry strut to stand between Alexa and Rachel

Rhodes before zooming in on her. "And you," she watched herself say to the sneering face of Rachel. "What are you? In high school? This is like a scene out of some lousy mean girls movie. Ridiculous." The woman's dumbfounded reaction was indeed priceless, making Kara grin as she watched the rest of the scene unfold. *A few too many White Russians almost got me punched in the face by a pro MMA fighter,* she thought. *Or was I standing up for Alexa because I care about her?* She had a feeling the answer was a little of both.

The video ended and before Kara could comment, Brady held up a finger. "Wait," he said. "There's more." After a second, he had queued up a second video of Alexa and Kara fleeing the scene, holding hands, as they dashed into a waiting elevator.

God, I hope that's as far as the video goes, she thought and then had a sick thought. "Brady, please tell me that's the last of video of me and Alexa last night," she said, and Annette covered her friend's hand.

"Don't worry," she said. "There's a hell of a rumor going on around your trip to the penthouse. But no video."

Kara swallowed hard. "And what is the rumor exactly?"

Brady shrugged. "That you had the ride of your life."

In the locker room, Alexa sat patiently on the massage table while her trainer applied white tape to her fists. He moved with practiced hands as one strip was applied after another. In a few minutes, Alexa was going to walk out and perform a final sparring workout in front of the media and a few hundred VIP fans. The display was nothing but a simple walk-thru of a few strikes and some grappling and was the last step aside from the ceremonial weigh-in before the fight night itself.

"And you're not epically pissed off at me?" Alexa asked, looking at Jess where she leaned one shoulder against the wall. "Because you're kind of freaking me out with this calm attitude."

Jess crossed her arms. "Epically pissed?" she replied. "No. But don't think I'm going to ever forget this. Cleaning things up after your stunt last night has been a royal nightmare."

"How does that feel?" the trainer asked Alexa. She punched one fist and then the other into her palms. The pressure was tight, but exactly as much as she liked.

"Feels good," she said, opening her fist so he could slide on the slightly padded and fingerless leather gloves she would wear over the tape. They were designed to protect her hands yet allow her the dexterity she needed to grab her opponent in a clinch. It was the only protection other than a rubber-like mouthguard that she would have in the fight tomorrow. Turning back to Jess, she sighed. "I know you moved mountains, and I appreciate all of it."

Once the trainer finished his tasks, Jess stepped away from the wall. "Can you give us a few minutes of privacy?" she asked the man. Alexa's small film crew had already left to set up for the sparring shots. "I need to talk to Alexa before she goes out."

"You bet," he said, gathering up his tape and supplies. "Meet you out there."

Not looking forward to whatever bad thing Jess was undoubtably going to say, Alexa watched him leave before meeting her manager's eye. "Okay," she said. "Let me have it."

"Have what?"

Alexa tilted her head while lifting a dark eyebrow.

"Don't pretend you're not about to give me hell for last night."

With a shrug, Jess stepped closer. "Actually, I'm not," she said. "But I am worried. Do you know what you are doing?" *Do I?* Alexa thought before answering. *Kara had consumed her thoughts for weeks. Last night was only a cumulation of pent up emotions finally coming out.* She smiled. *And wow did we.* "You're smiling so I'm assuming you're thinking there's nothing to worry about with your fight tomorrow." Jess narrowed her eyes. "Or you're thinking about having sex in the elevator."

"Honestly?" Alexa said. "I'm thinking I feel better than I have in months." She hesitated, analyzing her feelings for Kara. "Maybe even longer than that."

Jess didn't respond for a minute as she studied Alexa's face. "You really like her, don't you," she said. It wasn't a question, and she didn't wait for Alexa to answer. "I guess we will know tomorrow."

Rolling her shoulders and twisting her neck side to side, Alexa felt nothing but good. She was ready to beat Rachel Rhodes and put the final stamp in the record books of her championship career. "Everything will be fine," she said, standing. "We get through the grandstanding crap tonight at the weigh-in and then tomorrow it's game time." She wrapped an arm around Jess's shoulders. "One last rodeo. You and I made it this far, and I don't plan to let anything ruin our finale."

While she stood near the front of the room, Kara watched the main stage while the announcer rattled off another series of names, fight classes, and bodyweights. The tension was thick in the room as fighter after fighter approached the scale, only to have things turn worse when the pairs of opponents faced each while the cameras flashed. So far no one had come to blows, but she was sure it could happen at any second. Some of the fighters appeared to truly hate each other. *Or is that all an act for more publicity?* she wondered, although she thought the dislike between Alexa and Rachel Rhodes was very real. *I know I sure don't like her.*

Even though she was sandwiched between Brady and Annette, reporters continued to circle. Only Jess, who stood with Kara's group kept them at bay. Whenever one dared approach with a camera or microphone, Alexa's manager put up a hand to stop them. "No comment," she said. "Leave her alone." Even though Kara wasn't a big fan of people speaking on her behalf, in the current case, she was all for it. Ever since she entered the arena building, people stared and whispered, often raising their phones to take a picture or video. Kara could have done without all the new attention.

The only reason she was at the weigh-in was to support Alexa. Although they hadn't been able to meet anywhere all day, they sent text messages nonstop. Both agreed they only had to get through the next twenty-four hours. Once the fight was over and the excitement settled, they could find time to be alone, get to know each other, and see where things were headed between them. All Kara knew for sure was she was incredibly attracted to Alexa, and once she admitted that fact to herself, realized she had been since the encounter with the near car collision months ago. When Alexa asked her to come to the weigh-in, Kara hadn't hesitated. Aside from knowing Brady would be in heaven, she wanted to see Alexa and show her support.

A new energy swept through the room as the final pair of fighters were announced. "Oh boy, here we go," Brady murmured, and before Kara could ask any questions about what he meant, the announcer was calling forth the challenger—Rachel Rhodes. Like with the others, the woman came from the side of the stage, strutting with confidence, grinning as if she wasn't afraid of anything. When people cheered, she pumped her fists before pulling her red hoodie over her head. As she reached the stage, she stepped out of her sweats and was in nothing but a black and red sports bra and matching skintight athletic shorts. Rachel Rhodes was even more toned than Alexa. Her muscles rippled as she took the scale, flexed for the camera, and was declared ready for the fight. Suddenly, her gaze landed on Kara and when their eyes met, the woman winked.

Before Kara could even react, a wave of excitement came from offstage as the announcer was suddenly booming the words, "The reigning, the defending, undisputed bantamweight champion of the world! Alexa Knight!" Like her opponent, Alexa walked toward the stage but there was no showboating. Her green eyes were focused straight ahead while she peeled off her black zipper hoodie. A tingle ran through Kara as she thought of the woman's body on hers last night. Powerful, yet gentle too, a delicious combination, and she could not wait to get more. As she watched, Alexa stripped to her black and green sports bra and shorts, performed her weigh-in, and moved to stand face to face in front of Rachel. Her eyes filled with menace, Alexa pinned the challenger with her stare. Rather than act afraid, Rachel raised her fists as she smiled and moved closer. For a moment, Kara thought she might kiss Alexa they were so close, and then the announcer used his hands to push them apart. Hate for each other rolled off them in waves. Whatever happened tomorrow night, Kara recognized the fight would be epic.

Chapter Fourteen

As the music thundered through the darkened coliseum, it shook the floor under her feet, as Alexa made her last walk down the long corridor leading to the ring. Every note of the melody, ever word of the lyrics, resounded within her. Somehow her fighting theme song touched her more tonight than ever before. She had picked the music years ago, when she fought for the bantamweight title, and it was only fitting to listen to it at the end of her amazing career—*Legends are Made*. Around her walked her entourage, many who were with her from the beginning, and screaming fans hung over the edge of the seats to get a look at her as she passed by. Colored spotlights pulsed with the beat as they blazed around the space in every direction until all landed on her. Cameras captured her every step. Hands reached from the crowd wanting to touch her. Everything was organized chaos. *Will I miss this?* she wondered. *The rush of going into battle...* There was no time to decide. Ahead of her, in the octagon where she would fight, Rachel Rhodes already waited.

While the trainers and referee helped her with final

preparation before she entered the ring, Alexa focused on the task ahead. Her training, her pain, her sacrifices—all would pay off over the next twenty-five minutes. Five rounds of war. *Unless I can take her out early*, Alexa thought. *I know her strengths, but more importantly, I know her weaknesses. And she mistakenly thinks she knows mine.* Finally ready, she moved to enter the ring, and out of the corner of her eye, she saw her brother and Jess. They sat where they always did—front row, seats closest to her corner, but tonight she noticed something else. Kara was with them. Only through sheer willpower did Alexa steer her thoughts away from the woman and back to the job in front of her. Perhaps they shouldn't have brought her with them, but she guessed Anthony decided on it, instinctively knowing her presence was what his sister would want. Alexa couldn't deny having Kara close made her happy. In her mind, Kara was part of a bright future ahead of her. *So let me finish this first and be done.*

Taking the steps to the ring, Alexa gave a quick bow of respect and humility to the space where she would fight. The MMA octagon had changed her life and she was grateful, but when her eyes lifted, all she saw was Rachel Rhodes pacing the fence across from her. There was no cocky grin or grandstanding. The woman was all business, and even though Alexa knew she could beat the other fighter, she would not take her lightly.

Walking the fence on her own side of the octagon, she shrugged her shoulders to try and loosen the tension in her muscles while the ring announcer's voice boomed through the microphone. The fight was the main event of the evening, and as he set the stage for the audience, she looked through the cage's netting to find Anthony. Like with her song being a part of every championship fight and every victory, so was making eye contact with her brother beside the ring. Their green eyes, so eerily alike, held and she saw nothing but confidence in her twin's look. Every ounce of him believed in her, and because of it, Alexa believed in herself. After he gave her a slight nod, she glanced to his left, and she saw her manager, Jess. Calm, and reassuring as always. The start of every important fight was the same, but tonight there was one difference. Tonight, Kara sat beside Anthony, and Alexa could not mistake excitement flickering in her eyes. The woman may not have been an MMA fan before, but she was tonight. Only the sound of the announcer saying her name made Alexa turn away from the three people who meant so much to her.

While the crowd roared at her introduction, Alexa cleared everything from her mind but how she would attack her opponent. Finally, the referee waved them forward to touch gloves in a sign of sportsmanship, and when Rachel Rhodes refused, the crowd went crazy with cheers and boos. Not everyone was there to support Alexa, but she was used to that. People liked to see champions fall. *Not tonight*, she thought, preparing herself to attack when the referee's hands clapped. *It's time to finish this.*

"Fight."

Kara barely heard the referee in black yell at the top of his lungs. The crowd sounded ready to explode around her, their roar making the air reverberate. With the word, Kara watched Alexa spring from her side of the octagon, using her signature aggressive style Kara had grown accustomed too after watching all her fights. Only Rachel Rhodes was as quick and already waiting at the center of the ring. Unlike so many of Alexa's other foes who tried to avoid the aggressor's initial attack, this opponent seemed to welcome the charge as the two clashed in a rally of strikes. Everyone watching shot to their feet. Kara covered her mouth as the two women traded blows, neither willing to back up. *This is going to be over in seconds,* she thought. *But I'm not sure who's winning.*

Just when it seemed impossible they could both still be standing, Alexa landed a lightning-quick, outside calf kick, sending Rachel sprawling onto her ass. Kara, with thousands of people around her, screamed for Alexa to attack only her opponent was too fast, snapping back to her feet. The two faced each other again, but this time they circled, fists raised, looking for an opening. Just when it seemed neither knew what to do, the audience gasped when, in a flash, Alexa kicked Rachel Rhodes in the abdomen, sending her down to one knee. Like before, the minute Alexa tried to pounce, the other fighter jumped back to her feet and met the champion's attack with punches of her own.

As seconds ticked by, the women continued with bouts of circling, accented with flurries of punches and kicks from both sides. From her limited experience watching MMA with Brady, Kara knew a fighter won points by landing strikes and controlling the ring. So far, she couldn't tell who scored more or even who did the most damage. Flinching every time a punch or kick landed on Alexa, she worried—*is she doing enough? How much damage can she take?* The action was frustrating to watch. Rachel Rhodes refused to be overwhelmed every time Alexa tried to drive forward, while Alexa fought off every attempt at a takedown. Everyone in the coliseum knew the last thing Alexa wanted to do was to wrestle. Her strength was in how hard she could strike.

Heart pounding, ears ringing, and fists clenched from

anxiety, Kara was totally focused on the battle playing out before her. When someone suddenly grabbed her forearm, and started to pull her off balance, she whipped her head around. "What the hell," was on her lips until she realized it was Anthony who had ahold of her. He stared into her eyes, confusing Kara with his distraction when the outcome of the fight was still uncertain. Opening his mouth as if to tell her something, a bubble of startling, bright red blood formed on his lips. With a cough that shook his entire body, Anthony sprayed crimson across Kara's face before he started to sag toward the floor. He kept using Kara's arm for support, but she couldn't hold him. "Help!" Kara yelled. "Somebody help."

As another of her high kicks was deflected, Alexa's frustration mounted. Rachel Rhodes proved to be more of a mental challenge than she expected. All through her training, she knew the fight would be tough, but it was like the woman anticipated everything Alexa wanted to do. Back when they were sparring partners it made sense that Rachel would learn how Alexa liked to fight, but that was years ago. Working with her trainers, Alexa had made sure to consider that possibility by changing up her delivery. Apparently, the strategy wasn't working, and with every blocked blow or missed kick, Alexa grew angrier. Especially when her opponent answered each attack with a counter of her own. So far, to Alexa, it felt like they had traded strike for strike, and her only choice to get ahead was to wrestle Rachel Rhodes down to the canvas. It was the last thing anyone, especially the challenger, would expect.

Letting Rachel Rhodes press forward again, Alexa watched for her moment. All she had to do was drop her hands low to lure the woman in. When her opponent made the mistake of throwing a looping cross, Alexa jerked out of the way. Rachel Rhodes hit nothing but air, and the dramatic movement made her slip off balance. Knowing the mistake was her chance, Alexa dove under the swing and into her, grabbed her hips, and pushed the other fighter over backward. She heard the crowd's roar at the surprise attack. Still, Alexa wasn't going to make the mistake of thinking she could hold an experienced grappler like Rachel down forever, so she looked toward her corner for advice. There was no rule against them yelling directions to her, yet what she saw made her blink with confusion. A huddle of people had gathered near the ring. Someone was on the floor being tended to and when the mass separated enough to let the fight doctor squat down, in a split second, she realized the person was her brother.

Unable to speak right because of her mouthguard, when she yelled the word "Anthony" it went unrecognized. Clearly seeing Alexa was distracted, Rachel squirmed for leverage, lifting with her legs to push Alexa off, before rolling on top of her. Realizing what was happening, but no longer caring about the fight, Alexa tried to wriggle away when Rachel Rhodes punched her in the face with first her right hand and then her left. Dazed, Alexa couldn't even form the word "stop" as the blows rained down. Lifting her arms to try and ward off the damage, the challenger continued to batter her until finally the referee dove in to stop the fight.

The second she was free, and Rachel Rhodes raced around the ring, screaming her victory cry, Alexa's fight crew was at her side helping her sit up. Even with blood filling her mouth and one eye swelling so fast it made her blind on that side, Alexa tried to get up. "Anthony," she mumbled around the mouthguard before falling back to the canvas. "Where's Anthony?"

"The doctor is with him," her trainer said. "They are taking care of him. Let us take care of you."

Alexa tried to shrug them off. "No," she said, finally pulling out her mouthguard. "I need to see him. Get me up." Knowing better than to continue to argue, her trainer and cutman lifted her to her feet. At the same time, the referee motioned for her to come stand beside him so he could declare the winner. Rachel Rhodes hopped from foot to foot beside him, a giant grin on her face as she stared at Alexa. Not caring about ceremony, Alexa turned her back and limped toward the exit.

Suddenly, Rachel Rhodes was jumping past her to get in her face. "Where are you going?" she snarled. "Too embarrassed to watch me get my hand raised?"

Alexa started to push the woman aside, only wanting to be with her brother. Nothing else mattered. "Get out of my way."

At contact, Rachel Rhodes pushed her back and only because the referee and other people in the ring jumped to stop them did a second fight not break out. "Go ahead," the other woman spat at her as she strained against the many arms that held her. "Run away, you coward. But you got what you deserved."

Chapter Fifteen

Pacing in her hotel room, Kara grabbed at her curly brown hair. "They should have stopped the fight," she said, whirling on Brady who sat beside Annette on the small couch. "Right?"

Annette nodded. "Absolutely," she said, and Kara wasn't sure if she meant the words or was only trying to calm her down.

Brady apparently didn't get the hint. "Technically, what happened wasn't Rachel Rhodes's fault and the action was legal," he said. "So, stopping the fight would have been unfair to her. What happened to Anthony was outside the ring, and under those kind of circumstances—"

"Brady," Annette said, putting a hand on his leg, wisely interrupting. "Maybe you should check your phone to see what the internet is saying."

The interruption wasn't quick enough. "Are you kidding?" Kara said. "Her brother collapsed, and because of that she wasn't even trying to defend herself."

"Well, actually I think—" Brady started again, and Annette pointed at the phone in his hand.

"Search please," she said to him in a tone that left no room for argument, before looking at Kara. "Can I order you some food? I think you need a drink."

Kara growled and started to pace again. "What I need is to hear from Alexa," she said. Hours had passed and, so far, all her texts went unanswered. *Of course, that shouldn't upset me,* she thought. *She's certainly with Anthony at the hospital. Maybe getting medical attention herself.* Remembering how damaged Alexa's face looked as she knelt beside her brother, waiting for the paramedics, Kara winced. The woman had a bloody mouth she constantly had to hold a towel against to catch the bleeding, and horrible swelling around her eyes, especially the left. Even when Jess tried to get Alexa to let the doctor look, Kara watched the woman ignore her manager. Clearly, all Alexa's focus was on Anthony and her own pain meant nothing. Still looking at his phone, Brady cleared his throat, making Kara stop and stare at him. "What did you find?"

"Uh," he said, then dimmed his phone screen. "Nothing important."

Kara furrowed her brow. "What does that mean? Is there news about Alexa?"

Glancing at Annette as if he knew he was about to need support, he swallowed hard. "Not so much about Alexa," he said. "Actually, almost nothing other than that she was rushed to the hospital. Her brother isn't mentioned much." That didn't sound so bad to Kara. Alexa wanted to keep her brother out of the public eye as much as possible.

She waved for him to continue. "I can see on your face that isn't everything. Don't try to hide it. I'll hear about it all eventually." Then she had a guess—maybe the news was about Kara, the surprise girlfriend, being the reason Alexa lost. *Because I was a distraction over the last few weeks,* she thought. *And we slept together before the fight.* There were moments while she waited to hear from Alexa that she wondered if some of that might be true. *Did it make a difference? Or was the loss only because of Anthony's collapse?* It was impossible to know if Alexa was ahead in the fight when everything happened. Kara refocused on Brady. "Tell me."

The man let out a deep breath. "Okay," he said and held the phone up for her to see the screen. Rachel Rhodes was in the center of a small crowd, her groupies behind her, and talking into multiple microphones. The byline at the bottom of the small screen read 'Fighter accuses Alexa Knight of wrongdoing.'

Kara narrowed her eyes. "Turn it up," she said. "I definitely want to hear this."

"So, you're implying Alexa Knight threw the fight?" the interviewer asked, and there was an angry murmur from the crowd. "That's a pretty serious accusation."

With a concerned look in her face, Rachel Rhodes shrugged. "Watch the video," she said. "She got a signal from the crowd and then stopped fighting. Not a tapout either."

"Why would that matter?" the interviewer asked, and Kara watched the new champion stare straight into the camera.

"Because the payoff was twelve hundred times better if she lost a certain way." She paused, clearly for dramatic effect. "It had to be a TKO—a technical knockout."

Holding Anthony's hand, Alexa sat beside the hospital bed, looking into her twin's handsome face. *At least he looks like there's no pain,* she thought. She couldn't say the same about herself as the throbbing continued around her loosened teeth. The doctors said she was lucky her jaw wasn't broken. Still, everyone's primary concern was the damage to her left eye. Trying not to let the fact she had no vision in it at the moment bother her, she refused to let them examine her more thoroughly. Instead, she held ice to the swelling, and hoped for the best. Even though she had been there for hours, nothing would make her leave her brother's side.

Suddenly, her phone buzzed on the small table near Anthony's bed. A quick glance revealed who called—Kara. Knowing the woman must be worried, she was tempted for a moment to answer, but then let it go to voicemail. There had been texts earlier that she didn't respond to either. While she held vigil over her brother was not the time to try and deal with her feelings around Kara. She could already guess that some people speculated Alexa lost the fight because she was distracted by her. The rumor they had sex in the elevator had certainly spread like wildfire, so it was likely another one regarding Kara would too. *And did all of that distract me? Letting Kara into my life?* she wondered, before frowning. *No. That was not the reason things ended like they did.* As frustrated as she was in the fight against Rachel Rhodes, she hadn't been losing the match. *Only seeing my brother collapsed made any difference.*

Alexa heard the hospital door open behind her. Not ready to talk to anyone, she turned to tell them to leave, only to see a nurse had arrived with Alexa's parents following her. "Alexa," her mom said the minute she laid eyes on her daughter. "Oh, what have you done to your beautiful face? Come here."

Never being happier to see her mom and dad, Alexa stood to welcome their embrace. As her mother hugged her, Alexa felt some of the load she carried lift off her shoulders.

Although her parents retired to Arizona years ago, and did not like to watch her fight, they were still very close. After a minute, her mom pulled back and went to Anthony's bedside. She took his hand, and without a word, sank into the chair where Alexa had been. At the same time, her father laid a hand on Alexa's shoulder. "The doctor explained they will be taking Anthony into surgery soon. We will stay with him, but right now, you need to go."

"Dad, no," Alexa started, but he held up a finger to quiet her.

"He also tells me you won't let them examine your eye. You need to let them," he said, nodding toward the nurse. "She will take you." Alexa wanted to refuse, but as if reading her mind, her father shook his head. "I know you're a warrior, but you are still my daughter, and I am telling you to get this taken care of." He kissed her on the forehead. "We will all be here when you come back." Knowing when she couldn't win, Alexa followed the nurse out of the room.

When Alexa continued to let her calls go unanswered, Kara resorted to contacting Jess. Being cooped up with Brady and Annette and not having any information had gone on long enough, especially when Brady showed her clip after clip of nothing but bad news. Some people believed Rachel and called Alexa out. Others claimed she hadn't taken the fight seriously, too busy having sex in elevators, hence the loss. Regardless the reason, people were angry at the fighter, and Kara hated to see what was already happening to Alexa's legacy. *How quickly people will turn*, she thought and knew getting in contact with Jess was the only answer. She had to make sure they were aware of the firestorm brewing.

Sending a text, Kara asked if Jess knew anything about

Anthony. As much as she cared for Alexa, the prognosis of her twin was even more critical. If something happened to Anthony, she worried Alexa would never recover. She still wasn't clear about what took place at ringside. One minute, they were all cheering and excited over the fight, and the next the man was on the ground, coughing blood until his eyes rolled back and he passed out. It almost seemed like a stroke. *But he's so young for that*, she thought. *Unless there is an underlying health condition?* There hadn't been time to think about anything after he fell. Chaos had quickly ensued, especially when Alexa lost the fight. The crowd had gone completely crazy. Only thanks to a mass of security and fight personnel were they able to shield Anthony. The team protectively huddled around him and aside from possibly a few random pictures on cellphones, she didn't think there was a lot of evidence of Anthony's collapse. Not only because everyone had been one hundred percent focused on the fight, but no one knew who he was to Alexa. *Which could be backfiring.*

"He's going into surgery right now," Jess wrote back.

"And Alexa?" Kara typed. "How is she?"

Kara watched as three dots danced on her phone letting her know Jess was responding. "You haven't been in contact with her?" was the message.

With no other way to answer than the truth, Kara wrote back a simple "No." Then, after a pause, added. "She hasn't returned my texts or answered my calls."

"I see." Minutes passed. Staring at the two words, Kara didn't know what to think. *I see?* she wondered. *How am I supposed to interpret that?* Finally, the dots showed Jess was typing again. "Can you come to the hospital?"

Feeling the sudden burn of tears in her eyes, her heart soared at the idea she could not only see Alexa, but maybe lend her comfort. Kara wrote back immediately. "Yes. Where are you?"

After Jess gave the details, Kara was in motion. "Let's go," Kara told her friends, only to step out of her hotel room and straight into the lights of a cameraman and reporter. Clearly, someone from the hotel had tipped them off, and they had waited like wolves.

Immediately, a microphone was in her face. "Did you work with Alexa Knight to rig the title fight?"

"What? Of course not," Kara said, so surprised by the accusation she didn't know what else to say.

Before she could explain the claims made by Rachel Rhodes were ludicrous, the interviewer shot more questions at her. "But you knew about it? That your girlfriend was going to throw the fight." Kara reeled. The word 'girlfriend' also caught her off guard. Clearly, the media had decided that was her role, although Kara knew the title was unwarranted so quickly. She and Alexa were being painted as a unit, and the accusations against the fighter were splashing onto her.

Brady stepped in front of the camera, using his bulk to shield Kara. "That's enough," he said. "No more comments." Seeing the opening, Kara took it. Smart enough to know reporters would be camping out at the elevators again, she headed for the stairs. Going out the backway like she had the morning before would have to work. Kara needed to get to the hospital, to see Alexa and check if she was okay, but also to warn her. There were a lot of bad things going on.

Chapter Sixteen

Alexa opened her eyes, or at least one of her eyes, and tried to see where she was, but the room was darkened. When she slowly turned her head to look around, what she could see was blurry and unfamiliar. For some reason the disorientation didn't alarm her, and it almost felt like she wasn't even in her own body. It seemed like she was floating, but then again, she could feel the firmness of the bed underneath her. "Hey," she heard someone say from what sounded far away. "You're awake. Let me tell the nurse." There were footsteps and a door opening then closing. *How long have I been asleep?* she thought. *And where's Anthony? I need to see him.*

Trying to sit up, she heard someone come in the room, but Alexa's eyesight was still off. "Just lay back," a kind voice said, putting a gentle hand on her shoulder. "You need to rest a little while longer."

"Where's Anthony?" she asked, the words scratching her throat to come out in a raspy tone. Suddenly, she realized she was very thirsty. Still, nothing mattered but getting to her twin. "I need to see him."

"He's resting in his room, Alexa. The surgery to put in the VP shunt was a success," she heard Jess say and then her manager was close enough to the bed that Alexa could see her. Sort of. Something wasn't right with her eyes, and she reached to rub them only to feel a large wad of padding and gauze over her left one.

Feeling a little more relieved about Anthony with the update, Alexa forced herself to concentrate on her own situation. "What's happening with my eye?" she asked. For a fleeting moment wondered if the surgery failed and she was blind on one side of her face. *Don't panic. It's only the padding making things so I can't see*, she thought. *And I'm fuzzy-headed from whatever drugs they gave me. That's why I'm so thirsty too.* "Can I have a drink of water?"

The other person, who Alexa assumed was a hospital nurse, held a plastic cup with a straw near her mouth and she eagerly sipped. "The ocular surgery to fix your retinal detachment went well."

Frowning, Alexa wasn't sure she liked the sound of that. "Retinal detachment? Is that what they found?"

"Yeah. From when Rachel Rhodes punched you in the face a couple of dozen times before the fight was called," Jess added. "The referee was slow getting there to stop the fight in my opinion."

Alexa had a glimpse of a memory where Rachel Rhodes beat the crap out of her, and agreed the punching went on a little too long. *Best to let that go for now,* she thought. *My sight is more important.* "So, will I be able to see with my left eye again?" she asked as the nurse adjusted something behind Alexa's head that she couldn't see.

"I'll let the doctor know you're awake," she said, her voice giving away nothing positive or negative. "He should be in to visit you within the hour and answer your questions. For now, concentrate on resting." Then the nurse was gone.

Not thrilled with the lack of a direct answer but knowing only the doctor could tell her the details, Alexa focused on Jess the best she could. "Do you promise Anthony is all right?" she asked.

Jess took her hand and gave it a gentle squeeze. "Your parents are with him, and I sent them a text that you're awake," she said. "Please do what the nurse said and try to relax." The woman bit her lip, as if thinking something over, before telling Alexa the rest. "And Kara is here."

At the name, Alexa felt a tightness in her chest. Kara. She really wanted to see her, and yet, a part of her didn't. *Not yet. Not like this*, she thought. *I'm not ready for that.* Shaking her head, wincing from the movement, Alexa felt the start of a dull throb under the bandages. "I'm not in any shape to see her. Can you tell her I'll text her in a few days?"

"You're sure?"

Alexa thought about her answer for a beat. The two of them were barely starting to know each other, and the relationship was still fragile. Asking her to play nursemaid was too much. Sending the woman away was for the best. "Yes, I'm sure."

Sitting in the hospital's waiting room, Kara continued to scan her phone for news clips about the Knight versus Rhodes fight. Very little of what she found was in Alexa's favor. She learned quickly that even though she was popular as a champion, many people took glee in seeing her fall. "She always thought she was better than everyone else," one MMA bantamweight contender being interviewed said. "I mean, she was a champion in the ring. But out of the octagon..." The interviewee shook her head. "Really arrogant."

Kara hated the bad press but understood the perspective some too. Alexa, with her cool and quiet strength could come across as condescending. Even she had thought Alexa was arrogant when they first met. Because the woman didn't show emotion, it was an easy mistake to make. *But so far from the truth,* she thought, having witnessed Alexa's love for her brother and his for her. She had heard that about twins—a special connection. *All the more reason I'm going crazy sitting here waiting to hear about Alexa or Anthony.* One would not do well without the other.

Seeing movement at the large double doors leading back to the hospital rooms, Kara looked to see Jess coming toward her. "You might as well go home," she said, and Kara felt a stab of pain in her chest.

"Why? What does that mean?"

Jess shook her head. "I'm sorry, but Alexa doesn't want visitors right now."

Kara wasn't sure what to make of the statement. *Does she mean all visitors? Or only me? And does that all mean she is all right?* "But she's out of surgery and awake?" Kara asked, still dumbfounded by the news she wasn't welcome. "And what about Anthony?"

"They are both out of surgery," Jess said. "I can't go into a lot of detail out of respect for them though."

Kara furrowed her brow. "I see," she said, but wasn't sure if that was true. She was more confused than ever. "Can you at least tell me if they are doing okay?"

Jess nodded. "I can," she said. "But right now, the family needs space."

"You mean that as in Alexa needs space?" Kara asked. It

turned out, Jess was lousy at keeping a poker face. "Oh," was all Kara could do in response to the nonverbal confirmation of her concern. "Well, then I guess I'll go."

As Kara stood to rush out of the waiting room, Jess put a hand on her arm. "I'm sorry," she said. "If I'd know she didn't want visitors, I never would have suggested you come here." She sighed. "But on the phone, you also said you had something to tell me."

Kara had almost forgotten that aspect of her decision to hurry to the hospital. "Right," she said, fishing the phone out of her pocket. "There are some unpleasant accusations starting around Alexa." She searched her phone for the clip that was most damaging in her opinion. "And sort of against me."

Jess looked over her shoulder at the screen. Rachel Rhodes was back but in a different interview than before. She sat in a director's chair across from an eager-looking interviewer. He leaned in. "So, tell us, do you honestly believe Alexa Knight threw the fight to cash in on bets?" he said, sounding unconvinced. "How could she do that?"

The new champion shrugged. "Easy enough of a scheme," she said. "One person watches the odds moving up and down with an app on their phone or whatever. When the odds are at the best, she places a huge bet and then signals Alexa somehow."

The interviewer shook his head. "That sounds difficult. Who would be helping her then?"

Sighing with a clear amount of frustration at the interviewer's inability to connect the dots, she pointed a finger at him. "Investigate Kara Roberts, Alexa's girlfriend. She was ringside, and I'm sure you'll find something interesting there."

. . .

Her head swimming a bit as the remains of the pain medication wore off, Alexa had trouble grasping what Jess told her. "Let's talk about this later," Jess said, sounding frustrated. "I should have waited until you felt better."

"I feel fine," Alexa growled, not happy with how the conversation went so far. If she heard her manager correctly, Rachel Rhodes had accused Alexa of rigging the fight. "But I'm going to need you to explain what you said to me one more time. Because I know I heard you wrong."

Jess shook her head. "I think you heard me perfectly," she said. "The news is that bad." She explained the entire situation again, though Alexa still couldn't believe it. "And they drug Kara into this too?"

"Yes," Jess said, rubbing a hand over her face before pausing to look at the wall. Alexa could almost see her thinking. Finally, she turned to Alexa and her look wasn't reassuring. "You have to tell them everything about Anthony." Even before Alexa started to shake her head, Jess took her arm. "Yes, Alexa. That's the only way to explain what happened. Otherwise, the claims look real. Everyone saw you glance into the crowd before the fight turned on you."

"No." Pain throbbed around Alexa's eye, and she was getting desperate to check on Anthony again. Although her parents, Jess, and the nurses all reassured her that he was out of surgery and resting, it wasn't the same as seeing him for herself. In her weakened state, she worried they would withhold any bad details from her. "You're telling me no one has made this connection anyway."

"Some," Jess said with a nod, scrolling through her phone before holding it up to Alexa's good eye. Another video, that one clearly taken on the fly by someone in the crowd during the fight. She watched as Anthony grabbed Kara's arm before sagging to the ground. Thankfully, Kara was there and able to break his fall a little. The angle was behind Anthony, so the camera never saw his face clearly and then the scene ended. "That's the only one posted that shows his collapse. A few others show you rushing into the huddle around him, but nothing is clearly linking them together." With a sigh, Jess lowered her phone. "And Rachel Rhodes is speaking louder and with a more interesting story right now," she said. "Which is why you need to make a statement immediately before this gets even worse."

Only half hearing her manager as her mind whirled, an idea occurred to Alexa, and it made her stomach tighten with anxiety. "And Kara?" she asked. "Is she telling what really happened?" *Doing so would make total sense*, she thought. *Her name is being raked through the mud too.*

"Not yet," Jess answered. "And I'm not sure what she is going to do. With my phone on silent while I focused on you and Anthony, I didn't even know about it until she showed me in the lobby."

Picturing Kara, Alexa had second thoughts about not wanting to see her. "Is she gone?" she asked, and when Jess nodded her heart sank. *She cares about me and waited for who knows how long to see me*, she thought. *But I wouldn't let myself be vulnerable in front of her and said no. And now, with all this Rachel Rhodes disaster happening to her...* Alexa knew she would be lucky to see Kara ever again.

Chapter Seventeen

For the next two weeks Kara had two objectives: stay busy and keep her head low. The first seventy-two hours after Alexa's fight were the worst as reporters called her phone nonstop. The harassment got to the point she almost wanted to change her cell phone number. Blocking them did not seem to be effective as they simply used a different number to call again. But she didn't want to talk to anyone about what happened. She could have because she hadn't heard any word from Alexa or her manager telling her keep quiet. Still, instinct told her they would not want Kara to give out any details about Anthony's collapse. She knew how private Alexa was when it came to her twin brother. Even though it felt like they might never see each other again, Kara would not betray Alexa's trust. Instead, she sat at her desk, her cat on her lap, and worked on her documentary.

Going out to interview anyone at the moment seem like a bad idea, so she told her cameraman she had to take some time off and stayed home editing film. Some people might find the task tedious work, scanning video after video, but she enjoyed every second of it. Reliving the moments of the different interviews with doctors and their patients with leukemia fulfilled her. Her latest interview with the pediatrician was especially powerful. As she worked with the scene, picking the best soundbites, tears came to her eyes at the man's passion for his work. His attitude only inspired her to keep at the documentary, no matter how long it took.

During her self-imposed lockdown, the only person she talked to was Annette. Her best friend did what she could to console Kara, but even she didn't have advice on the best way to handle the Alexa fight situation other than keep her mouth shut. And as for what to do about Alexa herself, Annette simply told her to be patient. Not easy advice. Kara was not a patient person by nature, but she would do the best she could, and hope Alexa would eventually reach out.

Stopping the latest video clip, Kara rubbed her eyes and felt a headache coming on. As she contemplated if coffee might make it better even though it was getting late in the day, her cell phone buzzed. Expecting to see a message from at worse, another reporter, or at best Annette, Kara picked it up and then froze when she read the name on the screen. Alexa Knight. With shaking hands, she opened the text. "Can we talk?" was the message.

Without even thinking twice, Kara wrote back "Yes. But how?"

"Do you mind if I call you?" Alexa asked. "I don't think seeing you is possible right now."

Kara gave that request some thought. She wasn't sure if seeing Alexa was a good idea both because of the media and her churning emotions, but she would prefer face to face. For now, she would take a phone call. "Call me," she typed and then waited.

When there was no response and the phone didn't ring

for over a minute, she wasn't sure what to do. *Has Alexa dismissed me again?* she wondered, feeling the hurt from being rejected at the hospital all over again. That had been both embarrassing and painful. She felt they had a deep connection, but she could tell by the look on Jess's face that morning that Alexa simply did not want to see her. Finally, the phone rang. Taking a deep breath Kara pushed the connect button and held the phone to her ear. "Hi."

Again, another pause, until finally she heard Alexa exhale. "Thank you for answering," the woman said with such relief in her voice that Kara knew what had happened at the hospital was not how Alexa truly felt. "It's so good to hear your voice, but now I really want to see you."

While sitting with Anthony at the hospital in Los Angeles, Alexa considered her life. All while her brother, who they had transported to LA while still in a coma, slept. He had not woken since the surgery and the doctor's had no answer. All they could do was wait. Alexa did not know what she would do if she lost her twin. He was the person she loved most in the world, and a piece of her would be missing forever. So, she sat by his side, along with her parents, and prayed he only stayed asleep to give his body time to heal.

There was one good thing about the LA hospital. Security kept the reporters away. Turning off her cell phone, Alexa was able to put herself in a bubble and pretend the outside world and all the chaos did not exist. Only through Jess did she get updates and none of them were good. Rachel Rhodes continued her accusations. Some news channels had picked up on it, and there were rumors an official inquiry was pending. Worse, Alexa was being raked through the media and many of her one time fans turned against her. None of it mattered at the moment, because all she cared about was Anthony, and maybe when she took the time to admit it to herself, Kara.

Kara, she thought. The incredible woman who would not back down and repeatedly came to her defense. Alexa missed her terribly. *If only I had not sent her away when she came to visit in Las Vegas,* she thought. Even though Jess told her it was okay because of the situation, Alexa didn't think Kara would forgive her so easily. She had been able to ignore what she did for the last week but as she sat alone in the room with her brother while her parents went to get them lunch, she couldn't seem to get the woman out of her mind. Finally, she realized she needed to call her—to apologize if nothing else. Picking up her phone before she could change her mind, she sent a quick text. "Do you mind if I call you? I don't think seeing you is possible right now."

When Kara sent back the two words, "Call me," Alexa wasn't sure what to do. Both the willingness and the quick response caught her off guard. Thankfully, her parents were just returning. She kissed them both on the cheek and stepped outside into the hall. Not letting herself hesitate and lose her nerve, she punched Kara's number. Wondering if she would even pick up after the delay, Alexa was surprised when it was answered on the first ring. "Hi," she heard and felt her heart quicken. Her mouth was dry and for a second, she couldn't form words.

Finally, she forced something out. "Thank you for answering," she said. "It's good to hear your voice, but now I really want to see you."

"It's good to hear yours too," Kara answered with a gentle tone that started to let Alexa relax and think they were fine, only to have it quickly evaporate when Kara snapped out her next sentence. "But you have some nerve calling me after what happened at the hospital."

"I'm sorry," was all Alexa could say before Kara continued.

"How could you send me away like that?" the woman asked softly, and Alexa heard the pain in her voice. "You know I care about you. And Anthony."

"You're right," Alexa said. "I made a mistake." There was a pause on the line and Alexa was patient while she waited to hear what the woman said next.

Finally, Kara sighed. "How's Anthony?"

Alexa let out a long breath of relief. At least they were talking. "He's in a coma," she answered. "And hasn't woken since the surgery."

"Oh Alexa," Kara said. "I'm so sorry. What can I do?"

Alexa felt an even stronger tenderness toward the woman, because her first instinct was to comfort Alexa even after how she treated her. Suddenly, she desperately wanted to see Kara. "Can we meet?" Alexa said knowing it was a nearly impossible ask assuming Kara was dealing with the same sort of scrutiny from the reporters that she was facing.

"I don't know," Kara answered. "It's been crazy. Alexa, I didn't sign up for this."

"I know," Alexa said. "If I ever had any idea this would happen…"

They were both silent for a moment and before Alexa could decide what to say next, Kara said what Alexa longed to hear. "I want to meet you too," she said. "Can you sneak out of the hospital?"

"I'll find a way."

. . .

With the help of Annette and Brady running interference, and by wearing a baseball cap and sunglasses with her hair tucked up underneath, Kara was able to sneak out of her apartment undetected. Not easy considering there was one persistent reporter who had staked out a spot in front of her apartment building. While her two friends pulled up in their car to ask him directions and some other nonsense, Kara slipped away. Luckily, she didn't live far from the place that Alexa had suggested they meet—Nostra, the Italian restaurant. Kara hadn't even been able to work there for the past two weeks with all the scrutiny. At least Roberto had been understanding. Even though she had never discussed details with him, he clearly recognized she was somehow connected to Alexa and so received special treatment. The man had a definite soft spot for the fighter.

Reaching the back door, she gave a light knock. Roberto grinned when he opened the door to let her slip inside. "Clever disguise," Roberto said.

Kara smiled. "I was fresh out of clown masks."

The man shivered. "I hate clowns, so good," he said. "She is waiting for you in the break room."

"Thank you, Roberto," Kara said, giving his arm a squeeze as she slipped past him. When Kara walked in the breakroom, Alexa had her back to the door as if suddenly interested in the California state laws on minimum wage. Not sure what to do, Kara cleared her throat and when Alexa turned, even with one eye covered by an eyepatch, there was such appreciation in her gaze that Kara was even happier she had come. Instinctively, she moved across the room and pulled Alexa into a hug. The fighter stiffened at first but then relaxed into it, and Kara heard her suck in a breath that was verging on a sob. They held each other tightly for minute, and then Kara pulled back to look into the woman's face. "I missed you," Kara said. "I was angry at you, and this is all a crazy mess, but I missed you."

Alexa rested her forehead against Kara's. "I missed you too," she said. "I'm sorry for all this."

Leading them to the breakroom's small table, Kara sat across from Alexa but still held her hand. "No one could've predicted this," Kara said. "And eventually it will go away because people have a short attention span. What I really want is to hear about Anthony."

Alexa ran a hand over her face, careful of the eye patch and all the tension returned. "He hasn't woken up since the surgery, and the doctors are not sure why," she said. "Putting in the shunt apparently went smoothly and the pressure on his brain has greatly diminished but for some reason he won't wake up. All we can do is wait."

Kara squeezed her hand. "I'm so sorry," she said. "I know this must be devastating for you and your family, but you have to stay positive." She hesitated, not wanting to pry but wanting to know more. Alexa was a private person, especially about her family, but some things didn't add up. "Alexa, do they know why this happened?" The woman was quiet as she stared at their clasped hands.

Clearly the decision to tell Kara more was hard to make, but finally she nodded and met Kara's eyes. "Anthony has chronic leukemia."

Chapter Eighteen

As Kara told her about her documentary project, Alexa was amazed it was a film about leukemia. The coincidence was uncanny, but then it felt fated too. The woman had a real passion about the topic, and Alexa saw it in her eyes when she spoke about her interactions with the doctors and their patients. Everything Kara said touched her deeply and because of her experience with leukemia, the woman didn't give Alexa the usual blanket sympathy of "I'm so sorry" when Alexa confessed about her twin's condition. Instead of wanting to change the topic like so many others would, Kara wanted to talk about Anthony's current symptoms and what stage he was in. Best of all, they held hands the entire time. Alexa felt closer to Kara every second and was glad she had come to the restaurant, but the clock was ticking. She began to worry Anthony might need her.

Going on instinct she squeezed Kara's hand. "Come with me to the hospital," Alexa said.

Kara only hesitated for a moment before nodding. "If that's what you really want, I will."

"It is. Thank you," Alexa said. "I'd like to go now if that's okay. It's hard when I'm away from him."

"Of course," Kara said, standing. As Alexa followed suit, there were loud voices in the restaurant. Roberto's booming tone was easy to recognize, and he did not sound happy.

"Get out of here," Alexa heard him say. "This is none of your business." There was a murmur of someone else speaking but Alexa couldn't make out the words. Not sure what to do, and guessing the altercation had something to do with her, she stayed in the breakroom until finally there was a slamming of the door and Roberto came to join them.

His face was red, and Alexa couldn't think of a time she had seen him angry. "There's a reporter out front," he said. "And he's being very persistent."

"We will go," Alexa said, patting Roberto on the arm. "I don't want there to be any hassle for you."

"It's no hassle," Roberto said. "It was my pleasure to throw him out."

Alexa hesitated, and then wrapped her arms around the big man. "Thank you," she said, appreciating him more than she realized.

Roberto patted her on the back as if not quite sure how to react until Alexa pulled away and he smiled. "Let me get some food to go with you," he said. "I have something prepared for the family."

"You're wonderful, Roberto," Alexa said and followed him to the kitchen where he had already packaged some boxes.

He put them in a sack to hold out for her. "Let me know how Anthony is doing."

"I will," Alexa said as she started for the back door. Kara was behind her while they snuck into the alley behind the restaurant. Glancing in both directions, the coast appeared clear. "This way." They ran down the alley, because Alexa had wisely parked her dad's old truck a few blocks away. Although she often asked him to let her buy him something new, her dad loved the old truck. Under the circumstances, she was glad to have it for cover.

Pushing the key fob to unlock the doors, she heard Kara laugh. "This is your new ride?" she asked. "I wouldn't have pictured you in a big truck."

"It's my dad's," Alexa said with a smile. "I thought my Camaro might attract too much attention."

Kara nodded as she opened the passenger door. "Good thinking," she said while Alexa went around to her side. Before she could climb in, Alexa heard footsteps behind her.

Turning to look, she saw a man with a cellphone, and it was clear he was shooting a video. "Alexa Knight, what do you say about the accusations by Rachel Rhodes that you threw the fight to pay off gambling debts?"

"Gambling debts?" Kara heard Alexa respond after the reporter ambushed her. "What are you talking about?"

Furious, Kara raced around the truck and stepped between the man's phone and her friend. "Get the hell out of here," she growled. "What are you? Some sort of paparazzi looking for a bullshit reaction?" When the man only smiled, she wanted nothing more than to punch him in the face. *Which is what he would love to catch on video*, she thought, taking a deep breath to calm down. *As much as I don't care if my likeness splashes across the internet, Alexa will, and I won't give him the satisfaction anyway.*

She felt Alexa's hand on her arm. "Let's go, Kara," she said. "We have other things to take care of."

"Epic," the man said, still grinning. "The two of you together. It's my lucky day." He turned his full attention on Kara. "Maybe you'll answer my questions—how much did you help her with the scheme?"

Clenching her jaw while Alexa pulled lightly on her arm, Kara truly had to restrain herself. "You don't get it," she said. "There was no scheme. What happened was just because of—"

"Kara," Alexa interrupted, a hint of warning in her tone. "Let's go."

The man's eyebrows shot up. "Wait," he said. "Because of what? If there's an explanation, let me get it on record. I don't have to be the bad guy."

Kara shook her head. "Because of bad luck," she finished. She would never spill what really happened and invade Anthony's privacy, and she didn't trust the reporter anyway. He was only in it for the headlines. "Now go away. There are no soundbites here."

"Oh, don't be so sure of that," he said, shutting off the camera and backing away. "I hear you're a filmmaker of sorts. You know how it works."

Putting her hands on her hips, Kara narrowed her eyes. "What is that supposed to mean?" she said. "I do documentaries that show the truth. Not what you do."

He smirked. "Sure," he said, and then turned on his heel, leaving them alone.

"Well that sucked," Kara said, looking at Alexa.

The woman's face was a cold mask of restraint, but her green eyes were dark with fury. "We shouldn't have engaged with him at all," she said. "That was my fault. I was surprised by this latest twist is all."

Kara sobered, hating to say what she had to ask. "Is it true?" she said. "I know you didn't throw the fight, obviously, but, well..." She let her words fade away as Alexa's angry look shifted to surprise with a touch of hurt.

She shook her head. "No, Kara," she answered. "I don't gamble. Ever."

Realizing how harsh her question was, Kara reached for her. "Hey," she said, taking Alexa's arm before she could turn away to get into the truck. She felt the tension in the woman's muscles. "My gut said you wouldn't. But people surprise me sometimes. I needed to be sure."

She felt Alexa relax. "I understand," she said, looking Kara in the eyes. "I never want to surprise you, but I know I have."

Letting the mood between them lighten, Kara raised an eyebrow. "Like in the elevator maybe?" she said, her heart spiking up a notch at the memory. She was rewarded with a smile.

Alexa stepped closer. "Something like that," she said, before pecking Kara on the lips. "I will try to be more transparent going forward."

"Thank you," Kara replied, enjoying the feel of the woman's lips on hers even if for only a second. "I will do the same." They held each other's eyes for a moment, and Kara felt the chemistry between them sizzle a little.

Finally, Alexa gave a slow nod to break the powerful connection. "Ready to go to the hospital?" she asked, and Kara nodded in return. "Good, I want to see Anthony." She started to turn to the truck, but then hesitated. "Are you sure you're okay coming with me?"

"Yes," Kara replied. "There is no place I would rather be than with you."

. . .

Before she started the truck, Alexa reached across the console to take Kara's hand. "Thank you for always being so supportive," she said once the woman turned to look at her. "I missed you. It's been hard."

Kara face softened as she leaned closer. "I've missed you too," she replied, raising her hand to run across Alexa's cheek. "It was a rough time for me too." She gently touched the edge of her eyepatch. The caress of her fingers on Alexa's cheek made her entire body warm. "How is your eye? Does it hurt?"

"It did at first, but not really much anymore," Alexa answered. "I heal quickly, and I actually keep forgetting I have it on." She sighed. "Although, the doctor is concerned I will always have a slight blind spot in that direction."

Nodding, Kara leaned back but kept holding Alexa's hand. "Okay," she said. "Does that mean no more fighting then?"

Alexa frowned. "Fighting again was never on my agenda," she said, realizing after she did the answer sounded harsh, but she was not expecting the question. "Sorry. I didn't mean to come across like that."

Waving her hand as if to dismiss what she had asked, Kara seemed unphased by her tone. "I understand. I shouldn't have sprung it on you. But you haven't even thought about a rematch with Rachel Rhodes and setting things right?" she asked. "You would have beaten her. I know it." Alexa didn't answer right away. With all that was going on in her life with Anthony, her eye surgery, missing Kara, and all the accusations, she never considered fighting again. All along, in her mind, that chapter closed when she fought Rachel, win or lose. She would retire and walk away from the sport completely. *But I lost because of circum-*

stances out of my control, she thought. *Kara is right. I was going to win once I wore Rachel Rhodes down.*

There was one big problem with the idea regardless. "Even if I did consider it," she said. "I'm not a hundred percent sure the gaming commission would let me after these accusations." On that sad note, she started the truck. It was past time to go back to the hospital. Riding in silence for a mile, Alexa could almost hear the wheels turning in Kara's head. "What are you thinking about?"

"I'm thinking we need to find a way to clear both our names," she said. "It's such bullshit." She blew out a frustrated breath. "But I understand your situation. The media wouldn't let it go if you simply say your brother collapsed. They would dig until all of it came out."

Nodding, Alexa rolled to a stop at the light. "And even if I wanted to explain everything, which I don't, I can't until Anthony wakes up. I won't do anything without discussing it with him first."

Glancing over, Alexa watched Kara chew her fingernail. "Right," the woman said after a beat. "So, we wait until he is awake and see what he wants to do." As the light turned green and they started moving again, Alexa briefly wondered what Anthony would want to do. *Well, that's an easy answer, and I know it,* she thought. *He will do whatever he can to protect me. Just like I have always done for him.* She simply wasn't sure if that was the right thing to do.

Chapter Nineteen

Kara and Alexa held hands as they reached the front doors of the hospital. As the automatic doors slid open, Kara felt her phone vibrate in her back pocket. Pulling it out to look, she saw Annette's name on the screen. "Do you want to take that?" Alexa asked and Kara nodded.

"Do you mind? It's my best friend," she said with a smile. "Checking on me I think."

Alexa raised an eyebrow. "Is that necessary?" she asked, a hint of playfulness in her voice. "Were you expecting something bad to happen when we met?"

Giving Alexa's hand a squeeze, Kara laughed as she answered the phone. "No, I wasn't," she said before speaking to Annette. "Hi."

"You weren't what?" her friend asked with a cheerful tone. "Apparently something good from your laugh."

Leaning closer, Alexa brushed her lips over Kara's cheek. "Meet you in there," she whispered, leaving for the hallway leading toward Anthony's room. Kara enjoyed the sight as she watched her walk away. The confident posture as she moved, with a hint of power under the surface. *So very sexy,* she thought with a sigh.

"Okay, tell me what's going on, please?" she heard Annette say. "First you're laughing, then you're sighing like a lovesick pup."

Kara laughed. "Did it sound that obvious?" she asked. "I'm not sure about lovesick, but definitely attracted."

"So, I take it you're somewhere still with Alexa?"

"I'm at the hospital with her," Kara answered, moving toward a small waiting area where no one sat. "We just arrived and are going to check on her brother."

"Do you need to go?" her friend asked. "I was only checking to see how meeting her went." Annette chuckled. "I think I have my answer."

"Not yet," Kara answered, slipping into one of the vinyl cushioned chairs. "We had a good talk," she said. "I learned a few things about her, and Anthony, and what's going on." Her smile faded. "Unfortunately, there was a reporter stalking her and he ambushed us outside the restaurant at her dad's truck. With a new twist to the accusations." Just then, she saw Alexa's manager Jess coming in the front doors. Studying her phone, the woman didn't notice Kara watching her. After a beat, Jess let out a growl, shaking her head. *What's that all about?* Kara wondered. *More bad news?* "Annette, I'm going to go unless there's something new on the Brady marriage proposal front."

Her friend moaned. "Not a peep," she said. "But he's being so secretive lately. I know something is happening."

"Well, that's promising."

"I hope so," Annette said. "Text me later. I want more details about your visit with Alexa."

"I will," Kara promised, standing to intercept Jess as she turned for the hallway. The woman walked fast, as if fueled by her anger and Kara had to hurry to catch up. "Hey, Jess. What's going on?"

The woman slowed, glancing at Kara. "You tell me," she snapped. "I'd say it's none of your business, but from the footage, I can see you were there."

"Footage?" Kara asked a moment before she realized the ambush at the restaurant was all caught on video. "Oh."

"Yeah, oh," Jess said, picking up her pace again. "I am not even sure what to think. Last I heard you were out of the picture."

Not liking the woman's attitude, Kara matched her step for step. "Well, I am most definitely not out of the picture," she shot back. "We needed to talk, that's all."

Jess nodded but didn't look any happier. "Okay," she said. "I'm assuming she knows you're here?"

"Yes," Kara replied. "We came from the restaurant in her dad's truck." She motioned with the cell phone still in her hand. "I took a quick call before going to Anthony's room to be with her."

As they neared the hospital room, Jess stopped and looked Kara in the eye. "That's fine," she said. "If it's what Alexa wants, I'm willing to go along with it, but she's fragile right now. Remember that."

Sitting at Anthony's bedside, Alexa searched his face for any signs of change. *Maybe a little weight loss,* she thought although the serene look remained, as if he simply slept and wasn't in a coma. Two weeks had already passed and although no one said the words, people were beginning to worry about his prognosis. *Nothing can happen to him. I need him.* She would never admit it, but so much of her strength came from their bond. Like a lot of twins, it often felt like they were connected in an almost spiritual sense. *How often have we had conversations without hardly saying a word?* They simply understood each other at the deepest level, and she wasn't sure what would happen to her without him.

The sound of the room's door opening made her turn to look. She had taken over watching Anthony from her mother, sending her home to rest, so guessed the visitor was Kara. Seeing Jess with the woman was a surprise. Especially considering how neither of the two women looked particularly happy. *Have they been arguing?* she wondered. *Over what?* "Is everything okay?" she asked once the door closed. "You both look pissed."

Jess waved her hand dismissing the comment. "Don't worry about that," she said. "We need to talk about these latest accusations. Gambling."

Alexa shrugged. "It makes no sense to me," she answered. "I don't gamble."

Puffing out a frustrated breath, Jess looked at the ceiling. "I know that," she said. "So where did this leak come from?"

"Rachel Rhodes?" Kara chimed in as she moved closer to Alexa's chair. "Is this more of her hype?" The three women were quiet as the idea sank in.

Finally, Alexa shook her head. "I don't think so," she replied. "This is an outright fabrication meant to hurt me."

"And her other stuff isn't?" Jess snapped. "Come on. The bullshit about you throwing the fight is ridiculous."

"It feels different," Alexa said leaning back in her chair. A sudden thought made her stomach clench and she reached for Kara's hand. When the woman returned the gesture, Alexa looked her in the eye. "You believe what I said before, that it's all untrue, right?"

Kara squeezed her hand and sat on the arm of the chair. "I know it is exactly what Jess said. This is bullshit."

Letting out a long breath of relief, Alexa nodded. "Good," she said. "I need you on my side."

"Hopefully, at your side as well," she said holding her eye. "As long as you need me."

"Okay, that's enough of the googly eyes," Jess said, putting her hands on her hips. "I'm glad you are so into each other but there are real problems to focus on right now."

Knowing her manager was right, Alexa drug her eyes away from the comfort she found in Kara's. "What's the game plan?" she asked. "Can't we ignore it and let the next spectacle take over in a week?"

"Is that an option?" Kara asked, but Jess shook her head.

"I don't know," she answered. "We need to give a statement of some kind. Otherwise, you look like you're ducking the press."

Furrowing her brow, Alexa saw her point. "Like I'm hiding something," she said, never feeling more trapped. *I can't use my fists to fight my way out of this one,* she thought. *But I can't take it lying down either.* "If I do agree to make a statement, I want to do it right. Make a video to post, maybe an interview or something."

"I can help with that," Kara said, sounding excited. "It would be entirely professional and exactly the persona you need to present." Alexa watched Jess to see her reaction. The woman narrowed her eyes as she looked from one of them to the other.

Slowly, she nodded. "I can see how that could work," she said. "Then we could handle all the aspects. No surprises." Warming to the idea, Alexa glanced at Anthony's face and froze. His green eyes were open and studying them. "Anthony, you're awake."

He coughed. "I am," he said. "So, did you win?"

One minute they were strategizing about how to handle the accusations against Alexa, and the next was chaos. Alexa jumped out of her chair and grasped Anthony's hand. "Who won doesn't matter," she said, laughing as tears started to shine in her eyes. "You're awake."

At the same time, Kara moved to press the nurse's call button, all while Jess pulled out her phone. "I'll call your parents." Once the nurse arrived and the room quickly grew more crowded as more people joined them, Kara decided to excuse herself. The moment was special for Alexa's family, and she respected their space.

Touching Alexa's arm, the woman turned to her, a huge smile on her face and relief in her eyes.

"Hey," Alexa said. "Isn't this wonderful?"

Kara smiled. "I'm so happy for you," Kara said. "For everyone. But I'm going to go for now and let you take care of your brother."

Alexa covered Kara's hand with her own. "Thank you," she said. "For standing by me. It means everything."

Instinctively, Kara leaned in to kiss the fighter on the cheek. "You're very special to me," she whispered into her ear. "I am glad I was here, and we can talk later about the other stuff."

"Alexa," her mother said, clearly wanting something, and Kara took that as her chance to slip away into the hallway. Once she headed toward the lobby, she looked at her phone planning to call an Uber back to her car. Instead, she saw a half dozen texts from Annette. Not sure what to think, she read them one after the other. Each asked Kara to call her when she was free. *What's happened?* she thought. *Did Brady finally propose?*

Smiling at the idea, she called, and Annette answered on the first ring. "Kara," she said with a sob. Her emotions shifting from excitement to concern, Kara sent up a quick prayer that everyone was all right.

As Annette cried over the phone, Kara left the hospital, hoping to see a taxi. "Take a deep breath," she said to her best friend. "I need you to tell me what is going on."

"It's Brady," Annette managed to say, and Kara felt her heart stop for beat. *Not Brady,* she thought. *He can't be hurt. He's one of the good ones.*

When Annette didn't continue, Kara stayed patient even though her pulse raced. "What about Brady? Did something happen?"

Annette moaned. "Not exactly," she said. "I was going to surprise him with some carryout lasagna from that restaurant we found." Kara heard her take in a shaky breath. "He loves that food now. And that's when I saw him."

Shaking her head, Kara wasn't sure what to think. "Saw him how? Hurt?"

"No," Annette answered. "Not hurt. He was having dinner." Still not tracking the conversation, Kara was about to ask for more information when Annette sobbed again. "With another woman, Kara. A beautiful, sexy woman. Brady is cheating on me."

Chapter Twenty

Picking up the pace in her final minutes, Alexa sprinted on the treadmill in her personal weight room. Like the yoga space in her house, the setup for working out was designed specifically for her. Aside from a set of racked dumbbells in various weights, there were plenty of things to hit—some of which were about to be used in earnest. Alexa needed to let out some of her pent up frustration. After Kara left and Anthony promised he was okay, she headed straight to her home training space.

Breathing hard, with her heart pounding, she pressed the stop button and let the belt slowly come to a halt. Dressed in nothing but a sports bra and shorts, sweat made her body glisten, but she was far from done. Stepping off, she picked up her pair of padded, fingerless, fighting gloves and approached the heavy bag in the corner. Although she could have easily replaced the old bag with a new one over the years, she almost considered the worn and patched leather a friend. Alexa's first workouts were with it when her father hung the bag in their basement. Recognizing Alexa struggled with middle school drama and suffered from a quick temper, the man was smart enough to give her an outlet. That, combined with jujitsu classes, changed her life.

Running her fingertips over its cool surface, she took in a deep breath and held it to the count of four before exhaling slowly. Then, in a flash of motion, she threw a combination of punches, making the bag rattle on its chain. As it swayed away from her, Alexa followed the movement with a flying knee and then spun out of range of its return path only to attack from the side. If anyone were watching her, Alexa's speed and dexterity would shock them. And so would her tears.

For the first time in a long time, she let out her emotions. Even in solitude, Alexa hid how she felt, but not tonight. With a primal roar of anguish, she attacked the heavy bag with a vengeance, as if she could beat her own pain away. *How could anyone accuse me of such horrible things?* She thought. *And say I would rig a fight?* Her fists flew as her tears flowed down her cheeks. *That I would cheat and steal?* Her punches landed harder. *After all I have worked so hard for?* Her kicks threatened to split the bag at its seams. *After all I have sacrificed?*

Not until her muscles burned and her fury spent did Alexa pause, grabbing onto the bag not only to stop the sway, but for comfort. With her chest heaving, she rested her forehead on the leather. "Why is this happening?" she whispered, but the bag had no answer. After another minute, when her thoughts stopped racing and her breathing recovered, Alexa lifted her head. Patting the side of the bag in gratitude, she went for her towel. Wiping her face, she resolved there would be no more crying. The need for release had dissipated with every strike and her cool demeanor was back in place—Alexa the fighter, the champion.

Or ex-champion, she thought, clenching her jaw. As distracted as she was with Anthony in the hospital, Alexa hadn't taken the time to consider what she had lost until tonight. *Not only the fight, but perhaps my reputation.* She closed her eyes, trying to think of a way to fix everything. Somehow prove to Rachel's believers what she claimed was a lie. *But if I do what Kara and Jess suggest and make a video to tell my side, how can I protect my brother?* Anthony was still in the hospital, and no one knew for how much longer while the doctors ran more tests. He had tried asking questions about the fight and the aftermath, but Alexa downplayed the situation and would continue to until he was stronger. *For now, he needs to heal, not be in the middle of a circus.*

Annette blew her nose loudly into the wad of tissues Kara handed her. They were well into the second box of Kleenex and Kara still didn't quite understand what happened. After their phone call where her best friend shocked her with the news about Brady, she had calmed Annette down enough that her friend offered to come pick her up at the hospital. Not sure if that was the best idea considering how upset the woman was, but knowing she needed support, Kara agreed. Then, after waiting ten minutes, there was another brief call from Annette. "I'm sorry," she whispered but her voice still trembled. "I haven't left the apartment yet, and he's here."

"Why are you whispering?" Kara asked, keeping the disappointment of still being stranded and unable to be by her friend's side out of her voice. "And isn't that a good thing?"

"I'm hiding in the bathroom," her friend said. "What should I do?"

"Talk to him. Be direct and tell him what you saw, then ask what happened."

"Okay," Annette had said before hanging up. That was hours ago, and in the meantime, Kara had not only fetched her car but drove by to pick Annette up. Clearly, whatever Brady said in response to Annette's questions had not gone over well and an SOS "come get me" text from her best friend was all Kara needed. Unfortunately, getting a clear answer from the upset woman as to what Brady did wrong proved to be a challenge.

"And all he kept saying was you needed to trust him more?" Kara asked again. "With no more explanation about the other woman."

Annette nodded. "Yes," she sniffled. "I keep telling you. He was super evasive and wouldn't answer my questions." Frowning, Kara didn't know what to think. Brady was one of the nicest, and she would have said, most honest men she ever met. It floored her to think he would cheat on Annette. The two of them seemed perfect for each other, to the point Kara worried she would never find someone so special. Still, if he wouldn't answer her questions...*and acted evasive?* she thought. *How can I overlook that?*

Kara noticed Annette finishing her glass of wine and, glancing at the bottle, realized they were in need of a second. "I'll be right back," she said, standing from the couch where she had been sitting beside Annette. She snagged the empty bottle. "More wine seems in order."

"Wait," Annette said, touching Kara on the hip. "There's something I still haven't told you."

Puzzled, Kara sank back to the cushions. "What?"

Her friend sucked in a shuddering breath. "I asked him why he hasn't proposed to me yet," she said, then shook her head. "No, that makes it sound like a reasonable question. It wasn't when I asked it."

"I'm not sure what you mean," Kara said, taking Annette's hand.

Her best friend nodded. "I know," she said. "I'm not telling it like it happened. But I was so upset." She squeezed Kara's hand. "And hurting, so I wanted to hurt him too, and I... I was mean."

Kara tried to imagine her levelheaded, carefree friend as mean and didn't believe it. "I'm sure you weren't as bad as you think," she said. "What did you say?"

"I accused him of not wanting to marry me because he was with that other woman," she said. "That I was never enough for him." Those words struck a chord with Kara. Although Annette was beautiful and smart and was well on her way to being an amazing teacher someday, she had a tough time believing it. The woman's total meltdown had a lot to do with her self-doubt. Although she clearly loved Brady with all her heart, a part of her wanted Brady to marry her to prove she was worthy. *And was that too much for Brady to continue to handle?* Kara wondered. *Or is this something else?*

"Are you still up?" Jess's text asked, and Alexa looked at the clock. It was almost midnight, which wasn't a big deal for her to be awake, but a surprise to hear from her manager.

She furrowed her brow, feeling uneasy at the question. "I am," she wrote back. "But why are you?"

There was a long pause, making Alexa wonder if Jess

fell asleep or something before the phone buzzed again. "I'm sitting outside in my car," she sent.

Alexa blinked at the message. "Outside my house?"

"Yes."

Sitting up straighter on the couch, Alexa typed back. "And the reason you are sitting in your car outside my house is...?" There was no response for a few seconds until Alexa heard a tap at the front door. Starting to feel more than a little uneasy over how Jess was acting, Alexa went to answer it. *It wouldn't be about Anthony*, she thought as she walked down the hallway. *Someone from the hospital or mom and dad would call about that.* She opened the door to see Jess on the porch biting her lip. "Jess, what are you doing?"

"I wanted to talk to you. Can I come in?" the woman answered.

Alexa stepped aside and waved her forward. "By all means," she said. "But couldn't this have waiting until tomorrow? Or in the least, been a phone call?"

Walking past her toward the living room, Jess shook her head. "No," she said. "I've been thinking about this long enough, and I didn't believe you'd listen if I called."

"Okay," Alexa said. "Now I'm totally curious. And honestly, a little worried." They stepped into the living room. "Will this go better over wine?"

"Everything goes better over wine," Jess said. "But this might be short depending on your answer."

"I don't like the sound of this," Alexa said, moving to sit in her favorite armchair. "So, spill it."

Jess started to pace, back to working on her lip. "Fine, I'll cut straight to the chase. I want you to stop seeing Kara Roberts."

Not sure what she was expecting, a comment about

Kara wasn't even on Alexa's radar. "What does my relationship with Kara have to do with anything?"

Stopping to look Alexa hard in the eyes, Jess had never seemed more serious. "Nothing good has happened to you since you met her," she said. "Think about it. Your training was shit because you were distracted—"

"Wait a minute," Alexa interrupted, working to keep her tone neutral. "You can't blame Kara for that. She wasn't even around for most of the weeks I was preparing."

Shaking her head, Jess dropped onto the couch across from Alexa. "Kara was around plenty in Las Vegas," she said. "You screwed her in the elevator a day before the fight, for crying out loud."

"Two days."

"What?" Jess asked. "Two days?"

Alexa narrowed her eyes. "We were in the elevator two days before the fight," she said. "But that's none of your business. None of this is."

Jess's mouth fell open for a beat, then snapped shut as her face flushed pink. "Since when is stuff none of my business?" she asked, and Alexa couldn't miss the touch of hurt in her tone.

"You've been my manager a really long time," Alexa said. "And we've been friends even longer. But you're wrong about Kara." Pausing to consider her words, she tried to feel what Kara represented to her, hoping to be able to articulate it. "She is different. When I'm with her, I don't feel like I must be Alexa Knight, MMA star." She smiled, realizing that was exactly the answer. "With her I can be me."

Chapter Twenty-One

Creeping on tiptoe out of her bedroom, Kara hoped to get to her tiny kitchen and the coffee maker without waking her best friend on the couch. After a few steps, she realized there was no reason to worry. Annette was on the phone and not sounding happy. "Do I get to at least know her name?" she asked, and Kara surmised it was Brady on the other end. Even though she stayed up most of the night comforting Annette, details still were not clear on who did what and why.

The fact her friend refused to answer any of her boyfriend's texts or phone calls last night did not help matters. "At least consider letting him explain a little more," Kara had tried coaxing her, but with no luck.

"You weren't there," Annette said. "You didn't see how guilty he looked. Like he was caught red-handed." Kara didn't have any way to explain Brady's behavior, but she wasn't ready to give up on him as a good guy. The situation simply didn't make sense.

Unfortunately, the phone call happening this morning didn't sound like things were any better. "What do you mean it doesn't matter?" Annette cried into the phone. "It matters to me." She shook her head as she listened. "No, I'm not coming home until you're ready to tell me everything." Waiting to see the outcome of Brady's response, Kara sighed when Annette hung up without a goodbye.

Detouring to the couch to sit with her friend, Kara wrapped her arms around Annette, pulling her into a hug. "I'm sorry this is happening," she murmured against the woman's shoulder. "Is there anything I can do to help?"

Annette shook her head, and when Kara pulled away, there were fresh tears. "No," she said. "And I'm sorry to burden you with all of this. I know you have your own drama."

"Hey," Kara said, rubbing Annette's arm. "It's not a burden. And don't worry about all my stuff." She smiled and added, "I think we are starting to work toward a solution."

Pulling a tissue from the box on the coffee table, Annette blew her nose. "That's good at least," she mumbled through the Kleenex. "What are you thinking?"

"I think Jess and I have talked Alexa into making a video in her defense," she said. "We were discussing it right before her brother woke. But let's talk about it with some coffee in our hands. I'm dying for my morning caffeine fix."

She stood as Annette nodded. "I could use about a gallon of it," she said. "I didn't sleep much."

"I bet," Kara said, feeling her own heart hurt at her friend's misery. "Let's get some java going."

As Annette leaned back against her pillow and closed her eyes, Kara made her way to the kitchen nook. In a few practiced minutes, the coffee was started, and she felt her own phone buzzing in her pajama pants pocket. Taking a peek, she saw the caller was Alexa and felt a warm glow after how well they communicated the day before. Unlike Annette and Brady, they were in the stage of working things out. Pressing the button, she connected the call. "Good morning."

"Good morning," Alexa said, and Kara relished the comfortable sound in the woman's voice. Clearly, she was happy with their progress too. "I was thinking about you."

Kara liked those words even more. "And what were you thinking?" she asked, unable to hide the suggestiveness in her tone.

Alexa chuckled. "Some of that," she said. "Always. But also checking to hear how things are with your friend."

They had spoken briefly on the phone last night about Annette and Brady, but with her friend on her couch needing comfort, Kara hadn't taken the time to get into details. "Not so great," she answered. "They still aren't really talking."

"I see," Alexa said in Kara's ear. "Does that mean you will be staying home with her? Or can I see you?"

Kara peeked through the doorway at her friend on the sofa. She looked asleep, which Kara thought was for the best at the moment. Plus, she very much wanted to see Alexa. "I can for a little while," she answered. "Where are you?"

"Home," Alexa replied. "But I am on my way to the hospital soon. I can pick you up and we can go for coffee first?"

Kara smiled. "I would love that."

Alexa could not believe how much she looked forward to seeing Kara. After the short, but intense conversation with Jess late last night, Alexa had given serious thought about Kara Roberts. So much so, she tossed and turned a long time before falling asleep. What she told her manager was one hundred percent true—Kara was special to her. A different kind of special too. The attraction wasn't only sexual but rooted in the deep respect she felt for her. The fact she hadn't even known who Alexa Knight was when they met, not to mention she didn't care, meant a lot. Kara wasn't interested in her for her fame or money or power, but instead, wanted to be with Alexa for the person she was on the inside.

The sad part was Kara somehow became wrapped up in all the drama circling Alexa. Even before the fight, Rachel Rhodes had accused Kara of being Alexa's girlfriend and started the wheels in motion. *I have to find a way to get her clear of all of this,* she thought, pulling up in front of Kara's apartment building in her Camaro. Kara waited by the front door, and Alexa loved seeing her face light up when their eyes met. *Yes, I definitely need to get her out of hot water. Not only is it too soon to be thinking we are girlfriends, but she doesn't deserve to be dealing with the mess around me.*

Stopping, Alexa unlocked the door to watch Kara slide into the passenger seat. "Hi," the woman said. "I know it's crazy and we're still getting to know each other and everything, but I really missed you."

Instinctively, Alexa took Kara's hand as they drove away from the curb. "I feel exactly the same," she said. "And yes, it is crazy and early and everything, but I don't care."

Kara leaned across the console and kissed her softly on the cheek. "Good," she whispered, sending a chill through Alexa. A very hot and excited chill before Kara rested back in her seat. "Where are you taking us?"

"Actually," she answered. "There's a place I want to try —Landish Coffee. Part of a new local chain. Have you ever tried it?"

"Not this new one," Kara said, shaking her head. "But I've been to the original one on the Venice Beach boardwalk. Fabulous place."

Making a quick U-turn, Alexa headed them in the new direction. "Perfect." It wasn't long until they were seated at a cozy table in the corner, each with hot lattes. Looking around, Alexa noted the coffee shop was busy, but not overwhelming. She liked it and let her eyes settle on Kara.

The woman smiled at her. "Thanks for making time for me today," she said. "I know you're probably wanting to get back to the hospital."

After sipping the foam from her drink, Alexa nodded. "I do and I will," she said. "But I wanted to see you and thank you."

Kara tilted her head. "Thank me for what?"

"Standing by me through this bad stuff with the press," she said. "You didn't have to and could have explained what really happened." Alexa touched Kara's hand. "That you weren't part of it."

Taking Alexa's hand in hers, Kara sighed. "It has been crazy, but I will always stand by you, Alexa. I know you're a good person," she said. "Have you given more thought to doing a video?"

Hesitating, Alexa wasn't entirely sure of her answer. She had in fact given it some thought and liked the idea but would continue to protect Anthony as long as she could. She shook her head. "I just don't think—"

Suddenly, a man in an expensive business suit stood at their table. "Hey," he said pointing a finger at Alexa, and everything about him screamed threat. Pushing back her chair, she prepared to stand and protect Kara if he started to make any more aggressive moves. "I lost a big bet because of you, so you owe me ten thousand bucks." He got even louder. "You cheating bitch."

Kara couldn't believe what she was witnessing. A complete stranger was in Alexa's face over a stupid bet he lost. Ready to fly into protective-mode, Kara opened her mouth to tell him he was a jerk when a young blonde woman in a maroon Landish Coffee apron stepped beside him. "Andy," she said, in an even tone, that somehow sounded both friendly, yet hard as steel. Like she wouldn't put up with anything from him. "What has gotten into you? You're one of my regulars and never act like this."

Andy's posture relaxed, but not entirely. "I'm not trying to make a scene in your coffee shop, Ashley," he said. "I'm sorry." He went back to pointing at Alexa. "But you don't know who this is."

Ashley's eyes scanned over the table, meeting Kara's for a moment before focusing on Alexa. "You're right," she said. "I don't think I've seen you in here before, but you look familiar."

"She's the fighter Alexa Knight," Andy growled. "And she cheated me and thousands of other people out of their money by throwing her championship fight."

Kara had heard enough. "That's not true," she shot back. "Rachel Rhodes is making that up."

Holding her hands as if to block any more comments, the beautiful blonde woman shook her head. "I don't know what is going on, and I don't need to," she said. "But there will be no more yelling accusations, or you'll all have to leave."

For a moment, no one spoke, and then Andy turned on his heel. "You're lucky I have a meeting," he snarled, walking out the glass door. Once he was gone and the few other patrons who were clearly startled by the attack went back to their own conversations, Kara turned to Alexa who let out a long breath. *She always looks so calm when stuff happens*, Kara thought. *But was she as scared as I was over him?*

"Are you okay?" Ashley asked. "I don't understand why that happened."

Alexa sighed, and Kara heard both frustration and disappointment in it. "I'm embarrassed my being here made a scene in your coffee shop," she said. "But otherwise, fine. Thank you for stepping in." She looked at Kara. "Are you okay?"

Kara gave her a small smile. "Yes," she said. "But I hated that. We must do something to prove those are lies."

Ashley raised her eyebrows. "Is this happening other places?" Ashley asked, and Kara nodded.

"All over social media and some television," she answered, having a sudden sick feeling. "Alexa, have other people attacked you in person like that?"

Alexa gave a slight shake of her head while picking up her latte. "Not to my face," she said before sipping the drink. "But then I've been mostly home or at the hospital."

"Well, now that I've had a second to recognize you," Ashley started, a hint of playfulness in her voice. "They probably wouldn't dare." Kara appreciated the woman's help in diffusing the tension still in the air. "And before you leave, I'm going to need your autograph. My girlfriend is a marine and a huge fan."

Seeing Alexa smile a little at the comments, Kara welcomed the lightheartedness even more. "She has a point that people would be stupid to approach you directly," Kara said. "But that doesn't mean you shouldn't at least make a public statement."

"I'll think about it," Alexa said, and Kara let it go, knowing only Alexa could make the decision about what to do next.

Chapter Twenty-Two

Still unsettled from the interaction with the angry businessman in the coffee shop, Alexa drove Kara back to her apartment building. They rode in companionable silence, and Alexa appreciated Kara giving her time to process. She was aware of what Kara wanted to accomplish by making a video of Alexa explaining, but she still didn't know if that was what she wanted. *Maybe if Anthony is awake and feeling strong enough, we can talk,* she thought, missing her twin's shoulder to lean on. Growing up they always bounced ideas off of each other. *But this one is different. I can't have him making decisions only to help me.*

As they turned the last corner before reaching Kara's place, Alexa saw a woman with dark hair talking to a someone on the sidewalk. From the size of the person, she guessed it was a man, but couldn't see his face. "Oh, what's this all about?" she heard Kara murmur, helping Alexa place where she had seen the woman before—outside the Italian restaurant. *That must be Annette, Kara's best friend,* she thought. *And the man with her is the boyfriend?* Luckily, they didn't seem to be upset. *But not exactly in each other's arms either.*

"What do you want me to do?" Alexa asked as they rolled closer, not sure if Kara would want to give them privacy or investigate the situation.

Kara hesitated, making Alexa look over to see her pursing her lips. "Just pull up beside them," she finally said. "I'll stay in the car, so no one feels outnumbered." She looked at her. "Do you mind? I know this is taking time."

"I don't mind," Alexa answered. "These are your friends."

Kara squeezed Alexa's arm. "Thank you," she said before rolling down the passenger window and looking up the sidewalk. Alexa watched as Annette noticed the car and then saw her register Kara was in it.

After a word to the man with her, Annette approached the car. "Hey," she said when she got to the window. Alexa tried to read the woman's body language but couldn't quite determine if she was mad or sad. *Maybe both?* she wondered. *Kara said they were having a serious fight.* Looking past her, Alexa noticed the man turning to watch them and his body language was easier to interpret—worried about Annette. He was all but wringing his hands while his eyes followed her. Although she didn't know either of the pair well enough to base her feelings on facts, the instincts she had honed in the octagon told her the guy wasn't cheating.

Kara reached out the window and took Annette's hand. "Hey you," she said. "What is going on?"

"Brady wants me to come home," she said. "He drove over to ask me in person." Annette sighed. "I didn't want to have a fight in your apartment, so I came down."

"That wouldn't have mattered to me," Kara said. "But I

hope you are working something out. Are you going with him?"

Indecision showed in the woman's eyes, but then she nodded. "I will," she said. "If we can't work through this, I'll guess I'll... I don't know."

Kara shook Annette's hand. "You will pack more things and get back over here," she said. "And stay as long as you need the space."

Leaning in, Annette hugged Kara through the window. "Thank you," she said. "You're the best bestie ever." Pulling back, she caught Alexa's eye. "Hi, Alexa."

Alexa gave her a nod. "Hello."

"Seriously, Annette," Kara said as her friend stepped back. "You are welcome to stay."

"Okay," she said. "I'll text you."

Alexa watched as the woman walked away. "Do you want to come with me to the hospital?" she asked Kara. "Or can I drop you somewhere else?"

Kara rolled up the window. "I'd rather be with you," she said. "And I'd love to say hello to Anthony."

Walking into Anthony's hospital room, Kara was pleased to see him awake and talking to his parents. His coloring looked good and when he noticed them, his eyes lit up even more. *He's so much better*, she thought. *Like he really was only sleeping and is awake feeling refreshed.*

"Hi there," said the older man in the room, who Kara remembered as Alexa and Anthony's father. "You're just in time. I am headed out to get Anthony a breakfast sandwich." He chuckled. "Apparently the food here is not enough to fill him up." Kara liked the man immediately and didn't miss that he had green eyes like his children.

Not as vibrant, but still handsome. When his gaze fell on her, he held out a hand. "I saw you when we arrived that first day in Las Vegas, but I don't know if I caught your name."

"Sorry. Let me make formal introductions this time," Alexa said, putting a hand on Kara's lower back. "Mom, Dad, this is my friend Kara."

"And the person who kept me from landing flat on my face if I remember it correctly," Anthony said, grinning from the bed. "Thanks for that."

Kara smiled back at him. "Hey, the least I could do," she said, then sobered a little. "You scared me."

"He scared all of us," Kara heard their mother say a moment before she was enveloped in a giant hug. "I am so grateful you were there for him. Thank you."

Loving the warmth of the hug, Kara returned it. "You're welcome," she said. "I'm glad he's looking better."

"And feeling better," Anthony said. "Aside from starving I mean."

Alexa's dad held up his hands in surrender. "I heard you," he said. "I'm on my way. Isabella, come with me and let these kids have some time to talk." Alexa's mom let go, but still patted Kara's arm a half dozen times before following her husband out the door.

Once the door closed, Kara smiled. "Your parents are wonderful," she said, and Alexa nodded.

"They are pretty great," she said. "Always there for us." She looked at Anthony. "But brother, you really did scare all of us this time. A coma? Really?"

Laughing, Anthony shrugged. "You know me, always dramatic," he said. "But now you need to tell me what I missed. My cell phone is dead, and Dad wouldn't give me details, other than you lost, but I know something is up."

Kara watched Alexa hesitate, but Anthony wouldn't let her off the hook. "Seriously, is it that bad?"

"It's bad," Alexa murmured. "But nothing I can't handle. You need to work on getting better."

Anthony narrowed his eyes. "You and I both know I'm never going to get better," he said with no room for argument in his direct tone. "Not entirely. I have cancer so cut the bullshit and tell me."

Puffing out a long breath, Alexa nodded. "Rachel Rhodes is telling the world I rigged the fight and lost on purpose."

"What?" Anthony said, his mouth hanging open for a beat. "That's so stupid I can't believe anyone is buying it."

As Alexa seemed to deflate a little beside her, Kara put her arm around the woman's shoulders. "Unfortunately, lots of people are talking about it," she said. "And Alexa hasn't made a statement to say it's not true."

Anthony shook his head. "Why?"

"To protect you," Alexa murmured still looking at the floor. "You're why I was distracted and let her get me out of position. I saw you on the floor and nothing else mattered."

Running his hands over his face, Anthony seemed temporarily speechless. "So, rather than explain my condition and that I collapsed, you've put up with this shit?" he asked. "You didn't have to do that."

"I did," Alexa shot back, looking more like herself again. "You were in a coma. I wasn't going to make the whole thing about you."

Alexa held Anthony's hard stare. She needed him to understand why she had kept quiet, at least for the last couple of weeks. "Well, I'm not in a coma anymore,"

Anthony said softly but not breaking eye contact. "And my leukemia doesn't need to be a secret anymore if it will help you. I can handle the attention."

Giving a slow nod, Alexa looked down at her hands—so powerful, and yet she felt so helpless. "Even if I did tell the world you have cancer," she said. "They will claim I'm parading it out after all this time to distract from what Rachel is saying." Glancing over, Alexa saw Kara frowning, but not in an angry way. *She's absorbing what I said,* she thought. *And realizing I'm right.*

No one said a word for a long minute, then Kara started to nod. "Okay," she said. "I see what you're saying, but I think I know a way around that."

"How?" Alexa and Anthony said at the same time, and Alexa appreciated the fact their special connection was back. *My twin,* she thought. *Thinking alike.*

Holding up a finger, Kara smiled. "Yeah, I think this will work," she said and looked into Alexa's eyes. "Remember I told you about my documentary?"

Alexa blinked. "Yes," she said not entirely sure how Kara's work would help but feeling a glimmer of hope. "About leukemia, interviewing doctors and their patients."

"You're kidding," Anthony said, his eyes wide. "You're the one doing that?"

Kara's eyebrows went up. "You've heard of it?"

He nodded. "Of course," he said with a grin. "Word spreads during chemo and stuff. I think it's cool."

"Thank you," Kara said, and Alexa couldn't miss the excitement in her eyes. "Do you want to star in it?" Kara asked looking only at Anthony.

"Yes!" Anthony said, looking ready to jump out of bed and start immediately.

Alexa shook her head. "Whoa," she said. "You both need to hold on. What do you mean star in it?"

Beaming, Kara continued to explain. "I've been trying to find a way to tie all the scenes together," she said. "Audiences need a consistent thread to focus on or otherwise my documentary is nothing but a series of independent interviews." The woman clapped her hands from the excitement. "Anthony's experiences could be that thread."

Alexa looked at her brother. "Are you sure you want to do that?"

"I am totally sure."

Looking at Kara, Alexa saw a woman she truly cared for and trusted, but she was still confused. "I'm not against this idea, especially with you both so excited about it," she said. "But how will this help my situation?"

"That's the best part," Kara said, a twinkle in her eyes. "Tomorrow, I'll leak to the entertainment reporters I'm featuring Anthony Knight in my documentary." She smiled wide. "That will get the news out about his leukemia without you saying anything."

Anthony nodded at Kara's words. "Maybe I can even make a statement about being in it and how I am finally ready to tell my story," he said. "Try to really lay it on."

Finally understanding what the two planned, Alexa felt her chest loosen. She hadn't even realized how much anxiety she carried over keeping everything a secret. Still, she didn't know if it would get her out of the accusations. "But that won't necessarily explain what happened at the fight," she said, and Kara rubbed Alexa's arm.

"There is one more part to this," she said. "I know you hate it, but in a week, after people know about Anthony…" Kara bit her lip, clearly not excited about what else she had to say.

"What?" Alexa asked, and then connected the dots. First word about Anthony's cancer will go around. *And then I can explain why he collapsed and my reaction to it.* She sighed. "You want me to do a press conference and tell the world everything, don't you?" Kara nodded and Alexa had a big decision to make.

Chapter Twenty-Three

Nervously biting her lip, Kara tried not to let herself get psyched out by the number of people in the hotel conference room. When word got out about Alexa Knight holding a press conference, it seemed everybody in the sport's world wanted to be at it. *Nothing like a scandal to get attention*, she thought, then narrowed her eyes. *Which is exactly why Rachel Rhodes did it all along.* Kara was ready to put that woman in her place. The fighter had proved relentless with her lies about the fight's finish. Although there was no clear footage to prove it, she claimed Alexa didn't even fight back when Rachel Rhodes told her to protect herself from more damage.

Thankfully, Kara's announcement about Anthony Knight being the main feature in her documentary went over exactly as planned. For her, the situation was a win-win. Not only did she have a chance to help Alexa, but her film was getting good press from the addition of Anthony's story. She hadn't realized it before but using his battle as the centerpiece to weave all the other interviews around was priceless. Offers for distribution from a couple of production companies had already come in and it had been less than two weeks since the announcement. Kara's filmmaker career was suddenly on the fast-track.

The person who was the most excited though seemed to be Alexa. At first hesitant to have her brother in the limelight, once he made it clear that was what he wanted, she was all for helping any way she could. "I want to help finance it," Alexa said over a glass of wine at Nostra. "Not only is it the least I can do, but I really believe in your project." Being a smart businesswoman, Kara accepted the amazing offer.

All that didn't make what they were about to face with the press any less nerve-racking. When Alexa explained how her brother's illness caused him to collapse, thus distracting her, hopefully all the nonsense would end. They had yet to figure out where the gambling debts rumor started, but Alexa assured her they were completely unfounded. "I checked with Jess about my finances, and there's no issue," Alexa had explained that afternoon as she drove them to the E-Central, a downtown Los Angeles, boutique hotel where the press conference would be held. "Not to mention I've never made a bet in my life, so there's no possible way to have debts to pay."

"Then that will die down after today too," Kara said as they pulled up to the valet. "I'm sure you're so ready for this to be over."

Alexa took Kara's hand as they rolled to a stop. "No more than you," she said. "This has been a nightmare for both of us." *A nightmare that is about to be over*, Kara thought, waiting with Alexa at the doors outside the conference room.

Anthony was with them. Because he still suffered from dizzy spells, he was in a wheelchair, but insisted on being with them at the event for morale support. "We are team Alexa," he said.

As she watched, the final member of their group came through the door into the hallway. "They are ready for you," Jess said. "You remember what you're going to say?"

Alexa nodded. "I'm good," she said. "Let's get this over with."

With a nod, Jess pushed the door open and stood aside as Alexa strode through. Kara loved seeing the confident way she moved. No one would ever know how much everything had affected her. Pushing Anthony's wheelchair, Kara prepared to follow.

Before she took a step, her phone began it vibrate. Reaching to turn it off, she glanced at the screen to see it was Brady calling. *That's weird*, she thought. He had never called her before. She was surprised he even had her number. "Jess, can you help Anthony?" she asked. "I need one second to check this call."

"Don't take too long," Jess snapped as she moved them away. "This is important."

Not bothering to tell Jess she was aware of that fact, she answered. "Brady?" she asked. "What's wrong?"

"I can't find Annette," he said a hint of panic in his tone. "Is she with you?"

Keeping her eyes on the table, Alexa avoided looking into the cameras trained on her as she walked to her seat. *There must be fifty people in this room*, she thought. *This is ridiculous.* As seriously as she took the sport of MMA, it was still only a competition. People's lives were not on the line and considering her twin's diagnosis, the rumors going around about her fight were not that important. *At least not to me. But apparently, it is to them. So, let's get this over with.*

Taking her chair, she took a deep breath and let it out slowly. Glancing toward the wall, she looked to her brother and the others for support. Anthony gave her a nod and she saw Jess, but Kara was missing. *That makes no sense*, she thought, immediately worried something was wrong. A part of her wanted to go find out but leaving the press conference at that point would be an even bigger disaster. Forcing herself to focus, she pulled the microphone closer and cleared her throat.

"I'd like to make a statement," she said, seeing no point in wasting time. "In regard to my championship fight last month against Rachel Rhodes." The room went silent, and she felt her heart pounding in her chest. Although there was nothing like the adrenaline of preparing for a fight, of walking into a ring, of waiting for that first punch, what she felt right then was nearly as scary. Her legacy could come down to this moment. "There have been accusations made that I purposefully lost the championship fight with Rachel Rhodes. That is not the case. Those statements are false." A murmur went through the room. "As some of you know by now, my brother has an advanced case of leukemia, and he was ringside at the fight." Wanting to make sure her next sentence was crystal clear, Alexa finally stared into the cameras. "When he collapsed because of a complication from his illness, I saw him passed out on the floor and nothing else but getting to him mattered."

When she paused, a dozen questions erupted from the group, and to avoid chaos, she focused on one reporter. It was a man she liked and interviewed with in the past. *Hopefully he will ask a fair question,* she thought. *I don't need another ambush.* "Terry, what did you ask?" Before he could repeat his question, there was louder shouting from the back of the room. Refocusing, Alexa's stomach clenched when she realized Rachel Rhodes was making the commotion.

Pushing her way to the space in front of the podium, the woman pointed at Alexa. "You're trying to get everyone to believe the only reason you lost was because you were distracted?" she shouted. Alexa watched the cameras turn to capture everything Rachel was spewing. "I was kicking your ass and you know it." She shook her head. "Even if you didn't throw the fight, you still would have lost. Don't cover it up with bullshit excuses."

Alexa didn't bother to answer and prepared to stand. As far as she was concerned the press conference was over. She said what she came for and Rachel was nothing to her.

"Don't you try to walk away from me," Alexa heard Rachel growl. "Fight me again and prove me wrong."

Alexa paused, the room quieting in anticipation of her response. "Rachel," she said, leaning closer to the microphone so no one could miss her answer. "Go to hell."

The room erupted and Rachel charged the table. "You bitch," she said as people grabbed her to stop the attack. "You're afraid and you know it." Stepping away from the table, Alexa ignored the woman. She couldn't care less what she had to say and wanted to find Kara.

A female reporter bravely stepped in her path. "Wait, Ms. Knight," she said. "You are saying no to a rematch?"

"That's correct," Alexa said, pushing past the woman. "I'm saying no."

Hearing a commotion on the other side of the doors, Kara had trouble concentrating on what Brady said. The man kept repeating that he couldn't find her. *Annette is missing?*

she thought for the tenth time. *That doesn't make any sense.* "I can't talk right now, Brady," she said. "I'm at Alexa's press conference, but why do you think she is missing?"

"Because her school called," he explained, exasperation in his voice. "She missed an important exam, Kara."

"What?" Kara asked, feeling a sense of unease starting to work its way in. That was completely out of character for Annette. "And she didn't give a reason?"

"No. They've been trying to reach her on her phone all morning," he said. "And I have been too." She heard him swallow hard. "She hasn't answered or texted. Please tell me you know where she is."

Kara racked her brain. "Let me try her number," she said, trying to ignore the yelling she heard coming from the conference room. Whatever was happening in there did not sound positive, and she worried about Alexa while she worried about her best friend of over twenty-years even more. "I'll text you right back." Disconnecting before he could respond, she dialed Annette's cell. It went straight to voicemail. *Damnit,* she thought. *Where the hell is she?* "Annette, please call me as soon as you get this. I'm a little worried about you. Brady says you missed an important test." Hanging up, she tried to think of who else to call. She hated to alarm Annette's family. *Still, if she's with her mom that would make some sense after all the emotional stuff she's going through.*

Starting to search her directory, the conference room doors burst open. "What the hell are you thinking?" Jess snarled at her. "Don't you think supporting Alexa is more important than whatever you're doing?"

Blinking with surprise, Kara didn't know what to make of the outburst. "I'm sorry," she said, and after a beat felt her temper rise at the attack. "But this is important too."

Jess moved closer until she was in Kara's face. "You know, a lot of what's happened is because of you," she said. "I wish Alexa had never met you."

"That's enough," Kara heard Alexa say from the doorway. Glancing over, she saw the woman's green eyes snapping with anger as she pushed Anthony's wheelchair in front of her. "We talked about this, Jess. I don't want you to ever say that again."

Kara shook her head. "You talked about this?" she asked, not sure which part Alexa referred to—the fact things were Kara's fault or that Jess wished they never met.

"This is not the time or place to have this conversation," Alexa answered. "Let's go to the car before anyone follows us."

Jess shook her head. "You're blind when it comes to her, Alexa," she said. "And she's distracting you from everything we worked for. The fighter I knew would never have said no to that rematch."

Her head spinning from everything happening at the same time, Kara held up a hand. "I can't deal with this right now," she said. "No one can find my best friend, and I need to focus on that."

"Annette is missing?" Alexa asked, concern in her voice. "Since when?"

"Since this morning," Kara answered. "She missed an important exam at school."

Alexa started to push Anthony again. "Then let's go find her."

Chapter Twenty-Four

When Alexa and Anthony dropped Kara at her apartment building, Brady was waiting for her. She had quickly confirmed Annette wasn't there, and they decided the next step was to go check the places she liked to study. It made more sense for Kara and Brady to ride together, so Alexa kissed her goodbye. "Please call me if I can do anything to help," she said, looking into Kara's concerned face. "You'll hear from her soon. Stay positive."

Kara nodded. "Yes," she said. "You're right. I'll let you know when we find her." Pulling her into a hug, Kara held Alexa surprisingly tight. "I'm sorry I missed your press conference. We need to talk about what happened."

Hugging her back, Alexa relished having her arms around the woman—it felt right. "You were focused on more important things," she said. "And there's not much to talk about, but we can later."

"Okay," Kara said, stepping away to go join Brady waiting on the sidewalk. "I'll text you and keep you updated." Moving back to her car, she waited until she saw Brady and Kara leave in his car before Alexa pulled away from the curb.

Anthony had moved into the front seat to ride beside her. "That's scary business," he said. "Sounds like it's way out of the ordinary for her friend to disappear."

"Yes," Alexa said getting on the freeway to take them to her house. Anthony currently lived with her as he continued to recover. "I've only met her a couple of times, but she comes across as very reliable. Going to be a teacher actually."

Nodding, Anthony didn't respond for a mile. "Not to totally change the subject, but what the hell was up with Jess today?" he asked. "That was crazy."

Alexa wondered about that too because her manager and friend normally kept her emotions under control. "That's a really good question," she replied. "For some reason she doesn't like Kara. Blames her for things even."

"Seriously?" he asked. "I don't get that. You've never seemed happier than the last two weeks, even with all the garbage going on with the fight."

Warmed by the thought he saw that change in her, Alexa smiled. "She's good for me," she said. "Helps me remember who I really am and doesn't let me focus only on my MMA champion persona." She slowed down to take the off ramp. "Not that she's ever said anything specifically about it but being myself is a normal side effect of being with her."

"Yeah," Anthony said. "I get that feeling a little bit too. Kara Roberts is as real as a person can get." He laughed, and Alexa loved hearing the sound. Over the last two weeks since he came out of the coma, he grew stronger every day. All that remained from the episode was occasional but severe dizzy spells. He hated the wheelchair, but until the doctor cleared him one hundred percent, it was a safety precaution Alexa insisted on. "I think my favorite part is how she doesn't take any bullshit from anyone."

Alexa remembered when she first met Kara outside the Italian restaurant and had to laugh with him. "Oh, that is for sure," she said. "Since the first minute I met her." Simply enjoying having Anthony with her again, they rode in silence until turning the corner to her home. As they rolled closer, she saw the last thing she wanted to see—Jess waiting for her.

The woman sat in her car at the curb out front of the house. "Damnit," Alexa muttered, clicking the garage door opening. "I thought I was clear at the press conference."

Anthony put a hand on her forearm. "I know you're frustrated with her right now," he said. "But she's been your friend and ally for a long time. You have to at least hear what she wants."

With a sigh, Alexa knew he was right.

Disconnecting her fourth unsuccessful call, Kara dropped her phone into her lap. No one seemed to know where Annette was, and it had her worrying more by the second. "Nothing?" Brady asked from the driver's seat. They were headed to the university campus planning to check every possible place she would visit. Some of it was retracing what had been done, but they were out of new ideas.

Kara shook her head. "Nothing," she repeated back to him. "One of her study partners is going to try others in their group to see." She blew out a frustrated breath. "We will have to wait for her to call us back."

"Okay," Brady said, and Kara noticed his hands on the steering wheel. He gripped it so hard his knuckles were white. As worried as Kara felt, he clearly did as much if not more.

Still, this is his fault, she thought, not able to keep her temper in check anymore. "You need to start telling me what has been going on the last few weeks, Brady," she said. "After Annette saw you with the woman in the restaurant, she's never been the same."

The man winced. "I know," he said. "I thought we were okay again after she came home, but I guess I was so busy I missed how sad she still felt."

"How could you miss that?" Kara said, shaking her head in exasperation. "Are you having an affair or something like she thought?"

"No," Brady insisted. "I promise. Work has been crazy! And..."

When he didn't continue, Kara narrowed her eyes. "And? And what?"

He sighed. "I have been working three jobs."

Kara blinked. "What?" Kara asked. "Why?"

"Because I want to give Annette the wedding she deserves," he said, running a hand through his hair. "And I couldn't exactly tell her that."

Shaking her head, Kara tried to process what he said. "But you haven't even proposed yet?"

He barked out a wry laugh. "No kidding," he said. "I have a plan in the works for that too. You're not going to believe this when I tell you."

"Try me," Kara said, starting to put some of the pieces together. "I need to know all of it."

Nodding, Brady pulled into the giant parking garage on the university's campus. "You should have been in on it from the start," he said. "That was my first mistake." Kara didn't speak, wanting to see what else the man had to say.

"The woman Annette saw me with? She's an event planner. For like weddings and stuff."

Kara's mouth dropped open. "A wedding planner? But Brady—"

He held up a hand. "Don't get me wrong on that one," he said. "I was only arranging the engagement party. Not the wedding."

Leaning back in her seat, Kara took a moment to process everything. *Brady is working around the clock. The man is trying to give Annette the wedding of her dreams,* she thought. *And the woman Annette saw? A wedding planner, nothing more.* "Oh Brady, we need to hurry up and find her," she said, unfastening her seatbelt. "She's been a wreck over this, and you need to explain all of it to her."

"But the surprise...?" Brady started and Kara shook her head.

"We are past surprises," she said. "This needs to be resolved." Before Brady could argue, Kara's phone rang. When she saw Annette's name on the screen, tears came to her eyes. "Annette? Are you okay? Where are you?"

"I'm okay," her best friend replied. "I didn't mean to scare everyone... I was just... walking on the beach, soul searching."

Kara didn't care where her friend had been as long as she was safe. "Stay where you are and we will come get you," she said, glancing at the man beside her. Relief washed over his face. "Brady has lots of things to tell you, but it's going to be okay."

Alexa had half a mind to ignore Jess outside of her house and close the garage door, but Anthony was right. Jess was with her from the very beginning. No decision in her career since the very first pro fight was made without input from her manager. *So, why are we having such a disconnect about Kara?* she thought, walking through the house to the front door. *I don't understand it.* As she approached, the doorbell rang, and Alexa rolled her eyes. Sometimes Jess was too much. Still, she opened the door. "I thought we settled all of this on your last visit," she said to the woman on her front porch. "If you've come here to talk about Kara again, I'm not interested."

Jess shook her head. "It's not," she said, and the slur in her words gave Alexa pause. *Is she drunk? And she drove like this?* she wondered. That made no sense. Her friend rarely drank and never to the point of intoxication. Jess always claimed she never wanted to be out of control. That didn't seem to be the case today as she sneered at Alexa. "I have better things to talk about."

"I see," Alexa said, stepping aside. "Come in, Jess. Let me make you some coffee."

Giving a bitter laugh, Jess wandered past her and into the house. "Coffee won't fix this, Alexa," she said before seeing Anthony in the living room. "Anthony! I'm so glad you're here too." As Alexa followed her into the main part of the house, she made eye contact with her brother.

He raised an eyebrow. "Well, hi. Why are you so glad?"

Plopping down onto one of the easy chairs, Jess put her feet up on the ottoman and crossed her ankles. "Because we need to work together to talk some sense into your sister."

"I told you. I am not discussing Kara again," Alexa growled. "If that's all you have to say—"

"No, no, no," Jess said waving her hands. "Enough already. This is about business."

Feeling her shoulders relax at the comment, Alexa joined her brother on the couch across from her friend. "In that case, I am listening." Yet, before Jess could give her spiel, Alexa's intuition made a leap to another topic she wasn't ready for. "Unless this is about a rematch against Rachel Rhodes."

Jess's face fell. "Don't be like that," she said. "That is exactly what I want to talk about, and you know it."

"I already said no," Alexa said with a frown, unable to hide her irritation. "In fact, if I went on the internet right now, I'm sure there is a clip of me saying exactly those words on my way out of the press conference."

"There's a lot of things on the internet from that circus," Jess shot back. "Luckily, you being a coward isn't the highlight."

Alexa shot to her feet. "I think we are done," she said. "Jess, stay in that chair for an hour while you sober up. You're too drunk to drive."

Anthony held up his hands. "Whoa," he said. "Both of you take a deep breath." He looked hard at Jess. "Stop with the insults and explain why you are here." He pointed at Alexa. "And you sit down and listen."

Only because he was her brother and she loved him did Alexa sit. "She has sixty-seconds."

"Fine," Jess said. "I don't need it. This will be quick—there's an offer on the table if you're willing to step into the ring with Rachel Rhodes again. It has a big payout attached." She met Alexa's eye. "A very, very big number."

Chapter Twenty-Five

After a whirlwind of an evening of finding Annette at the beach, Brady immediately proposing, and then lots of tears, Kara was emotionally spent. All she wanted was a shower followed by a big glass of wine. While texting Alexa to let her know the good news, she kicked off her shoes and went to turn on the hot water. Only a loud meow by Oliver made her divert from her mission and walk into the kitchen. "Oh, big guy, I'm so sorry," she said, noticing his dry food bowl showed a hint of white ceramic at the bottom of the dish. It was far from empty, but that was never good enough. "I'm pretty sure you would have lasted the fifteen minutes for me to shower though." Purring, he weaved in and around her legs while she replenished his supply. "Better?"

When Oliver settled in to eat, Kara sighed. If only the rest of the world was as easy to please as her cat. She had yet to talk to Alexa about the press conference. All she knew was from Jess's angry accusations that Alexa had turned down a rematch because of her. *And I do not understand all that crap*, she thought, finally getting to the bathroom. *How is any of what has happened because of me? I didn't ask for any of this.*

Resolving to deal with Jess later, she cranked on the hot water and stripped. With her hand under the water, she waited for it to get warm. Just when it seemed good enough and Kara started to get in, the door buzzer to her apartment sounded. *Oh, you have got to be kidding,* she thought, looking around for her phone and realized she left it on the kitchen counter. If someone had called her or sent a text in advance of arriving, she hadn't seen it. For all she knew, Annette and Brady might have not settled things after all. *I have to answer it.*

Slipping into her robe, Kara hurried to the door and peeked through the peephole. Alexa Knight stood in the hallway. Blinking with surprise, she quickly opened the door. "Alexa," she said. "This is an unexpected surprise."

Raising an eyebrow, the woman looked Kara up and down. "Hopefully not a bad one," she said. "Did I interrupt something?"

Kara laughed. "Only me trying to take a shower," she said. "Seeing you is much better."

With her dark eyes twinkling at the compliment, Alexa motioned toward the inside of the apartment. "Can I come in?"

After a brief hesitation while Kara tried to remember if she had picked up all her dirty dishes, she nodded, letting Alexa inside. "Of course," she said, relatively secure there was nothing out that would embarrass her. Although they spent a few nights together at Alexa's house before Anthony came to live with her, tonight was the first time the woman had come over to Kara's. "I'll go turn the water off and then pour us some wine."

"Don't delay a shower if you want one," Alexa said, her voice taking on a huskier tone. "I can wait. Unless…"

A warm tingle ran through Kara. "Unless, what? What are you thinking, Ms. Knight?"

Alexa moved closer until their bodies nearly touched. "I'm thinking of how you look inside this robe," she said. "And how much I want to remove it."

Tilting her head, Kara looked at the woman through half closed eyes. "And if I want you to?" she asked, a pulse starting low in her body. "Will you shower with me?"

As an answer, Alexa took the terrycloth in her hands and pulled Kara against her. "Yes," she breathed a moment before kissing her.

With steam swirling all around them, Alexa watched the hot water cascade over Kara's sensual body. The woman's eyes fixed on her as if enjoying every second of Alexa's attention. "Are you going to join me?" she asked, and Alexa slowly nodded as she started to undress.

"Wait for me. I want to bathe you," she said, trying control her pounding heart. "If I may."

Kara hummed, closing her eyes as she tipped her head back to let the water wet her hair. "I'd like that," she murmured, and Alexa stepped into the shower.

Every part of her wanted to rush, but she forced her hands to move slowly as she picked up the shampoo. "Turn around," she said, and Kara opened her eyes to lock with Alexa's. No words needed to be said to convey the desire crackling between them. "Please." Without a word, Kara turned under the water and waited. Slowly, Alexa filled her palm with the pearly liquid before moving closer. The nearness of their naked bodies made it hard for her to concentrate.

She paused to control herself, making Kara look back over her shoulder. "Are you okay?" she asked, starting to turn.

"Oh yes, you have no idea," Alexa said, running her soapy hands into Kara's curly, wet hair. As she felt the strands across her palms, she thought of that first meeting in the conference room at ESPN headquarters. She noticed Kara's hair then, how it threatened to break loose from her ponytail at any second. The wildness attracted her then no matter how much she tried to deny it and caressing it in the shower only attracted her more. Everything about Kara fascinated her.

The woman sighed. "That feels so amazing," Kara said. "I could stand here and let you do that all night."

Smiling, Alexa kept working her fingers. "And nothing else?" she asked. "I'm not sure that was what I intended."

With a little laugh, Kara surprised her by reaching back and grabbing her hip to pull their bodies closer together. "I think you are going to get exactly what you intended." It was Alexa's turn to hum with pleasure as her body grazed the curve of Kara's smooth backside. Only soapy water was between them, and Alexa had to focus to stay on task as she started to rinse her hair. Letting her hands drift with the bubbles, Alexa ran her fingertips across the swell of Kara's breast. When she grazed a tight nipple, the woman gasped. "You're making me crazy."

"Am I?" Alexa whispered in her ear. "Does that mean you want me to stop?"

Kara's body shuddered. "Don't you dare."

With a small smile of satisfaction, Alexa slid her hand lower, relishing the feel of Kara's soft, slippery skin. "Good," she said, moving her fingertips in a small circle a breath above the hair between Kara's legs. "Because I don't think I can."

Hearing Kara's breath starting to come faster, Alexa sank her hand lower into her wet curls and brushed across the woman's swollen lips. "Oh God, you're such a tease," Kara moaned, and Alexa felt her body reacting as well. Both were on the knife edge of desire, eager to touch and be touched. No moment could compare to the thrill of having so much sexual tension. Kara pressed her body against Alexa's teasing fingers. She moaned. "Please keep going." Unable to hold back a moment longer, Alexa slid lower until she grazed the woman's clit, making Kara gasp again.

Alexa added more pressure. "Here?"

"Yes," Kara moaned. "Yes." The woman's body trembled as she braced herself against the wall with hot water coursing down the front of her. "Faster." Without hesitating, Alexa did what she asked, while pressing her own body into Kara's.

Kara moved with her, and Alexa whispered in her ear, "Come for me." For a moment, everything stood in the balance, and then, with a cry of ecstasy, she did.

Lazing in the bed after another round of sex, Kara played with a strand of Alexa's long dark hair. "I don't know how you make me come so fast," she said with a sigh. "Or so often."

Alexa chuckled, taking hold of Kara's hand, and kissing her fingers. "You do the same to me," she said. "And some."

Liking the sound of knowing she pleased her partner, Kara snuggled closer. "We are good together," she said and when Alexa didn't answer, she raised her head to look into the woman's face. *Was that too much?* she wondered. *But it's true.* "Did that make you uncomfortable?"

Alexa returned her look, seriousness reflected in the deep green of her eyes. "No," she said. "I'm not uncomfortable. Only thinking about what you said. And I agree." She moved closer to brush a kiss across Kara's lips. "One hundred percent."

Feeling her body relax again, Kara settled against Alexa's shoulder. "Good," she said. "I was worried for a second Jess had gotten to you."

With a sigh, Alexa wrapped her arm around Kara's body to hold her close. "I promise that won't happen," she said. "I honestly don't know what's going on with her. She came by the house again." For a moment, she hesitated and then continued. "And I think she was drunk."

"Really?" Kara asked, unable to envision Jess intoxicated. The woman was never out of control. "What did she want?" Then the answer came to her. "Was it something about a rematch?" They had yet to discuss the press conference. Kara planned to watch what she could on social media after her shower but was pleasantly sidetracked. A tingle ran through her at the memory of the shower. *Very pleasantly sidetracked,* she thought, wondering if she was ready to focus on Jess and MMA yet.

Before she could decide, Alexa nodded, bringing her back to the conversation. "It was. She really wants me to do it. And for a lot of reasons."

Kara frowned knowing Alexa was not interested in fighting again. In fact, with the injury to her eye, she shouldn't. "But you still said no, right?" Hearing the woman blow out a frustrated breath, Kara took her hand. "Talk to me."

"I didn't answer either way," she said. "Rachel Rhodes

called me out at the press conference and apparently has done nothing but trash me on social media since." Alexa's whole body stiffened. "She's calling me a coward."

Feeling her temper rising at the thought, Kara worked to keep her tone even. "That's simply how she acts," she said, trying to be the voice of reason. "You can't let her bait you into doing something you don't want to do."

"Yes," Alexa said. "You're right. But there's more. The MMA promoters are willing to put together a huge purse if I agree to another fight." Kara was confused, thinking money was the last thing Alexa needed. *But I could be wrong,* she thought. *All those crazy allegations about debts.* She furrowed her brow. *Alexa said there was nothing to those though.* As if reading her mind, Alexa kissed Kara on the forehead. "If you're worried I need the money, don't be. But I had another idea."

"What is that?" Kara asked, and Alexa squeezed her hand.

Kara could feel the energy around Alexa's idea thrumming through her. "I agree to the fight," she said. "Set the record straight regarding Rachel Rhodes, but even more importantly, I can put the money to good use."

Caught up in the woman's excitement, Kara rolled to look into Alexa's beautiful face. "How?" she asked, and Alexa smiled.

"Donate it all to cancer research."

Chapter Twenty-Six

Pulling into the parking lot at Griffith Park Observatory, Alexa saw Jess already parked and out of her car. Dressed in running tights and a tank top, she looked fit and ready to exercise. *And not particularly hungover considering,* Alexa thought parking the Camaro. *I guess we will see.* The Hollywood Reservoir Loop trail was no cakewalk. Meeting there for a morning outing was Alexa's idea. She needed to discuss her decisions with her manager and hoped a little physical exertion would help calm Jess down. Still, there wasn't anything she had to tell her that should upset the woman. A rematch was what Jess wanted. *Let's see how she feels about the rest of it.*

"Good morning," Jess said as Alexa climbed out of her car. "This is a great idea. And a perfect way to start a Saturday."

Raising an eyebrow at her friend's enthusiasm, Alexa noticed the day was warm already. "You're certainly in a good mood," she said, taking off her hoodie to leave it in the car. "I wasn't sure you'd say yes when I sent the text this morning."

Jess bent her leg, grabbing her ankle to stretch her thigh muscle. "Why wouldn't I?"

Alexa snorted a laugh. "Well, aside from the fact you were drunk at my house yesterday evening," she said. "You've been a bit pissed at me lately."

"Ah, I'm over it," Jess said while she rotated one ankle and then the other. "It is what it is. Time to enjoy retirement."

Pausing, Alexa didn't know what to think of Jess's one-eighty. "And if I told you I changed my mind about fighting again?" she asked, starting to stretch. "Wouldn't you be interested?"

Jess stopped moving and looked at her. "Have you?" she asked, clearly hopeful that was the case.

Alexa rolled her head left and then to the right, loosening her neck. "Let's get started and I'll tell you everything on the trail," she answered. "I think it's going to get too warm soon."

"Fair enough," Jess said, leading them to the trailhead. "I can't wait to hear this. Just when I resigned myself to the idea." Smiling at her friend's renewed enthusiasm, Alexa started them at an even pace. The paved trail was wide enough to run side-by-side. After a few minutes they found their rhythm and Jess restarted the conversation. "Don't leave me in suspense. What's going on?"

"Well, not to start this off on the wrong note, but I talked all this through with Kara last night after you left." Alexa couldn't see, but she was pretty sure Jess rolled her eyes.

"Okay," the woman said. "So, you were talking to her, and?"

"And I have decided to accept Rachel Rhodes's offer for

a rematch," Alexa answered. "As long as the promotors stick with that number you quoted me."

Jess started to nod. "I can make sure that happens," she said between breaths as the trail steepened quickly. "This will be big, Alexa. I don't think you realize." She didn't say anything for a second making Alexa glance over to see if everything was all right. Her friend looked lost in thought, clearly calculating all the different scenarios. "If we're going to do it right, there will be a lot of publicity. We need to make sure the entire world knows that you're defending your honor." Alexa listened as they ran around a wide corner on the trail. "Are you going to be okay with that?"

Not loving the idea, but knowing Jess was right, Alexa nodded. "I understand," she said. "If Rachel wants a circus, make it a circus under our terms."

Jess puffed out a laugh. "Oh, I can do that."

Alexa liked her friend's confidence. "There's one more thing," she said. "To add even one more twist." When Jess didn't respond, she kept going. "I want to donate the money."

Catching Alexa by surprise by stopping in the center of the trail, Jess coughed out an answer. "You're going to do what?"

Confused, Alexa turned toward her. "Donate it. Every cent," she said jogging in place. "I don't want the money from this. It all goes to cancer research."

Staring at her, clearly dazed by the decision, Jess shook her head. "You can't do that," she whispered. "Not that much."

Alexa frowned. "Of course, I can," she said. "It's the right thing to do."

For a moment, it looked like Jess would argue, but then she seemed to snap out of whatever upset her. "Right," she said, starting to run again and Alexa fell into step beside her. "Of course, you can."

While she waited in the building's laundry room for her load to finish, Kara listened to Annette over the phone. "He went to work at his second job," her friend said. "Delivering food, of all things. I told him he didn't need to keep doing that, but he insisted."

As she leaned against the dryer, Kara wasn't surprised he kept at it. "Brady is as good as they come," she said. "He really wants this for you. For you both."

"I know," Annette said. "He's so amazing. I love him so much."

"And now you know why he's been so tired and distracted," Kara said as the dryer buzzed that it was finished. "You have no idea how happy I am that everything worked itself out." Holding the phone against her shoulder, she opened the machine's door. "Watching you two struggle was tearing me apart."

Annette sighed. "You were the best friend I could ask for through it," she said. "I felt entirely supported. I honestly believe you would have let me move into that little place."

Laughing, Kara started piling warm clothes into her laundry basket. "Oliver might get his nose out of joint over it, but I meant it," she said. "You'd do the same for me."

"Always."

Kara started for the stairs to go back to her apartment. "So, did you get any more details on what Brady is planning for your engagement party?" she asked. "I'm excited."

"No," Annette said with a laugh. "Even though he poured out his heart, he's keeping those details to himself."

Jogging up the steps toward her third floor apartment, Kara racked her brain trying to figure out what Brady would have come up with. "And you really have no idea?" she asked, starting to breathe heavier as she got closer to her floor. "Annette, we really need to get back into racquetball. These stairs are kicking my ass."

Annette laughed. "We totally need to, but you could have taken the elevator," her friend reminded her when suddenly Kara's phone pinged in her ear.

"Hold on," she said. "I'm getting another call." Before Annette could answer, Kara looked at the screen. It was a local number, but not one she recognized. She was about to silence it when she hesitated. Something in her gut told her to go ahead and answer. Putting Annette on hold, she connected the call. "Hello?"

"Kara? It's me, Anthony," she heard a man's voice say.

Feeling a twist of concern, Kara stopped climbing. "Anthony, what's wrong? Is everyone okay?"

"Whoa, nothing is wrong," Anthony said. "Sorry to call you out of the blue, but I promise everything is fine."

Kara felt her body relax. "It's okay," she said, finishing her trip up the stairs. "I didn't know why else you would call me." She laughed, realizing how that sounded. "I mean, I'm always happy to talk to you, it's just..."

She heard Anthony laugh too. "You don't have to explain," he said. "I get it. But I am calling because I need your help."

"Help? Okay, for what?"

"Alexa's birthday. It's in two weeks and I want to celebrate it."

Reaching her apartment, Kara typed in her keycode to open the door. "Of course, I will help," she said, liking the idea of Alexa having a birthday. Then it dawned on her

Anthony's would be the same day. "But it will need to be a double-sized event to celebrate you too."

She could almost hear him grin over the phone. "I won't say no to that," he said. "I always love a party."

Back from her run, Alexa went straight to her fridge. As she had hoped, an ice-cold, high-protein smoothy waited for her. "Thank you, Anthony," she called, taking the drink with her to settle on one of the stools at the counter. After a minute of no answer, she frowned. "Anthony? Where are you?" It seemed unlikely he left without texting her. *And someone would have had to pick him up*, she thought, a sudden feeling of unease creeping into her chest. Leaving the smoothy, she went to his bedroom, and the door was ajar. "Anthony?"

As she moved to push the door open, praying her brother was simply asleep, she paused when the room was empty. *Where the hell is he?* she wondered, returning to the kitchen to get her phone. Before she could pick it up, the thing buzzed with a new text. Anthony's name showed on the screen. "Can we get Italian from Nostra tonight?" his message asked.

Alexa had to check her temper knowing he hadn't meant to scare her. "We can do that," she wrote back. "Where are you?"

"Mom and Dad picked me up for my doctor's appointment," he sent, and Alexa mentally smacked herself on the forehead. She had completely forgotten and felt a wave of guilt.

All the excitement around her decision to take the rematch and donate the money made Anthony's appointment slip her mind. "I'm sorry," she wrote. "I can't believe I forgot."

"No worries. I could have reminded you but after you didn't come home last night..." He included a row of laughing face emojis.

Alexa couldn't help but smile. "Fair enough," she sent. "Text me when you're headed back."

A quick thumbs up emoji came back. *I can't believe I missed that appointment*, she thought, walking toward her bedroom. Stripping off her sweaty tank top, a shower sounded perfect. Thinking of one brought a smile to her face as she pictured Kara naked under the hot water. *Even if I did forget, I can't say it wasn't worth it.* Yet, before she could even get the water started, the doorbell rang. *If that's Kara...* the coincidence would be too weird. Still, the idea of seeing her made Alexa's stomach tighten with anticipation.

Opening the door, Alexa realized the person on the front step could not be further from Kara, and the excitement she felt turned ice cold in a second. Rachel Rhodes stood on her porch. Knowing she should close the door without saying a word, the sight of the woman on her property made the hairs on the back of her neck stand up. "What do you want?" she hissed, and Rachel narrowed her eyes.

"Nice outfit," she said pointing at Alexa standing at the door in a sports bra and running shorts. "Expecting me?"

Alexa stiffened. "I'll ask you once more and then I'm slamming the door—what do you want?"

"Take it easy, Alexa," Rachel answered. "I would have called but I knew you wouldn't answer so I came in person."

Not caring to hear more, Alexa started to close the door. "You're right," she said, and Rachel held up her hands to make Alexa pause.

"Fine. I'll keep this short," Rachel said. "Jess let word out about your accepting the fight."

Not thrilled Jess did it so quickly and without a heads up, Alexa still kept a straight face. "I would have thought that would make you happy."

Rachel sneered. "Oh, it does," she said. "That's a lot of money. I wanted to tell you to your face, without all the lights and cameras, that I plan to crush you." The woman's eyes shimmered with her passion to hurt Alexa.

Unwilling to give the woman any satisfaction for her ambush, Alexa gave a wry laugh. "Good luck with that," she said and slammed the door.

Chapter Twenty-Seven

The next week went by in a rush, but Kara didn't mind. Busy mapping out the documentary with Anthony, things started to come together. "This is going to be a powerful film," Alexa said as she surveyed the storyboard tacked to the wall in Kara's apartment. "How long do you think it will take?"

Standing beside her, Kara pursed her lips. "I'm not entirely sure," she said. "With the extra money, I am arranging a full crew. Unfortunately, my usual lead cameraman is booked until the end of the month."

Alexa turned to her. "And he's worth waiting for?" she asked, and Kara nodded.

"Very," she said. "Plus, he's been with me since the beginning of the project." She laughed. "I don't want to cut him out now that I can actually pay him what he's worth."

Putting her arms around Kara, Alexa smiled. "That's why you are such a special person," she said. "You always do the right thing." Warmed by the woman's touch, Kara leaned into Alexa and kissed her. The last week had been special because of the amount of quality time she was able to share with her. Although neither said it, the fact things were about to get crazy once the world knew about the upcoming rematch remained. Kara didn't understand how it would change things exactly but guessed Alexa's training would be more intense than ever. *Will she still have room for me in her life?* she wondered. *I don't want to be a distraction like Jess claimed I was, but I don't want to lose her either.*

Pulling back to study her face, Alexa's brow furrowed. "What are you so busy thinking about?" she asked. "I can tell something is in your head."

Kara sighed. "Just wondering what will happen when Jess arranges the date for the fight," she said. "And the advertising starts."

Looking into Kara's eyes, Alexa clearly had something important to say that Kara wasn't aware of yet. "Well, that's one of the main reasons I came by this morning," she said. "Jess was able to talk the promoters into giving me an early date to fight."

"How early?" Kara asked, feeling a twist of anxiety in her stomach.

Alexa let out a deep breath. "One month." Blinking in surprise, Kara didn't know what to say. One month wasn't nearly enough time for all the preparations needed. Not to mention Alexa needing to train. For the last fight she took nine weeks and that would be cut by over half.

She shook her head. "How can you actually do that?"

When Alexa stepped away breaking contact, Kara felt a strange sense of loss, as if her body already guessed what was coming. "I'm meeting with my training team in an hour," she said. "We will map out an aggressive program. Ten hours a day."

"Okay," Kara said, hating the instinct to cling to Alexa,

but unable to stop. "What does that mean for us?" She gathered herself. "I didn't mean for that to sound needy, but I want to know what's realistic."

Alexa ran a hand over her face. "I hate this," she said. "It's not what I wanted, and you have to believe me." Feeling unexpected tears burn her eyes, all Kara could do was nod. She had always worried the day might come Alexa didn't have time for her anymore.

She lifted her chin, forcing back the pain of being abandoned, even if it was only temporary. "Of course," she said. "I understand. This is something you must do. I won't stand in your way."

"Kara..." Alexa said, reaching for her, but Kara stepped back.

"You should go get ready to talk to the trainers," she said. "I want to get back to work on the documentary."

Dropping her hand, Alexa's face filled with sadness as she turned to leave. "It's not forever," she said. "Only a month."

A lot could happen in a month, and there were no guarantees, but she wouldn't give up either. "Right, not forever," she said, following her to the door. Alexa opened it and then paused in the doorway as if ready to say something more, but Kara had enough. There was no sense dragging it out. "Good luck, Alexa. I'm here if you need me." Without another word, Alexa was gone.

"Okay, it's done," Alexa said into her Camaro's Bluetooth as she pulled away from Kara's apartment building. Every instinct was to go back inside and apologize to Kara for acting so stupid. Having the woman out of her life was the last thing she wanted. *But it had to be done,* she thought as she ground her teeth in frustration. *This next month will be intense.*

"It was the right thing to do," Jess said over the speaker.

Frowning, Alexa wasn't so sure. "Explain to me again why I upset the woman I care so much about?"

She heard Jess sigh. "Because things are about to become a circus," she said. "And Kara doesn't deserve to be mixed up in that." When Alexa didn't comment, she went on. "You're doing this to protect her, Alexa."

Rolling to a stop at a red light, she thought through what her manager said. *I'm doing this to protect her.* She remembered the last thing Kara said. "I'll be here if you need me." Alexa felt her chest tighten. *What if I need her already? Why does my life have to be so complicated?* Frustrated, when the light turned green, she roared the Camaro's engine and shot off the line, hitting sixty by the next light where she squealed to a stop. "What the hell was that?" Jess asked, bringing Alexa back to the moment. "Are you trying to get another speeding ticket? You can't take any more bad publicity."

"You're right," Alexa replied, blowing out a frustrated breath. "Part of this whole thing is to repair my reputation." The accusations from Rachel Rhodes and all the reporters rang in her mind. Then she remembered something else. "Jess, did you ever find out anything behind the gambling bullshit?"

Taking the onramp to head to the gym to meet with her training team, Alexa thought the call had disconnected when Jess didn't answer. "Not really," Jess finally said. "I'd kind of forgotten about that rumor. Why? Did someone approach you again?"

The freeway was jammed, an absolute parking lot, and Alexa's temper threatened to get away from her. "No,"

Alexa growled. "It was so out of left field." When a car suddenly cut in front of her, she gripped the steering wheel hard enough to turn her knuckles white. "I need to hang up. Traffic is a mess and I want to concentrate."

"All right," Jess said. "And Alexa..." She hesitated before going on. "Don't hate me over any of this, okay?"

Raising an eyebrow, Alexa waited to see if she was going to say more. "I don't understand," Alexa finally answered. "Why would that ever happen? I know you only want the best for me. Even when it comes to Kara."

"Yes, that is exactly what I am doing," the woman said. "Never forget that. I'll talk to you later. Drive safe."

Still not sure what to make of Jess's tone, Alexa thought about asking more, but then let it go. "I will," she replied, starting to say she'd see her tomorrow at the gym, but her friend had hung up. Wondering if maybe she should call her back and follow up after all, a car suddenly stopped in front of her. She slammed on the brakes, swearing at the bad traffic, and forgot about Jess for the moment.

Trying to focus on something other than Alexa, Kara worked at editing film for her documentary. She was less than an hour in when the next scene was a preliminary interview with Anthony. As soon as he showed up on her screen, his handsome green eyes captivated the camera. *And look exactly like Alexa's*, she thought, angrily snapping off the monitor to hide the picture. When tears threatened, she decided editing would have to wait for later. "Damnit," Kara said, making Oliver, who slept on the desk near her keyboard, open one eye. Noticing, she ran a hand over the tabby cat's back. "Sorry, buddy, I didn't mean to disturb you." She sighed. "But I think I might need some wine. And not only a little."

Wandering to the kitchen, Kara couldn't help but think about everything Alexa had said before she left. It wasn't so much the words that upset her, but the message behind them. *I am a distraction and not wanted around*, she thought when a sick thought made her stop walking. *What if she's bought into the idea that I was part of why she lost the fight?* "No, she would never think that," she said aloud to the empty apartment. "Not the Alexa I know." *But how well do I really know her?* the little voice in her head said. It seemed like the answer was a lot because she knew her brother, her manager, even her parents some. She started walking again, intent on getting the wine as her mind whirled with scenarios.

After pouring a healthy serving, and with her glass of wine in one hand and the bottle in another, Kara sat on the couch. Her laptop rested on the coffee table, closed but seeming to lure her attention. Other than watch video with Brady and listen to his retelling of Alexa's fighting history, Kara never learned about the woman's past. *How wrong would it be to google her?* she wondered, feeling a hint of guilt at even thinking about digging through Alexa's past. She sipped the wine and stared at the laptop. *Maybe I should ask Annette and see what she thinks. Would snooping make me a bad girlfriend?* Frowning, Kara considered that last thought. *But was I ever really her girlfriend? And if I was, did she just breakup with me?*

"Screw it," she said, and slid the computer onto her lap to turn it on. After a minute, she typed Alexa Knight into the search field and hit enter. There were a lot of fighting articles, references, and links to videos on YouTube. One thing intrigued her though. A picture of Alexa at some sort of awards event dressed in a killer, fitted black suit that showed off her perfect body, but what truly caught her eye was the title—*Fighter or Heartbreaker?* Clicking on the link to read more, when the results came up, Kara did a double-take. The screen was filled with pictures of Alexa with at least a dozen different beautiful women.

Skimming the article, she continued to drink the wine in bigger and bigger sips. "Alexa Knight, MMA bantamweight champion, continues her streak of dating and then dumping sexy women." Kara's hand started to shake as she scrolled. A bigger picture of Alexa with a gorgeous brunette filled the screen. The candid photo caught them laughing over drinks at a beach bar somewhere. Reading the caption underneath, the wine suddenly made Kara feel sick. "Charlese Senger, another woman left by the wayside as the fighter heads into training camp in preparation to defend her belt." Slamming the laptop shut, Kara couldn't stop the hot angry tears from coming. *I've been so stupid,* she thought. *I'm simply another conquest.*

Chapter Twenty-Eight

With music blasting throughout the training gym, Alexa went through the complex motions of a Brazilian Jujitsu workout. Her sparring partner grunted as Alexa twisted in a flash of movement and pulled on her arm. After a second, the woman tapped her hand hard against Alexa's side. "Stop," she cried. "That's too much."

"Damnit," barked her trainer while Alexa immediately let go. "I love the enthusiasm, but we are only going through the moves, not breaking her arm."

Helping her partner up from the mat, Alexa tried not to overreact at the man's words. "Sorry about that," she mumbled to the other woman.

She rubbed her arm, flexing it at the elbow. "It's okay," she said. "I want you to beat Rachel Rhodes as much as anyone."

Alexa gave her a half smile. "Thanks," she said. "But I'll be more careful until then." She turned to the trainer. "I need a break. Two minutes."

"Okay," he said. "Get some water. Find your focus."

"Thanks," she said, climbing out of the ring and going to her duffle bag in the corner. Holding her breath, she looked at her phone, hoping against hope there was a text. Nothing. It had been a week since she saw or heard from Kara, and it was all her fault. The way she acted in the woman's apartment, being so dismissive, when her heart felt completely the opposite was too much to let go. *But Jess was right*, she thought. *This has been a circus.*

Every day when she arrived, no matter if it was the front or backdoor, reporters waited. They weren't all sports focused either. It seemed the championship rematch had taken on larger proportions. The press painted the fight as an epic battle between lifelong rivals but with a twist. Apparently, Rachel had let it slip they were once lovers. It wasn't an accident, of that Alexa was certain. The internet ate the details up and wanted more. From somewhere, a photo of them together in a serious lip-lock surfaced and memes were everywhere. Plus, all the recent footage between them, including in Las Vegas where Kara jumped in and defended Alexa, was all over social media. The Vegas incident had over a million views alone. Jess said there was no such thing as bad publicity, but Alexa didn't agree. It was only a week, and she was sick of all the craziness. Not to mention all the attention made it hard to focus on training.

"Times up, Alexa," her trainer yelled across the room. "Let's run through some speed drills. You seem a little sluggish today."

Blowing out a frustrated breath, Alexa tossed the phone back into her bag. "One second, I need the bathroom first." Without waiting for an answer, she went in the locker room only to hear the scurry of footsteps. *What the...?* Alexa thought, looking in the direction of the noise.

Her eyes fell on the slight swaying of a shower curtain. In two steps, she was across the space, ripping the plastic aside. A man with a camera stood inside and from the wide look of his eyes, he was about ready to wet himself. "Who the hell are you?" Rather than answer immediately, he raised the camera and took a shot. In a flash, Alexa had ahold of the camera which was on a strap around the man's neck.

He let out a squeal as she jerked him forward. "Don't hurt me," he said. "I'm only trying to make a living."

At his confession, Alexa put two and two together. "You hid in here to take a picture of me in the shower?" She shook her head in complete disbelief. "When did you sneak in here?"

"Last night after the cleaning crew left," he said. "I slipped in when they weren't looking."

"Wait, you've been in here all night and all day?" she said, releasing her grip. "To take a picture of me naked?"

He rubbed the back of his neck and nodded. "It will be worth a fortune," he said. When Alexa only stared at him, he grinned. "So, what do you say? One shot? Help a guy out?"

Through clenched teeth, Alexa pointed toward the exit. "Get out. Now," she said. "Or I will snap your neck." Not needing more motivation, the creep left, while Alexa covered her face with her hands. Feeling every possible emotion, it was all she could do not to scream.

Getting in contact with Charlese Senger took a little longer than Kara thought it would, but it turned out the woman had been in Hawaii on a kayaking adventure all week. Her agent politely explained she didn't want to be disturbed.

Then, out of the blue, she sent Kara a text. "Do you like sushi?"

"Absolutely," Kara answered and a few hours later they were sequestered behind gold, silk curtains in the back room of a West Hollywood restaurant known for its fabulous sushi as well for being discrete. The Hollywood elite couldn't eat out like everybody else otherwise fans would be relentless. Kara appreciated that fact more than ever after the craziness of Alexa's world. Even still, reporters called her for reactions to every recently exposed bit of news. All she said was 'no comment' and hung up but seeing how bad the publicity was around the fight made Kara feel sorry for Alexa. She had to be hating every second of it.

After they ordered a few different delicacies and the sake was delivered, Charlese settled in on the red cushions. "So, Kara Roberts," she said. "I'm afraid I didn't recognize the name, but when my agent filled me in, I thought we needed more than a phone call."

Kara raised an eyebrow. "That's intriguing," she said. "Not that I mind. It's not every day I'm asked to dinner by a Hollywood A-lister."

The woman laughed and the sound was charming and sexy, a combination that made her career. "Well, thank you, I think," she said. "I'm hoping it's a good thing."

Smiling, Kara picked up a small, white cup and sipped her sake. "It is," she said. "But don't be surprised if I ask for an autograph on a napkin before we leave."

"And I may do the same," Charlese replied. "I googled you after the tipoff by my agent, and your documentary sounds excellent. I'm surprised Anthony is doing it." She gave Kara a small smile. "Or that Alexa is letting him. Is that how you met?"

"No. I was part of ESPN's docuseries team set up to

film her journey to the big fight," Kara answered. "It didn't go so well."

Charlese tilted her head. "How so?"

"Well, for starters, I didn't know who she was," Kara laughed. "I don't follow MMA."

Her eyes widening, Charlese leaned back. "Oh, I so wish I was there for that moment," she said. "But let me guess, it was Jess who reacted the most?"

Thinking back, Kara tried to remember exactly how that first meeting went. "Not so much at first," she answered. "But once Alexa showed interest in me beyond a professional relationship, Jess totally ran interference." She shook her head. "That woman blames me for everything that's happened."

Charlese reached across the small table and took Kara's hand. "Don't let her get in your head," she said. "Jess has her own agenda." She looked Kara hard in the eyes. "Let me guess. You wanted to talk to me because Alexa broke up with you to go train for the next fight." Feeling a surprising amount of hurt over the reality of what Alexa did, all Kara could do was nod. Letting go, Charlese shook her head. "That bitch, and I don't mean Alexa. Jess forced that. She did it to us too and although that didn't matter too much because Alexa and I were better as friends, Jess needs to be fired and thrown out on her ass."

Sitting in the dark drinking a glass of ice water, Alexa contemplated her life. For starters, she wished she had wine instead of water but that would not be good for training. After that, she missed the hell out of Kara but calling her would be selfish. Even if the woman answered, Alexa didn't have anything different to offer her. The training was more than a circus, it was a nightmare. *The kind with scary clowns,* she thought, remembering the man in the shower. If she hadn't come across him accidently, there was no telling the pictures he would have taken of her. Then, a photo of Alexa in all her glory, would be all over the place.

Finally, tomorrow was her and Anthony's birthday. Normally she planned something for them to do together, but amazingly, Anthony was busy. "We can celebrate it after you're done training," he had said. "Then we can really party." Although she would never admit it, his decision hurt. She didn't expect much, but at least to go to dinner or have a cake at home. Something. In the end, only Jess wanted to spend the evening with her. *Oh well, dinner at Nostra will be nice,* she thought. *A big plate of carbs before I have to start cutting weight.*

As she contemplated which of Roberto's dishes she would order, if not two, she heard a key in the lock and the front door opening. After a moment, the living room lights flipped on, half blinding her. "What the hell," Anthony said with a start. "You scared the crap out of me, sis. Why are you sitting in the dark?"

"Sorry," Alexa said. "I was enjoying the quiet after another crazy day."

Anthony came to sit beside her on the couch. "That bad?"

After sipping her ice water, Alexa nodded. "Someone tried to take a picture of me in the locker room's shower."

"What?" he said, a flush of anger coming to his face. "How the hell did they get in?"

"Snuck in with the cleaning crew last night," she said with a shake of her head. "How's that for dedicated?"

They sat in silence for a minute before Anthony

jumped up. "I need a drink after that news," he said, pointing at her hand. "What is that?"

"Ice water."

Anthony frowned. "Can't you have anything else?" he asked. "Under the circumstances?" Alexa studied her glass. *Do I admit I am sticking to water for more than only my training?* she wondered. *That if I get even a little drunk, I'll be calling Kara asking her to take me back?*

She sighed. "Sticking to water," she said. "Seems like a good idea."

Rubbing his chin, Anthony looked ready to say more, but then wandered toward the kitchen. "I hope you plan to at least have a drink tomorrow," he mumbled barely loud enough for Alexa to hear.

"What do you mean? Because it's our birthday?" she asked, forcing herself to sound normal and not reveal the disappointment she felt. "Yeah, maybe a glass of wine at dinner. Jess is taking me out."

Returning with a beer in hand, Anthony sat on the couch across from her. "That's a good idea," he said. "Nostra?"

Alexa smiled. "Where else?"

Chapter Twenty-Nine

When Anthony called, Kara assumed he wanted to discuss times for their next set of interviews.

"So, what time are you getting there?" he asked, confusing Kara entirely.

"Get where?" she asked. "I thought we would meet here next week and go find a quiet spot for the interview with—"

She heard Anthony gasp. "Kara, don't you dare tell me you forgot," he said. "You helped me with the secret birthday invites for crying out loud."

Furrowing her brow, it took Kara another second before she realized her mistake. "Oh, Anthony," she said. "I can't possibly—"

He interrupted her again. "Don't you dare cancel on me." Kara closed her mouth and didn't know what more to say. Going to Alexa and Anthony's birthday was something she planned weeks ago. A lot had changed since she helped arrange a private party at Nostra.

Shaking her head, she tried to make herself clear. "Anthony, I think your amazing," she said and paused. *And*

I think your sister is amazing too, she thought before continuing. "But in case Alexa hasn't explained things to you, we aren't together right now." *Or ever again?* She didn't like to think about that option. Her heart still held out hope although after speaking with Charlese she was even more confused. The actress had provided information about Alexa in much more detail than Kara had known before. Some was bad, but ninety percent of her explanation was positive. According to Charlese, Alexa Knight had many complexities, but at her core was a good person. Someone who could be warm and loving under the right circumstances.

"Alexa did tell me some things," Anthony said, bringing her back to the moment. His voice gentle and Kara felt herself caving already. "But you're still her friend, right?"

Kara sighed. "I am," she said. "And I always will be, but are you sure she would want me there?"

Anthony had assured her Alexa would be happy to see her which was why Kara hurried through the rain with Annette and Brady to the backdoor of Nostra. A perky teenager with dark hair and the family's signature green eyes opened the door and greeted them. "You're just in time," she said, excitement in her voice. "Jess sent a text that they are leaving Aunt Alexa's house right now."

Climbing the two steps, Kara ducked inside to get out of the stormy weather. "Aunt Alexa?" she asked not realizing Alexa and Anthony had other siblings.

The girl smiled. "Well, I'm Danielle and we are actually cousins, but it's easier to call her my aunt." She waved them forward through the kitchen. "Come with me. We have everything set up in the banquet room." Following Danielle, Kara and her friends quickly joined the three dozen other people in the large space.

Anthony spotted them as they came in and hurrying over, pulled Kara into a hug. "Thank you so much for coming," he said, giving her a squeeze. "I promise you won't be sorry."

"I better not be," Kara said with a smile, but was only half kidding. If Alexa ignored her, Kara thought she might curl up in a ball and cry. She missed her and thought about her all the time, constantly wondering over the last week if Alexa thought about her too. The whole thing had her nerves on edge.

When Annette took her hand, Kara felt herself relax a little. "You're going to be okay," she whispered into Kara's ear. "And they've made this room look wonderful. Pushing all the tables and chairs back to make a little dance floor even."

Looking around, Kara had to agree. The streamers and balloons were fun, with a bar set up in the corner and a waiter preparing to serve drinks. The setup had the makings for a fantastic party. She could only hope Alexa was in the mood to have one.

"This weather sucks," Alexa growled to Jess. The rain and wind only made her bad mood worse. Anthony left earlier without hardly even a goodbye. So far, her birthday wasn't much fun. "Maybe we should ditch this idea, and I can go back inside to chill with a good book."

"On your birthday?" Jess asked as she drove down the water soaked streets. Traffic threatened to grow ugly with the weather. Los Angelenos did not do well in inclement circumstances. "No way. The least I can do is buy you dinner at your favorite restaurant."

Alexa sighed. "If you insist," she said. "But only if I can have wine. I need a drink."

Reaching to touch Alexa's arm, Jess shook her head. "I know it's hard but not while you're in training," she said. "I won't even let you look at the wine menu."

Grimacing, Alexa didn't comment until they neared the restaurant. "Looks empty tonight," she said. "I'm glad to see people are smarter than us and staying home."

"Can you be in a worse mood?" Jess said as she parked out front of Nostra. "Try to have some fun, okay?" Alexa snorted a laugh. As much as she enjoyed her manager's company, fun seemed a stretch. She would be happy with a quiet dinner. Roberto might have a small slice of cake for her or something, but otherwise the night would be like any other.

Trying to make the most of it, Alexa nodded. "You're right," she said. "I'm sorry. Thank you for getting me out of the house."

Shutting down the car, Jess unfastened her seatbelt. "That's better. Now, come on. Hopefully, we can get to the door without drowning." Alexa agreed. The weather was crappy. *Figures it would suck on my birthday,* she thought and then mentally kicked herself. Her attitude only made things worse. A minute later, they rushed inside the familiar restaurant. Smelling the scent of Italian spices and sauce, Alexa relaxed. She did love Roberto's cooking.

Rather than find a regular booth, Jess walked through the dining room toward the back. "Where are you going?" Alexa asked. "I'd rather sit by the window."

"And watch the rain?" Jess asked. "No. I want to try back here."

Frowning, Alexa followed until they were at the slightly

ajar door to the banquet room. "Seriously, where the hell are you going?"

Jess grabbed her arm and pulled her forward. "Just come on." Surprised, Alexa almost stumbled and then she was in the room. It was dim and she blinked. In another second, the lights flashed on, and a large group of people all yelled "Happy Birthday!"

Stunned, Alexa stood in the doorway. Her parents were there, and of course Anthony with a huge grin on his face. Plus, her uncle and aunt, cousins, her training crew, and... Kara. The woman looked straight at her, making Alexa's heart stop for a beat. Kara. *She came to my birthday party,* she thought, thrilled at the realization, but then saw Annette and Brady with her. *With a support team. I can't blame her.*

Anthony crossed the room to join her. "Well, say something," he said, handing her a drink. "Did we surprise you?"

Shaking her head, still filled with disbelief, she let her eyes roam over the group again until they landed on Kara. "More than you can imagine," she said before turning on him. "You have some explaining to do, brother. So, when you said you were too busy and that we would celebrate later, you were planning this?"

He grinned. "Yes," he said. "With Kara's help."

A million emotions ran through Kara as she watched Alexa process the surprise. For a moment, their eyes locked, but she couldn't read anything in their green depths. *At least she didn't turn around and leave,* she thought. *And she doesn't seem upset, which is good.* In fact, the only person who looked perturbed was Jess. Her stare was not as hard to read. Clearly, the woman assumed Kara would not attend.

Well, guess what Jess? I'm here and you're not going to push me around anymore.

Fired up by Jess's attitude, Kara strode across the room until she was within a foot of Anthony and Alexa. "Great job, Anthony," she said before letting her eyes drift to meet Alexa's. "Happy Birthday. I hope you like the surprise."

Alexa slowly nodded. "I like it very much," she said. "Thank you."

Just then, music started to play. A few people took to the small dance floor and Kara's nerve started to waver. "Well, good," she said, beginning to backpedal. "I think it's time for me to find a drink."

"Yes," Jess interjected from beside Alexa. "Definitely time for you to go away and do that."

Turning her head to glare at the woman, Kara had a retort on her lips when Anthony cleared his throat. "Okay, ladies, let's all get along and enjoy the party."

After a beat, Kara nodded. "You're right," she said. "Alexa, have a great party." With that, she turned on her heel to go find a drink. *A very strong drink*, she thought as Annette slipped into step beside her.

"You okay?" she murmured, and Kara didn't dare react somehow knowing Jess still stared at her.

"I need a drink."

When they approached the bar, the waiter smiled. "Hi," he said. "What can I get you? Wine? Beer? Champagne?"

Kara shook her head. "Got anything stronger back there?" she asked and watched the man raise an eyebrow.

"I do," he said. "Mr. Knight had me stash a bottle of grappa for a late night toast."

"Kara..." Annette started but Kara ignored the warning.

She needed some liquid courage if she were to survive the evening. "Slip me a double shot of that with some lemon," she said. "In a wine glass though. Let's not alert the media."

He smiled. "Totally understand," he said and turned his back to the room for a moment. Then he was back with the wine glass. Only an inch filled the bottom, but it would have to do. Putting a five in his tip jar, Kara retreated with Annette to stand beside Brady.

The man's eyes were wide. "Can you believe this?" he asked. "I'm at Alexa Knight's birthday party."

Annette slipped a hand under his arm. "Try not to gawk, sweetheart. Alexa's a friend of ours now."

He nodded. "Right," he said. "It's just there's been so much press and the big fight..."

"Let's forget all that for a night, if you don't mind," Kara said, taking the moment to drink the liquor all at once. It burned, but she forced herself not to cough. In an instant, a warmth bloomed in her stomach. *I'm going to be fine*, she thought. *Alexa can ignore me all she wants*. Unable to help herself, she let her eyes drift back toward the door, but only Anthony and Jess stood there. *Where did Alexa go?*

Glancing around, she didn't see her as the music turned to an eighties rock ballad. More people joined in on the slower dancing, including Alexa's parents. "Dance with me?" Annette asked Brady who swallowed hard but then held out a hand. Kara couldn't help but love how hard he worked to make Annette happy. Her friend turned to Kara. "Are you okay for a minute?"

Kara waved toward the dancing. "Of course," she said. "Have fun." The moment the two left her, Kara felt a presence at her side.

Before she could look, a familiar voice sent a chill down her spine. "How about you?" Alexa asked her. "Want to dance?" With her heart pounding hard, Kara was unable to say a word. Alexa held out her hand for Kara to take before leading her to the floor. Not sure if it was the alcohol or simply being close to Alexa again, but Kara felt slightly dizzy. To steady herself, she wrapped her arms around Alexa's neck. The closeness was enough to drive her a little crazy, but luckily, they weren't somewhere that attacking Alexa would be appropriate.

Still, the look in Alexa's eyes shined with the same desire. "I miss you," Kara said before she could stop. *Damn that grappa,* she thought, kicking herself when Alexa didn't answer.

Embarrassed, she started to pull away, but Alexa held her tight. "I miss you too," she said. "So much. I can't stop thinking about you."

"Really? You promise?"

"Yes," Alexa said. "I don't want to keep going on like this."

Kara stared at her, almost unable to believe the wonderful words. "What do we do now?"

"I am going to ask you something completely selfish," Alexa said. "But I'm moving my training to an undisclosed location. I have no choice with all the publicity, but I want you to come with me. Will you?"

Kara didn't even need a heartbeat to answer. "Yes."

Chapter Thirty

Walking into the small, but more than adequate training facility, Alexa was reassured she made the right choice. Getting far away from Los Angeles was the only way to keep the media hounds at bay. For the first time in a long time, she felt herself relax. No one would ever think to look for her in a small coastal town at the northwest tip of Oregon. In fact, she had never heard of it. Standing beside her, Kara seemed to be reading her mind. "What's the name of the town again?" she asked.

"Astoria," the trainer said. "I grew up here and I promise nobody will bother us."

Considering Alexa and Kara were staying at a bed and breakfast a few blocks away, she agreed it was the last place anyone would look. "Good," she said. "If another camera was pointed my way, I think I would have lost it." When they had checked into their two rooms, the hostess didn't bat an eye. Either she had no clue who Alexa was, or she acted respectfully enough not to mention it.

Ushering them in, the woman started with a quick tour of the historically preserved Victorian mansion. "Welcome to Hamilton Manor, I'm Cynthia, and I'm here to assist you with whatever you need," she said as she led them through the different rooms. Never having been inside any place like the mansion, Alexa was fascinated from the moment they stepped through the doorway. Greeted by a grand staircase with polished wooden steps and intricately carved banisters, Alexa felt like she had been transported to another time in history. The feeling didn't diminish when she visited the parlor, small library, and dining room with a table big enough for twenty.

Only the kitchen held modern conveniences. "Staying here is such a good idea," Alexa said as they walked inside the room. "It's all beautiful."

"Thank you," Cynthia said. "We are a historical landmark and have worked hard to preserve everything in keeping with the 1880s when it was built." Waving a hand at the stainless steel refrigerator, she smiled. "But some things had to be a little modernized. Including the bathrooms and beds."

"Of course," Kara said. "But you would never know it wasn't the 1880s while inside this house."

Taking a pair of old fashioned skeleton keys with brass tags from hooks on the wall, Cynthia handed one to each of them. I've put you in adjoining rooms connected by a bathroom. I hope that's okay?"

Wanting Kara as close as possible, Alexa thought the arrangement was very okay. "I'm fine with it," she said, glancing at Kara who looked as pleased with the idea.

"Perfect," Kara said. "I can't wait to see the bedrooms."

"They are lovely and easy to find," Cynthia said. "Top of the stairs on the left. Numbers are on the doors, unless you want me to show you?" Alexa shook her head. She had to get to the gym before too much more time passed but wanted a few minutes alone with Kara.

If nothing else, but to tell her how grateful she was that Kara paused everything with her documentary and came along. "I think we're fine," Alexa answered as Kara nodded.

A few minutes later, Alexa watched as Kara unlocked her door and let them in to one of the bedrooms. "Oh, wow," she heard Kara gasp and Alexa had to admit, the room was gorgeous. *And very romantic,* she thought as a familiar tingle ran through her. A large four-poster bed took up much of the room and seemed almost to tease Alexa. Visions of picking Kara up to lay her back on the bed filled her mind. The desire to undress her slowly, touch her everywhere, taste her... it was all she could do not to moan. Instead, she sighed knowing before anything could happen, she had a long day of training ahead.

Hanging out at the training space, Kara watched Alexa go to the locker room to change, at the same time she felt her phone buzz. Looking, she saw the text was Anthony. "I just got here. Where are you guys?"

Excited that Anthony would be in town during Alexa's training, she smiled as she typed. "Gym," she said and put in the name and the street. In ten minutes, Alexa's twin strolled through the doors. He looked good, better than Kara had ever seen him. The last two weeks his dizzy spells had completely subsided letting him return to living a relatively normal life.

Putting his arms around Kara, Anthony pulled her into a quick hug. "Made it," he said as if the results were in question. "That's a hell of a drive from Portland Airport."

Kara tilted her head. "Why didn't you take the jump to

the little Astoria airport?" she asked. "It would have saved you a lot of time."

"Oh no," he said, shaking his head. "I have enough trouble in first class on the regular-sized planes. You'll never get me on a puddle jumper." He shrugged. "Besides, it was a pretty drive. They have a hell of a lot of trees up here."

Kara noticed that when they flew in too. "Very true," she said. "I think the whole town is pretty. I can't wait to look around." She looked past him. "Where's Jess?"

"She didn't make the trip," he answered. "At the last minute, she told me to take an Uber to the airport because she wasn't going to be able to pick me up." He wrinkled his nose as he scanned the training space. "Well, this should be enough for Alexa to work with, about the size of the one she started her career in, but it doesn't smell so great."

At that, Kara agreed considering the mixture of leather and sweat. "Alexa went into the locker room to dress down," she said, knowing the best thing she could do was get out of the area else be a distraction to the fighter. Back in the bedroom, she hadn't missed the burning desire in the woman's eyes. It had been all she could do to not rip Alexa's clothes off, and she was pretty sure that chemistry wouldn't calm down unless she made herself scarce.

Kara turned toward the door. "Let's go find some lunch," she said as Anthony fell into step with her. "Did you check in already?"

"I did," he said. "The hotel seems nice enough."

Pausing, Kara looked at him. "You're not staying at the bed and breakfast either?"

Anthony smirked as he shook his head. "I'm staying with the rest of the training team," he said. "I only arranged for you and Alexa to stay at Hamilton Manor. Thought you two could use some privacy."

Loving how considerate Anthony was, Kara took his arm and gave it a squeeze while the kept walking. "You're the best," she said, and he laughed.

"Well," he said. "It was that or risk hearing the two of you in the middle of the night."

Unable to help herself, Kara blushed but felt a heat low in her body too. *Will that be something worth worrying about?* she wondered. *Or is training going to make Alexa stay between the lines?* The absolute last thing she wanted was to interrupt the woman's agenda because the big fight with Rachel Rhodes was only nineteen days away. *And Alexa must be ready.*

After changing from her street clothes to a pair of shorts and a fitted tank, Alexa carefully wrapped her hands with strips of gauze. One of the trainers would cover them with tape once she was ringside. Although the process seemed minor, taping her hands just for practice, it was critical to protect them. The gauze and tape did next to nothing to pad her punches but rather was used to support the small, fragile bones in her hands. It wasn't uncommon for a fighter to suffer a break in the middle of a fight. Earlier in her career, after a spinning backfist that landed on her opponent's jaw, she had fractured her left hand. Luckily, the strike damaged her opponent's face more, and Alexa finished her before the end of the round. When asked about battling through the pain in her post fight interview, Alexa had shrugged. "I won't let little things like broken bones stop me from becoming a champion," she said, then looked into the camera, calling out the MMA promoters. "So, give me my shot." Six months later, she won her first belt.

As Alexa started on her other hand, her cellphone

rattled on the bench beside her. Checking to see who called, the screen on the phone was suddenly blurry. Blinking to clear her vision, Alexa realized the trouble was on her left from the eye that had surgery. With a sense of panic, she shook her head, but the problem remained. "Shit," she muttered, rubbing the closed lid, and opening it again. Thankfully, after another few seconds, most of the blurriness was gone. But not all of it.

I'll worry about that later, she thought, seeing it was Jess calling her. Alexa tapped the speaker. "What's up?"

For a beat, Jess didn't answer making Alexa think she missed the call. "What's wrong?" her manager finally asked. "You sound funny."

"I'm fine," Alexa lied. *How does she know me so well?* she thought. *There's no way I'm telling her about my eye.* "Just wrapping my hands to go train. Did you land?"

"Actually... no," Jess answered. "I'm not coming up, or at least not for now." Alexa frowned. In all their years working together, her manager was always around during training camp. She helped keep Alexa focused and motivated.

Suddenly, she guessed the problem and stopped wrapping her hand for a moment. "Jess, if this about Kara—"

She heard Jess give a wry laugh. "Actually, Kara has nothing to do with this. You already know how I feel on the topic."

"Yes, I do," Alexa said, but even more puzzled. "So then, what's the problem? I need you up here." Her manager didn't reply for long enough that Alexa glanced at the phone on the bench to see if they were still connected. "Jess?"

"You'll be fine," the woman answered. "Focus on what matters and listen to the trainers. If I can make it to Astoria, I will." Then the call ended, leaving Alexa staring at the screen. *If I can make it, I will?* Alexa repeated. *What the hell is going on?* Getting ready to call Jess back, she heard someone come into the locker room. Her first thought was another reporter stalked her, until she remembered where they were and how secret the location. *No one knows we are here. I don't need to worry.*

"Alexa?" came the voice of her sparring partner as she walked around the lockers. "What are you doing? The guys are getting pissed."

With a nod, Alexa refocused on her priority number one. "Sorry," she said standing to follow the woman out to the ring. "I'm coming." The hard core training was about to begin.

Chapter Thirty-One

As Alexa moved gracefully around the ring, keeping her sparring partner at a distance using front kicks and jabs, Kara watched from the sidelines. Although she steered clear of the training facility much of the time to allow Alexa to concentrate fully, when she did come in, seeing the fighter's skill and power thrilled her. The force behind her strikes, the speed in which she moved, and precision of her attacks seemed almost superhuman. Most importantly, every routine Kara witnessed seemed better than the last. Overhearing the trainers, Kara learned Alexa never looked better. The time in Astoria had been a win.

Kara enjoyed every minute while they were there. Spending much of the time over the two weeks with Anthony helped them bond even more. Pages and pages of notes on scenes to film when they returned filled Kara's notebook. Even some candid video with her phone of the twins interacting would make the documentary. The connection between Alexa and Anthony filmed perfectly and she would use it to show how important family support was when living with leukemia.

Amazingly, Jess never made the trip, but Alexa said her manager had set up everything for their return. Rather than fly into Los Angeles, they would go straight to Las Vegas tomorrow to start the mandatory three days of pre-fight promotion. After the serenity of the last two weeks, Kara dreaded rejoining the circus, but doing so was part of the required routine.

"It's almost over," Anthony had reassured her over a microbrew at Astoria's local taphouse. The place was one of their primary hangouts and usually they sat outside with a view of the Columbia River, but a storm had rolled in during the morning. "With a decade of practice, Alexa can handle the media attention."

"Unless they turn on her," Kara said, running a finger around the rim of her pint glass. "Everything is so upside down right now."

Anthony took her hand and gave it a gentle squeeze. "With your support she can handle anything." At that moment, Kara hadn't been so certain, but watching Alexa finish her last day of training by throwing her partner to the mat again and again helped reassure her.

Clapping his hands, Alexa's trainer finally took mercy on Alexa's opponent. "Okay, let's call it a day," he said. "You're as ready as you're going to get."

"Thanks," Alexa said after slipping out her mouthguard. "I think." Suddenly the sound of thunder shook the building and the lights flickered. Looking toward the ceiling, Alexa grinned. "I'll take that as a good sign."

As she climbed out of the ring, Kara had a water bottle waiting for her. Unable to help the feeling of arousal seeing the woman all toned and glistening, Kara gave her a sultry smile. "You look amazing," she said softly, watching Alexa's eyes widen a little. Although they had slept in the same bed a few nights, so far kissing was as far as they went. It was important Alexa save her strength and focus for training. But with preparation over and days until the fight... she bit her lip.

Before either of them could say a word, Anthony approached. "Hey, sis, let's go have dinner to celebrate," he said putting an arm around Alexa's shoulders before pulling back, and wrinkling his nose. "After you hit the shower." He grinned. "Then I'll sneak you a beer."

"Um," Alexa said, holding Kara's look for a moment longer. All the desire Kara felt reflected in them, but then she smiled an apology and shrugged. "Sure. Let's do that."

"Great," Anthony said, pulling his cellphone from his pocket. "I'll call and get us all a table."

As he walked away to make the call, Alexa stepped close. "Soon," she said, making Kara's body tingle as the sudden sound of rain pounded the roof. It seemed to match the feeling of her heart because Kara couldn't wait.

Even in the mad dash from the crew's van to the restaurant's front door Alexa was half soaked. She had been warned that Astoria's weather was known for wicked rainstorms, and the last two weeks of sunshine had spoiled them. Mother Nature seemed ready to make up for the short drought in one day as the rain came down in sheets from the storming gray skies. Still, everyone was in high spirits and laughing as they crossed the threshold. Looking at Kara, Alexa saw the woman's curly hair was more out of control than ever from the wind and rain and she loved the wildness of it. Working to contain it, Kara took a hair tie from her pocket and pulled the mass together to put in a ponytail. Loose strands refusing to be tamed framed her damp face, making the sudden desire to kiss Kara so strong Alexa sucked in a breath. *I'm incredibly attracted to her*, she thought, once again grateful the woman took time out of her life to stay with her through training. *After this coming week is over, I'm going to make sure she knows what she means to me.*

"This way, please," the hostess said pulling a half dozen menus from the podium before leading them toward a long plank wood table along the windows. The design went along with the fishing vessel motif of nets and floats, and Alexa liked the rustic feel of the place.

She put her arm around Anthony's waist as they walked at the back of the pack. "Great choice," she said. "Let me guess, you picked it because they have killer tasting crab legs?"

Her brother's addiction to shellfish after two weeks in Astoria was no secret. "You know it," he admitted, smiling. "And thanks for coming along. I know you were thinking along different lines when I asked."

Laughing, Alexa pulled away enough to look him in the face. "Was it that obvious?" she asked, and he nodded.

"I thought you two might burst into flames at any second," he replied. "But getting some calories in you before letting the two of you disappear motivated me to interrupt." He paused as they neared the table, then leaned in closer to not be overheard. "You and Kara have so much chemistry, I'm a little jealous."

Taking her seat, Alexa considered his comment. *We really do*, she thought, looking at Kara who sat beside her. *Like I've never felt with anyone.* "What are you and

Anthony conspiring about?" Kara murmured only loud enough for Alexa to hear. "Or is it better I don't know?"

Alexa smiled. "He apologized for interrupting us at the gym," she said and loved watching a flush of color reach Kara's cheeks. "Seems to think we have chemistry."

Suddenly, Alexa felt Kara's hand touch her thigh sending a charge of electricity through her. "And do you agree?" the woman asked, a sexy glow in her eyes.

Licking her lips, Alexa had trouble focusing on the question. "Do I agree to what?"

Holding her look, Kara raised an eyebrow while she slipped her hand slightly higher. "Think we have chemistry?" she asked, and all Alexa could do was nod. As happy as she was to be with everyone for a celebratory dinner, every minute without being naked in bed with Kara would be torture. "Good. Because so do I. Eat quickly." Without another word, the woman took her hand away, picking up a menu to study. The missing contact was almost more erotic, making Alexa long for it. She cleared her throat, scanning her own options. For some reason, she was suddenly ravenous, but not sure what she wanted was on the menu.

After holding hands like teenagers in the backseat of the crew's van, Kara could not get upstairs in Hamilton Manor fast enough. Unfortunately, progress was delayed when Cynthia met them at the door with oversized, amazingly soft, and thick towels. "I saw you pulling up," she said, handing them each one. "And guessed you'd need something to dry off with." Her guess was a good one as the rain, which continued to pour relentlessly all evening, drenched them on their race up the walkway and steps. Kara didn't need a mirror to know her curly hair was a wild, wet mess, and although eager to go to her room, took the offering gratefully.

Wrapping the towel around her shoulders, Kara nodded. "Thank you so much," she said. "This storm is crazy."

Cynthia smiled. "Not as crazy as you might think," she said. "We get squalls through here often enough." Picking up two flashlights from the sideboard beside the stairs, she held them out. "You'll want these too. Generally, we lose power for a few hours at some point, and it can get very dark in those rooms."

Not minding one bit how dark things might get very soon, Kara still took the flashlight. "I'm sure we will be fine," she said. "But thank you."

"Thank you," Alexa added. "You're very thoughtful."

"Of course," Cynthia replied. "I have some kerosine lamps lit and there's a fire in the hearth if you'd rather stay down here until this storm blows over."

Kara didn't need to look at Alexa to guess her answer. "I appreciate that," Kara said. "But I think I'll head upstairs and change into something warm and dry for now."

"Understandable," she said. "You're welcome if you change your mind. We have boardgames and books available."

Almost ready to laugh at how long it was taking to get upstairs when her entire body thrummed with excitement for Alexa, Kara squeezed Cynthia's forearm. "Thank you again," she said, and without another word nearly ran up the stairs with Alexa right behind her.

Before Kara could even unlock it, Alexa pressed her against the heavy, wooden door. "I'm dying to touch you," she murmured into Kara's ear. "Everywhere."

Kara moaned with anticipation as she fumbled with the

key. "I want that," she said, finally making the lock work so they could stumble together inside. The door was hardly closed when Alexa whipped the towel from Kara's shoulders and pressed her back until she collapsed on the high, four-poster bed.

Relishing the power she felt radiating off of Alexa, Kara squirmed up against the pillows splayed along the headboard and waited. "I'm ready for whatever you want," she said, her voice thick with need.

With narrowed eyes, Alexa growled. "Take off your clothes," she said. "I want you naked." Not hesitating, Kara shrugged off everything she wore in less than a minute, until there was nothing left but a lacy black bra and panties she wore exactly for that moment. Alexa looked her over. "That's not everything."

"Does that mean you don't like them?" she asked with a tilt of her head, excited to see the fire in her lover's eyes grow hotter. In answer, Alexa pulled off her clothes until her amazing body was naked. Never able to get enough of looking at the fighter's physique, Kara felt a pulse between her legs.

Alexa slid onto the foot of the bed. "I do like them," she said. "Very much. But if you don't want them to be ruined, take them off."

Lifting her chin, excited almost to the point of pain, Kara waited. "Then ruin them," she whispered. Alexa didn't hesitate and moved with the sleek power that made her a champion. In a second, the panties were torn aside and two of her fingers plunged inside Kara. She let out a cry at the suddenness but relished the feeling of being so wanted. Moving her fingers in and out, Alexa smashed her lips against Kara's, forcing her lips open with her tongue. The force that rippled through Alexa and into Kara made her wild. She grabbed at Alexa's shoulder, who caught her wrists in one strong hand before driving them over Kara's head.

With Alexa's fingers inside her, the weight of her body pressing Kara down, and her wrists clasped together, she suddenly felt completely helpless. She whimpered against Alexa's mouth, never having been touched so deeply and with such intensity. Barely able to stand the pleasure, she bucked her hips against the rhythm of Alexa's hand until the woman curled her fingers and touched a spot inside her no one ever had. The passion was too much to hold back, and she felt herself melt into an orgasm that shook her entire body. Everything else faded away and for the first time in her life, she felt entirely fulfilled. Somehow, Alexa was everything.

Chapter Thirty-Two

Pausing before walking backstage at the large press conference event, Alexa took a deep breath. *Here we go*, she thought, squaring her shoulders, and striding into the open space half filled with fighters, but the first person who greeted her was the event's head promoter. "Alexa," he said with a wide smile. "Welcome back. You look good. Feeling hungry? Ready to get that belt back?"

"It will be the fight of the night," Alexa said, smiling back. "Get ready to sign me that check." He laughed. Although the man was known to be a cutthroat businessman with his own interests always coming first, his charisma was impossible to resist. Plus, Alexa owed him a lot for signing her to a contract back when she was a raw fighter.

He laughed. "Happy to," he said, with a pat on her shoulder before moving on to the next person to greet. Alexa looked around at the people waiting with her. All types of fighters made up the group. Some of the deer-in-the-headlights newbies had their managers with them, some midlevel fighters stood quietly apart clearly trying to get in the zone, and other veterans strutted around doing some high fives with colleagues. The co-main event fighter was even signing an autograph for one of the photographers mixing among them to take candid pics.

The promotors were wise enough to have a thick, black curtain between competitors though—red corner on one side, and blue on another. Alexa guessed Rachel Rhodes was already waiting on the other side. If she had to guess, the woman was of the strut around, high five group. What the fighter lacked in class and skill she made up for with bravado. Luckily, Alexa knew she could beat the crap out of ego. The opportunity couldn't come soon enough for her. She wanted everything to be over. *And then I can focus on Kara and my family and things that actually matter,* she thought. Considering the sport had been her entire life for years, she was surprised how little she cared about it now. Perhaps with time she would answer some of the requests already surfacing from small networks, and even a podcast, for her to be an MMA announcer. *It's not like I need the money though, so I'll have to see how it feels and if it fits into my future.*

Standing to one side of the main group, Alexa looked up from studying the floor when someone came to stand beside her. "Ready for another round of the dog and pony show?" she heard an old friend and fellow fighter ask. Alexa smiled. Rocky Milo was one of the long-time veterans and although not in a championship bout, he was still ranked well. Amazingly, almost three years had gone by since she last fought on a main card with him. It was nice to see a friendly face.

"Hey, Rocky," she answered. "One last time for me. No matter what happens."

The fighter nodded. "You'll be missed," he said. "And

don't worry, those of us who know you don't believe the bullshit Rhodes is doling out."

"Thank you," Alexa replied. "I appreciate you saying that. I won't lie, it's been rough." She sighed. "I even had to go to a secret place to train. How crazy is that?

Grimacing at her words, Rocky put a hand on her shoulder. "But we are warriors, and we persevere, right?"

Thinking about his words, Alexa slowly nodded. "Right," she agreed, and what he said was true. The average person could not fathom the effort and sacrifice that went on behind the scenes, or the struggle to be the best that lingered well past the end of each fight. For all of Alexa's adult life, she gave over a hundred percent of her focus to being a champion—in and out of the ring. First as she aspired to become one and then keeping the belt once she had it. Other female contenders came and went while she remained the top of her league. *And I beat them all*, she thought, a deeper fierceness starting to ignite inside her. *The last fight was only bad luck, with bad timing. It won't happen again.* Rachel Rhodes had no idea what sort of force headed her way.

Sitting with Anthony inside the filled auditorium, Kara didn't think she had ever been more nervous. *And it's all just beginning*, she thought, worried by the actual fight she would be a wreck. For Alexa's last fight, Kara didn't witness the large press conference where all the fighters on the card sat at tables and answered questions peppered at them from the audience. "Tell me again," she said to Anthony. "What exactly is going to happen?"

"Other than a lot of bickering?" he said with a grin. "Don't be so worried. Alexa's done over a dozen of these."

He put an arm around her shoulders and gave a little hug. "This is not her first rodeo." Kara tried to take comfort from his words. The man was right, and yet, she felt very uneasy. She couldn't shake the feeling something bad was going to happen. *Is she making the right decision doing this fight?* she wondered. *Does she really need to?*

The word was out that all Alexa's proceeds from the fight would go to charity. Making that decision was a good one, not only because of what the millions of dollars would do in helping research continue, but it helped her image reclaim some of its glamor. She remembered Brady explaining that Alexa had been one of the most popular female MMA fighters in history. Her mysterious, complex persona made both men and women gravitate toward her. "But, of course, some people are haters simply because someone is successful," Brady had said. "When they found a crack in Alexa's image to exploit, they went for the throat."

A lot of that died down once Alexa could explain her actions, but the stain would never be gone. The best she could do was show the world losing to Rachel Rhodes was a fluke. *By crushing her on Saturday night,* Kara thought, feeling her stomach clench with more anxiety. As much as she believed in Alexa, fate already proved anything could happen. Blowing out a breath to calm herself, she watched the main promotor stroll onto the stage covered in tables draped in black cloth. Over a dozen chairs lined up behind the tables on the different tiers, each spot marked with a name placard set beside individual microphones. Kara saw the one for Alexa Knight. First row, near the center. On the other side of the podium was one for Rachel Rhodes.

After making a quick welcome speech, the promoter stepped aside to let the fighters be announced. One by one they were called from backstage to take their seats. "She'll be next to last," Anthony said. "Before Rachel Rhodes, because this time Alexa is the challenger."

Just like he predicted, all but two chairs were filled when the announcers voice boomed over the speakers listing Alexa's many accolades. "And here is, the one, the only, Alexa Knight," he finished making the crowd roar. Loud boos intermixed the cheering, making Kara bristle.

"Do they usually boo her?" Kara whispered into Anthony's ear.

He shook his head, and she didn't miss the sad look on his face. "Not like that."

When Alexa heard her name announced, she walked through the gap in the black curtains to take the short flight of stairs to the stage. The minute she appeared, and the bright lights struck her, what she heard made her pause for a beat. There were boos coming from the audience. Not that she hadn't been booed before at times throughout her career, but they were rare. Even as an early challenger, she was generally the fan favorite. Tonight though, there was a definite shift, and she felt the pain to her core. No punch could have stung more. Still, she would not give the naysayers the satisfaction of seeing how she felt and instead gave the cameras her characteristic smirk and a quick wave to acknowledge the crowd. All part of her signature style that she wasn't about to change for the last fight of her career. As she made her way to her chair, she let the pain harden to become fuel to motivate her toward the ultimate goal—having her arm raised at the end of the fight Saturday night.

After a quick handshake with the promoter, she sat, and the announcer started his introduction of Rachel Rhodes.

Her list of accomplishments was significantly shorter, but hearing the woman called a champion made Alexa clench her jaw. Anyone with half a brain would have to know that title was a farce. While Alexa stared straight ahead not willing to give any sign she cared what happened, Rachel Rhodes took the stage. There were a large number of boos for her too and Alexa took some solace knowing not everyone was fooled by her competitor's charade.

"Okay," the promoter said from the podium. "First question!" The crowd cheered as a young man in a black t-shirt and jeans approached the microphone at the base of the stage.

He grinned, clearly loving all the attention. "My first question is for Ms. Knight," he said, and Alexa held her breath. *Will they go for the jugular right out of the gate?* she wondered, staring the man down. Noticing her looking at him, she saw him swallow hard. *Now he's all nervous... at least I can still make that happen.* "Uh, Ms. Knight. Are you..." He looked around and Alexa could swear she saw him starting to sweat. *Just ask it already.* "...at all concerned about the allegations you lost the last fight on purpose?" At his question the crowd erupted, and that time the boos were even louder, but Alexa hoped some were pointed at the young man as much as her.

She pulled her microphone closer. "No, I am not," she said. "On Saturday, everyone will see how stupid that rumor is when I easily beat my opponent."

"Your opponent? What? You can't even say my name?" she heard Rachel Rhodes bark into her microphone. "I guess I intimidate you that much."

Knowing every camera switched back on her to catch a reaction, Alexa still didn't look at Rhodes, but made an exaggerated roll of her eyes. "Or maybe I don't want to waste the breath," she said, making a snicker ripple through the crowd. "Pretty sure everyone here knows who I'm beating Saturday."

"Like you did last time? Funny, because I see your belt sitting on the table right here in front of me."

Unable to keep the hint of a smile from crossing her face at her opponent's slip, Alexa leaned back in her chair. "That is funny, you're right," Alexa said. "That you see *my belt* in front of you." She took the time to look over and loved seeing the red flush in Rachel Rhodes's face. "Hope you're keeping it warm for me, Rach, because I'm coming back for it."

Chapter Thirty-Three

The bright Las Vegas sun half blinded Kara even with her sunglasses on. "I don't think I can do this," she said, suddenly pulling out her earbuds and sitting upright in the poolside lounger at the hotel. "I can't stay still."

Annette, who lay in the lounger beside her, put a soft hand on her shoulder. "You need to try," she said. "It's hours until the fight and you must relax."

Flopping back, Kara growled. "How can I relax? I'm a jumble of nerves." Truly, it felt like every part of her body tingled with anxiety. She had no idea how she would stand waiting the next six hours until the evening started. Especially without Alexa nearby. After a large breakfast, the fighter had kissed Kara goodbye. The rest of the day was about finding her warrior focus, and with Kara around, Alexa said she couldn't. "When I'm with you, the last thing I am is a warrior," she explained. "All I want to be is loving." The woman smiled. "Which is how it should be."

Kara had nodded. "That's what I want," she said. "Of course, it is."

"Good," Alexa said, gently kissing her on the lips before murmuring what Kara felt too. "But I'll miss you." Then, she disappeared to be with her trainers and prepare. That had been hours ago, and Kara had no idea where she was, although the last thing she wanted to be was a distraction. All of which left her to hang out with her best friends and Anthony.

In no mood to gamble with the guys, Annette had suggested working on their tan. "Close your eyes and turn up your music," Annette suggested. "Try to take a nap."

Thinking napping was impossible, Kara blew out a frustrated breath. "Not a chance," she said. "Maybe I need a drink."

"Good idea," Annette said, raising a hand to signal the poolside waiter. "What do you want?"

I want to know how Alexa is doing, Kara thought, but instead focused on her options. One thing she learned while in Las Vegas was no cocktail selection was off limits. The bartenders appeared able to make anything requested. Today, however, she went with the usual once the handsome young man in white shorts and a baby blue polo shirt reached them. "Pina colada, blended, please," she said. "Extra fruit."

"Well, that sounds boring," Annette said with a laugh. "But same with me."

After the waiter left to get their drinks, Kara second guessed her decision. "Maybe having alcohol right now is a bad idea," she said. "I mean if I need to go somewhere. Like if I have to run an errand."

Annette sighed. "Kara," she said. "Not only has Alexa been through this routine a bunch of times, but she has an entire team to take care of her." Closing her eyes, Kara tried to absorb her friend's words. "Just enjoy your drink, and let's talk about something else. Like me, for example."

At Annette's comment, Kara smiled. "Yes, let's," she said. "Tell me about his proposal again." After a lot of persuading by Annette and Kara, Brady had finally been willing to forgo the engagement party idea in lieu of a bigger honeymoon. The change didn't keep him from making the event as romantic and memorable as possible. While in Astoria, Annette described the basics to her over the phone, but Kara hadn't heard every aspect of the proposal or seen any pictures. Being the best friend, having those details was critical. *Plus, being excited for her will help me stop fretting about the fight tonight,* she thought. *I need to think positive and know Alexa can handle everything.* Listening to Annette, she tried hard to believe it.

Alexa was focused, she was ready, and couldn't wait to get the fight started. There was only one thing wrong—Jess was nowhere to be found. As much as Alexa tried to block out the distraction of her manager being out of touch, it lingered at the back of her mind. There had been no contact since the strange phone conversation while in Astoria. Alexa worried about her to the point she asked Anthony to track her down. So far, no matter who he contacted he wasn't successful. For some reason, Jess had gone to ground, and Alexa didn't understand why.

In her place, Anthony kept her company between her stretching and warm-up sessions. He respected her need for silence at times and then blaring music the next. The intensity of the pre-fight wait was a ritual every fighter had to withstand. Soon they would go to the arena to dress and have her trainer tape her hands.. All a part of the process.

As the siblings debated the meaningless topic about which of Roberto's pasta dishes at Nostra tasted the best, there was a light knock at the door to the training room. Anthony raised an eyebrow. If it was the trainers, they would have walked in without apology. "Want me to get it or leave it?" he asked. Alexa's mind immediately went to Kara. Although the woman seemed to completely understand the reasons to be apart until after the fight, there might still be a reason she visited. *Something important*, she thought and nodded toward the door. "Check who it is."

Anthony lowered the wooden chair he was leaning back in and stood to walk to the door. He cracked it open. "Who is it?" he said, looking through the gap. Alexa watched him tilt his head, clearly puzzled.

After a second, a man's voice answered. "It's Marco, I'm looking for Jess," he said. "I need to get ahold of her." Anthony turned to Alexa and shrugged.

Not liking the idea of a distraction to entirely disrupt her mental prep, Alexa still wanted more information on Jess. *And maybe Marco has some*, she thought with a wave of her hand to signal opening the door all the way. Once Anthony did, a broad-shouldered, dark-haired man, dressed in a black suit stood in the doorway. The stereotype was so profound, Alexa almost laughed. The man was straight out an episode of the once popular TV show *The Sopranos*. Then she sobered. *Why is this guy looking for Jess?*

"Can I help you?" Anthony asked and the big man looked past him.

When he saw Alexa sitting in the armchair, he nodded. "Sorry to interrupt ya, Ms. Knight," he said. "But I'm looking for your manager."

Alexa sighed. "So are we," she said. "I'm sorry, but I haven't heard from her in over two weeks." Frowning, she pinned the stranger with a look. "And to be honest, I'm worried about her."

"I see," Marco said, rubbing his chin sporting a serious five o'clock shadow. "Well, that's pretty unfortunate." He looked from Anthony to Alexa and then up and down the hall. "Unless you can help me?"

Not liking the sudden twist in her gut, Alexa stood and moved closer. "What do you want?"

"Maybe I should come in," he suggested and after a kneejerk reaction to send him packing, Alexa thought twice.

Clearly, he knew something they didn't. "Come in," she said and once Marco was inside Anthony closed the door. "I don't need this distraction right now, so tell me what you want and then go."

Marco nodded. "Right," he said. "I always go through Jess for this so it's a little awkward." He swallowed hard. "Especially since she forbid me from ever talking to you directly because... well, you know..."

Her head swirling a little but every negative instinct firing, Alexa didn't follow. "No," she said. "I don't know. Start talking."

As if sensing he was in a dangerous situation, Marco started to back toward the door. "Actually," he said. "I'll wait for Jess."

"No," Alexa said, her voice cold as ice. "You'll say it now. What do you need from Jess?"

"Shit," Marco said, looking caught in a trap. "Okay. I need to know what fights she wants to bet on."

Although she was only half focused on the action around her, Kara could tell the evening of fights was an exceptional one. The crowd was deafening, often on their feet, and overall fired up, meaning the battles in the octagon were especially violent. Flying knees, spinning elbows, reverse triangles—all the weapons of the warriors showcased that night.

The bits of the fights Kara did absorb featured impressive feats of strength, resilience, and skill. After all the time spent around the sport in the last months, Kara realized those three elements were the keys to success. But the most important attribute of all was that the fighter had to have heart. The will to win seemed able to throw the balance in any battle. Even the most battered warrior in the ring could come out of the contest with a submission or a knockout if they never lost the fire inside them to win. Alexa tried to explain the phenomenon one night over dinner. "It's belief. Like the ultimate mind over matter scenario. Unless you are literally knocked out cold, anyone can win if they commit themselves to it enough." Kara couldn't admit to ever wanting something so much, but unlike the last fight, Alexa had that fire for this bout against Rachel Rhodes. She would step into the cage with one thing and only one thing on her mind—victory.

Ringside, Kara stood beside Anthony as they had before. On the other side of him was an empty seat though. Jess was still missing in action, only Kara started to think Anthony knew something about it. When they took their seats, and the manager still hadn't appeared, she mentioned the odd situation. "Yeah," Anthony said, his eyes scanning the room as if he was completely distracted. "Pretty sure she won't be making it."

"Do you know why?" Kara had asked. "Did Alexa hear from her?"

"Not exactly," Anthony murmured, but before Kara could follow up with more questions, the music for a fighter's entrance blared and drowned out her words. As the night went on, she thought about Jess less while her anxiety climbed. One more fight before Alexa's championship bout. The co-main event of two heavyweights. Anthony explained earlier the fight would not go the five total rounds. "These big guys throw bricks and can knock the other person out with one punch. Plus, they usually don't have the cardio to go for the whole twenty-five minutes." Kara kept all those details in mind as the two men entered the ring. Alexa's fight could be soon.

Just as Anthony predicted, the big fighters threw looping swings meant to destroy the opponent with one strike. While she watched, there was movement to her left and for a brief second her heart stopped at the idea Anthony was in trouble again. Looking over, she saw Alexa's brother was fine, but someone had appeared next to him. Without a word, Jess took her seat.

Chapter Thirty-Four

Even after Anthony left to meet Kara and take his seat ringside, Alexa couldn't find a way to refocus on the fight ahead of her. *How could Jess do this?* she thought over and over. She had a million questions. *When did it start? And why?* Ever since the beginning, Alexa was generous with her winnings. No one on her team lacked for money, but especially Jess. They were partners. Each decision, certainly professionally, and often personally, was made with Jess at her side. *But gambling?* Her mind whirled. "Alexa," her trainer said after taping her hands. "Whatever is in your head right now needs to go. Or you're going to get your ass kicked."

Alexa could only nod. The man, a long-time friend too, was absolutely right. He had looked into her eyes and seen her lacking the fire she needed. Betrayal was a bitter pill though, and Alexa could hardly keep from vomiting thinking about all the ramifications Jess's actions could have on their lives. While she closed her eyes and tried to put everything in a box to examine later, she heard the dressing room door open. "They are ready for you, Ms. Knight," one of the fight staff said, and Alexa stood from the bench to join her team for one final walkout. No matter what happened tonight, she would never make this journey again. Unlike last time where there was nostalgia, all Alexa felt was relief. In an hour, the fighting chapter of her life would close.

Walking along the hallway to step out into the venue, she heard music begin to play. Her music. *This is how legends are made*, she sang along in her mind. For the first time she wondered what her new legacy would ultimately be. Before the loss to Rachel Rhodes and all the accusations, she would have been on a pedestal. *But there is no way to know what the future holds for me now.*

As she started down the path to the ring, the crowds were as crazy as always. Screaming masses, clapping, and chanting her name. *But there are boos in there too*, she thought unable to block any of it out. The tunnel vision, the insane ability to focus she was famous for was lacking. For the first time in her career, Alexa felt a sliver of doubt. Taking a deep breath, forcing herself to get back in the game, she made her way toward the pre-fight staging area when suddenly a splash of cold liquid hit her in the face. The smell of beer filled the air and shocked, she spun in the direction of the attack. A laughing face stood out from the crowd and the man made the mistake of pointing at her because in a flash, Alexa grabbed his outstretched arm and drug him from the seats.

With a yelp of fear, the heckler fell on his ass at her feet. The crowd went crazy as the cameras caught and displayed on the jumbotron every moment of the interaction. "I should break you in half, you piece of shit," Alexa screamed into his face, making sure she was heard over the sound of the masses.

"Screw you, bitch," the man yelled as he scrambled to

his feet. "You're gonna get your ass kicked. I'm not afraid of you." Suddenly all the rage Alexa felt over her predicament came roaring through her. She had never been more ready to crush someone in her life. *But it's not this asshole,* she thought as adrenaline filled her veins. *It's going to be the real bitch in all of this. Rachel Rhodes is going to pay.*

With a sneer, Alexa stepped past the scumbag to finish her walk to the ring. "Thanks," she said as she went by him, and the old focus needed to win was back. "That was exactly what I needed."

Kara stood on tiptoe to try and see over the crowd. She heard Alexa's music start, ready for her to make her walk to the octagon. Suddenly, everyone went wild, and Kara wanted to find out what all the screaming was about. "Oh, shit," she heard Anthony say and turned to follow his gaze. Alexa was on the jumbotron. Someone in the crowd had thrown a beer on her and in retaliation, the fighter pulled him out of the stands.

Kara covered her mouth with her hands. "Oh my God," she said, every instinct in her wanting to rush over and punch the guy herself. "Who would do that?"

Shaking his head, Anthony looked as ready as she was to go defend his sister. "A stupid asshole," he growled, but then Alexa walked past the man and continued toward the ring. For some strange reason, a smirk appeared on the woman's face. A very dark smirk, and any doubts Kara had about Alexa being ready were erased. What she saw in that moment was a look she never wanted to see again—Alexa, the predator. If she had even an ounce of goodwill toward Rachel Rhodes, Kara would be worried for the woman. *But*

I'm not, she thought with a smirk of her own. *Let Alexa wipe the mat with her.*

Finally, Alexa lined up to enter the ring, and Kara watched her walk to the stairs. Just like last time, she looked over and Kara watched the woman make eye contact with her brother. Then, her eyes drifted to Kara's, and although there was nothing gentle in the look, Kara understood and gave Alexa a nod. Finally, Alexa looked at where Jess always sat, and Kara watched her eyes widen only the slightest. *She is surprised to see her,* Kara thought, still not sure what the situation was with Alexa's manager but by now knowing it was bad.

Turning away, Alexa went into the ring and started to swing her arms to keep them limber while they waited for the inevitable arrival of the champion. As much as Kara expected it, the sound of music playing again made Kara flinch. Rachel Rhodes came at them. Once again, the crowds went berserk and watching on the big screen, Kara saw the champion strut down the aisle waving to the people in the stands. Cameras flashed and no one threw beer, but still there were boos. Kara took some hope from that. Maybe after tonight people would see Rachel Rhodes for what she truly was—a liar and an unworthy champion.

While she waited for the woman to enter the ring, Kara only focused on Alexa. Taking in how strong and dangerous the fighter looked in the green sports bra and black shorts, there was suddenly a commotion to her left. Turning in the direction of the noise, she was shocked to suddenly be face to face with Rachel Rhodes. The fighter had diverted from the walk up the stairs to the ring to talk to Kara. "Hey," she yelled. "When I'm done kicking Alexa's ass, how about you and I go for a ride in the elevator?"

Before Kara could even react, her people pulled Rachel

Rhodes back in line, but not before Alexa noticed. In a second, the woman was on top of the fence while her trainers grabbed at her to keep her from jumping at Rachel. There was bedlam in the auditorium as people took sides on who to root for in the match. Shaken, Kara made eye contact with Alexa who still sat on the rail. The look held for a second before Kara mouthed the words "beat her." With a nod, Alexa slipped back into the octagon. It was time to fight.

The introductions were a blur. All Alexa could see was Rachel Rhodes across the ring from her. The woman strutted side to side, a big grin on her face, as if she actually believed she was a real champion. *Well, in about thirty seconds, she is about to think differently*, Alexa thought, her dark smirk back. Unlike her competitor, she had no need to pace or even move. All she did was glare, putting all her fury into laser focus. Rachel Rhodes might not be the single reason for all the bad things that happened to Alexa over the last few months, but for the moment, she would pay for it.

Finally, the referee pointed at her. "Ready?" he asked, and Alexa gave him the requisite nod. He asked the same of her opponent and when Rachel Rhodes nodded, he raised his hand. Then, with a drop of his arm, the fight was on. Unlike the first fight where she trained to counter any knowledge Rachel Rhodes might have from their previous sparring rounds, Alexa stuck to the gameplan she used from day one of her career. She stormed across the ring at her opponent intent on overwhelming her. As if expecting no less, Rachel Rhodes spun away but not before Alexa caught her with a blazing fast spinning kick to her midsection.

There was nothing fancy about the move and it would never make a highlight reel, but Alexa was well aware the damage strikes to the body could do. As her trainer told her often, "Kill the body and the head will die."

Dancing away, Rachel Rhodes seemed content to spend the round feeling each other out, but Alexa wasn't interested. She rushed her opponent again and again, relentless in her attack of punches and kicks. All the blocks and defenses Rachel Rhodes used in the previous fight could not stand up against the kamikaze-like attitude. Even if a counter strike did land, Alexa would not be deterred and as her punches found their target, Rachel's head snapped back again and again. Only a minute of the first round had passed and the outcome already seemed clear—Alexa was too much for Rachel Rhodes to handle for long.

As Alexa pushed her opponent up against the fence to deliver one knee after another to Rachel Rhodes' ribs, she heard the announcers. They weren't talking about who would win, but how long Rhodes could withstand the punishment. "This is the Alexa Knight we haven't seen since early in her career," one of the broadcasters said. "And I don't think I've ever seen her so determined to win."

Those words were all Alexa needed to step back and start landing punch after punch into Rachel's body. The fight would be called by the referee at any second, but before Alexa could finish her, Rachel Rhodes pushed off the cage to try a last attempt at a takedown. As if she had rehearsed it a dozen times, the fighter's right hand reached for Alexa's face and jammed a thumb into her left eye.

With a cry of pain and rage, Alexa stumbled back. Unable to help herself, she closed her eyes and Rachel Rhodes dove at her. As they fell to the mat in a twisting ball of arms and legs, Alexa expected the referee to intercede.

Eye pokes were a foul, but when no break came, Alexa found herself on her back with Rachel Rhodes on top trying to drop punches into her face. It was the last place she ever wanted to be, and through blurred vision Alexa knew if she didn't fight back in another second, the referee would call the fight the same way as last time.

Oh, hell no, she thought. Even if she could barely see to land punches, Alexa had other weapons and she let instinct take over. Grabbing Rachel Rhodes' arms and pulling her in to stop the strikes, she let her overeager opponent fall into her own trap. When Rachel Rhodes overcommitted her weight forward, Alexa used a quick twist of her hips to flip their positions. With her opponent suddenly on top, Rachel Rhodes tried to wrestle free, but Alexa slipped onto the other fighter's back. A quick double punch to Rachel's face to make her jerk her head back, and Alexa snaked an arm around her neck, cutting off her air supply. Using one of the sport's most basic moves, the rear naked choke, she only had to wait. As tears wept from her damaged eye, Alexa finally felt Rachel Rhodes slap her arm and tapout. The fight was over, and with a primal roar of victory, Alexa had won.

Chapter Thirty-Five

Returning with two cups of hot coffee from the nearest all-night diner, Kara met Anthony in the waiting room at the hospital. She sank into the plastic chair beside him. Although she already knew the answer because Anthony would have sent her a text if things had changed, Kara asked anyway. "Any news?"

Anthony took one of the coffees from her. "Nothing," he said with a yawn. "I'm hoping that only means the doctors are busy and not that something is seriously wrong." Nodding, Kara felt the same. After Alexa had her hand raised at the end of the great fight, the ringside doctor insisted she go to the emergency room about her left eye. Kara knew it was bad when Alexa didn't even argue. When she gave Kara a hug, she didn't seem able to open it. Her trainers rushed her to the hospital, and in all the excitement, Kara did notice one thing—Jess had vanished again.

Finally with a quiet moment, Kara wanted some answers. "Okay," she said. "Tell me what you know about Jess and her weird behavior."

Can't Fight Love

Anthony hesitated. "I'm not so sure—" he started and Kara fixed Anthony with a look.

"I'm not asking for every gory detail," she said. "Just the highlights."

The man rolled his eyes. "The highlights are bad enough as it is." Frowning, Kara wasn't sure what to make of that statement. *How bad is it?* she wondered. *Did Jess kill someone or something?* Finally, Anthony sighed. "She's been using Alexa's money to make bets on fights."

Kara almost choked on her coffee. "What?" she asked. "You can't be serious."

"Oh, I'm serious," he said. "A bookie who looked like he was right out of a gangster movie came to Alexa's locker room looking for Jess."

Thinking through what he said, Kara frowned. "As in today, before the fight?"

He nodded. "Yes," Anthony said. "Not long before I had to leave to come find you and sit down." Kara could hardly believe what she was hearing. *Alexa's manager and long-time friend?* she wondered. *But that's such a betrayal.*

Kara leaned back in her chair, holding the coffee cup to her chest. "And we don't have any other details about why she did it or anything?"

When Anthony didn't answer, she looked at him only to see he stared at the door of the waiting room. "Well," he said. "I guess we can ask her ourselves."

Not sure what he meant, Kara followed his gaze only to see Jess standing in the doorway. "Oh," Kara said, even more surprised to see her after hearing what she had done to Alexa. "Hello, Jess."

Expecting a scowl, Kara was surprised when the woman's reaction was nothing but a sad sigh. "Hello," she said, her shoulders sagging. If Kara needed a word to describe how she looked, it would be defeated. "How's Alexa?"

"You're kidding, right?" Anthony growled. "You think you have any right to walk in here and act like you give a shit?"

Nodding, Jess looked at the floor. "I know you're angry," she said. "I would be the same if I were in your shoes."

With the shock of seeing her wearing off, Kare felt her temper rising too. "But you're not in our shoes," she said. "How could you steal from Alexa? She loves you."

A hint of the old fire flickered in Jess's eyes and Kara saw her clench her jaw. "And I love her too," she said. "You don't understand and frankly, Kara, I don't need to explain it to you of all people." Kara opened her mouth to respond, but Jess held up a hand. "Never mind. I only came here to say goodbye to Alexa."

Resting her head against the pillow, Alexa closed her eyes and felt an overall sense of relief. After talking with the doctor and hearing that she didn't need surgery, she knew she had dodged a bullet. After Rachel Rhodes's intentional eye poke, and she would never believe otherwise, there had been no way to know how bad the damage was until they could get to the hospital. "Just a scratch across your cornea," he had explained. "I'll prescribe you eyedrops. Check in with your doctor in Los Angeles when you're back to check for infection." Alexa could live with that.

The big weight on her shoulders about the fight was gone too. *I beat her, even after she cheated*, she thought with a smug smile. *Choked her into a tapout no less.* Although submission wins were not her specialty, Alexa liked this one. There was something satisfying in how she won. Total domination. *And now I can retire a champion.* She would have to relinquish the belt once she announced it officially, but that didn't bother her. All the great fighters faced the same thing at the end of their careers. Walking away at the top of her game was the best way to go out.

A gentle tap on her hospital room door made Alexa open her eyes. When Anthony walked in, a smile crossed her face. It grew even wider when she saw Kara was with him. "Hey, sis," Anthony said as they came to flank her on both sides of the bed. "The nurse said you were good to see visitors. What did the doc say about your eye?"

When Kara offered her hand. Alexa took it and relished the warmth of the touch. "Nothing major and no surgery," she said, relief in her voice. She kissed the back of Kara's hand. "Not even the sexy eye patch."

With a smile, Kara gave her hand a squeeze. "You made a very sexy pirate," she said, but there was something in her tone that made Alexa furrow her brow.

"Is everything okay?" she asked, looking from Kara to Anthony. She watched the two of them make eye contact before Anthony gave a little nod.

Kara returned her look. "Jess is outside in the hall," she said. "And wants to talk to you."

A million emotions raced through Alexa at the mention of her manager's name. "She's here?" she asked, still trying to absorb the news.

"Yes," Anthony said. "There is something she feels like she needs to tell you." Alexa looked at her hand clenched in Kara's, not sure what she wanted. Jess had betrayed her, perhaps ruined all Alexa envisioned. If the gaming commission thought she was involved with betting on fights, they would strip her of everything.

Making up her mind, Alexa nodded. "Okay," she said. "Send her in. But I want to talk to her alone."

"I'll tell her," Kara said before she bent to kiss Alexa on the lips. "But we will be right outside."

"Thank you," Alexa said as the two turned to go. After a second, Jess walked into the hospital room. With dark circles under her eyes, she looked worn out, and Alexa took a certain satisfaction in knowing what she had done kept her up at night. "I'm surprised to see you, Jess."

Jess stared at the floor for a beat before meeting her gaze. "Hello, Alexa." The two of them stared at each other for a minute. They had been friends for so long and traveled a bumpy road to the championship together.

And now it ends like this? Alexa thought, feeling an overwhelming sense of sadness. "If you have something to say, say it," she said, not wanting to look at her anymore. It hurt too much.

"I wanted to say goodbye," Jess said. "And let you know I have been working with an attorney the last two weeks to fix as much of this as I can."

Alexa shook her head. "What does that even mean?"

"I signed affidavits absolving you of any part of the gambling," she said. "And used all my savings plus took out a loan against my house in Malibu to put back every penny I used for my addiction."

Furrowing her brow, Alexa thought through what the woman said. "Your savings? A loan?" she asked. "How bad is it?"

Jess took a manila envelope from under her arm and laid it on Alexa's lap. "All the details are in there," she said. "But I promise, you are in the clear on every level." She started to back toward the door, and Alexa saw tears on her cheeks. A burning in her own eyes made her blink. "I wanted to tell you that before I go. I love you, Alexa. You made the best champion."

"Wait," Alexa said, making Jess pause. "Did you ever bet on my fights?"

With a small smile, Jess shook her head. "Never," she said. "I promise." Then, the woman was gone.

Walking through Los Angeles International Airport, Kara reveled in how good it felt to be back home. Astoria was beautiful, and Las Vegas had been exciting, but there was something about the City of Angels that drew Kara. The creative energy. She longed to get back to her documentary, and the whole flight back she and Anthony talked about how they could promote the film once it wrapped. If things went as planned, all the filming could be done by the end of next month. It made her heart skip at the idea the project she worked so hard on for so long would actually be finished. Soon she could be showing it at the many indie film festivals, and then they would have to wait and see what the world thought.

Holding hands, Alexa was beside her while Anthony hung back with Brady and Annette. Kara looked forward to seeing what the world held for her and Alexa. Their relationship had been a rollercoaster and with things ready to settle, Kara looked forward to quiet time with the woman. *I can't wait to get to know her better,* she thought. *When the world isn't crazy around us.*

As she considered how nice the quiet would be, two women stopped in front of them with phones out. "Oh my God," one woman gushed. "It really is you." She actually squealed, grabbing her friend by the sleeve. "I told you it was Alexa Knight." The friend nodded so hard Kara was slightly alarmed she would sprain her neck. *So much for quiet time*, she thought, but smiled. People recognizing Alexa for the great fighter she was would not end, and she accepted that as part of their relationship. "Can we take selfies with you?"

Alexa looked at Kara. "Sorry," she said, but Kara waved her on.

"It's fine," she said. "Actually, I can take a picture of the three of you if you want."

The two girls squealed again. "Yes!" They moved in close to Alexa to pose and the taller of the two shook her head. "I can't believe this. And I was telling Britney how pissed I was over what Rachel Rhodes did to you."

Kara raised an eyebrow as she lifted the phone to frame the shot. "What do you mean?" Alexa asked, lifting her fists in her signature stance.

"The eye poke," the other girl said. "Everybody knows she did it on purpose."

After Kara took the picture and the two girls wandered away babbling about how awesome it was to meet the fighter, she caught Alexa's eye. "What was that?"

Before Alexa could answer, Brady stepped forward, phone in hand to show them a video playing over social media. "They aren't kidding," he said. "It's all over the internet. Fans are calling out Rachel Rhodes for the foul." As Kara watched the phone in his hand, a slow-motion closeup of Rachel Rhodes raking her fingers over Alexa's eye could not look more on purpose. "I think she's pretty done in MMA."

Strangely, the news was less satisfying than Kara would imagine. "I hope we don't have to cross paths with that woman again," she said, and Alexa took her hand.

"We won't," she said, starting to walk toward the exit,

when suddenly the two fangirls were back. They looked shyer, and Kara had no idea what was wrong. *Another photo?* she wondered. *Did I screw up the last one?*

Before she could ask, one of them held out her phone. "I'm sorry, but can we have one more picture?" she asked, and Kara looked at Alexa who shrugged.

"Sure," Alexa said, stepping away from Kara to pose again.

Britney waved a hand. "Oh, wait," she said. "We want one with you and your girlfriend too."

Alexa paused, looking at Kara who saw a twinkle in the fighter's green eyes. "Well?" she asked. "Want to pose with me, Kara?"

A smile spread across Kara's face. "I would love to," she said. "Girlfriend."

Epilogue

Leaning across the car's center console, Alexa kissed Kara on the lips. "Thank you for understanding," Alexa said as she unclipped her seatbelt. "I know we have somewhere important to be, so I will keep this quick."

"Very important," Kara said, but her tone was softened with a smile. "I know you haven't seen Jess in almost a year, but her timing..."

She hesitated and Alexa took her hand. "I agree," she said. "And I don't like how she is handling this either, but I promised to give her a few minutes." Alexa climbed out with a last look at Kara. "Be careful driving."

Kara's smile widened. "Of course, I will," she said. "It's not often I get to drive your fancy Camaro. You're only trying to pacify me."

With a little laugh, Alexa started to shut the car door. "I think you're right," she said. "But it was more convenient than making two trips. Go pick up Annette and Brady's replacement guestbook, ideally with the bride's name spelled right this time, and I'll text you." Stepping away from the curb, she watched Kara give a little wave and then Alexa's favorite car sped away.

"You even let her drive your car," she heard Jess say coming up behind her. "This must truly be serious."

Alexa turned, coming face to face with the woman who was once her closest friend. "We are," she said. "Now that her documentary has taken off, and I still haven't signed an announcer contract, we've had time to get to know each other. I plan to ask her to marry me once her best friend's wedding and honeymoon are over."

Jess held her stare for a beat and then nodded. "I knew you would," she said. "She is special somehow. Does something to you."

"Makes me better than I am," Alexa explained. "And not as a fighter, but as a person." When Jess didn't respond, Alexa nodded toward the outdoor tables around the cafe nearby. "Let's go sit down. You wanted to meet here to tell me something that you didn't want to say over the phone." Walking together, they slipped into chairs, and Alexa waited to see what Jess would do next. It was her show. For a minute, Jess tapped her finger on the tabletop, and Alexa thought the woman might not go through with whatever she planned.

Finally, she looked up, eyes squinted a little, as if afraid of what she might see in Alexa's reaction. "I'm moving to London tomorrow," she said. "I wasn't going to tell you because... well..." She shrugged. "Why at this point would you care? But I needed to try and explain the gambling to you." Shaking her head, she laughed. "Totally self-serving decision honestly, now that I think about it."

"Probably," Alexa said. "But I have wondered. If you needed money, I would have always given it to you. All you had to do was ask."

Jess shook her head. "That's the part you will never understand. Gambling isn't really about money," she said. "Or at least not for a lot of us."

"Us?" Alexa asked with a frown.

"Yes," Jess said. "Us. I've spent the last months in a support group for people who can't stop gambling." She looked Alexa hard in the eye. "It's an addiction as powerful as cocaine to some."

Alexa furrowed her brow. "Gambling is?" She couldn't quite believe it.

But before she could argue, Jess held up her hand. "I won't try to explain all the science behind dopamine and brain function, but yes, gambling is highly addictive," she said. "You will never understand it because you had your own high—fighting. The excitement, the risk, the reward." Jess gave a wry laugh. "I would get so excited over your fights. They were my life, but when they were over, I felt lost until the next one. So..."

"You bet on others?" Alexa asked, trying hard to understand. *What if I needed to maintain the thrill of the fight all the time?* she wondered. *How far would I go to keep that high?* Slowly, the pieces came together. "I had no idea, Jess. I'm so sorry."

Shaking her head, Jess looked into the distance. "No," she said. "Don't say that. This was all my choice, and I could have told you a million times." She sighed. "I'm the one who is truly sorry, Alexa. I borrowed your money to cover my bets too. That's how bad I got."

Neither of them said anything for a few minutes, both seeming to need to absorb the moment. "But you got me out of trouble over it," Alexa finally said. "So at least there is that."

"I wouldn't have been able to live with myself if I pulled

you down with me," Jess said. "But there's nothing for me here anymore. No one will work with me, so I'm leaving to try and rebuild my life." Alexa didn't know what to say. The two of them created a legacy together, and Jess would never be allowed to bask in what they accomplished. Even if the woman did betray her, Alexa couldn't hate her.

Reaching, she grabbed Jess's hand. "Hey," she said. "No matter what you've done or why, they can't take away the fact we made it to the top." She felt tears burn her eyes. "I would never have been a champion if not for you, Jess. We were invincible."

Tears slipped down Jess's cheeks as she squeezed Alexa's hand. "Yes," she said. "We were." In a rush, she stood, pulling her hand away to wipe her tears. "I'm sorry. I didn't mean for this to be a big emotional scene, but I needed to try and explain." She bent to kiss Alexa on the cheek. "I love you. And I want you to find nothing but the greatest happiness with Kara and your new life."

As the woman started to walk away, Alexa felt a million emotions. "Jess," she said, making her pause and look back. "Why did you always dislike Kara so much?"

Jess paused, looking over her shoulder. "Because she is better for you than me," she said. "And in the end, you can't fight love." Without another word, she walked down the sidewalk away from Alexa until she was out of sight.

THE END
Want more?
Sign up for my newsletter (http://eepurl.com/dx_iEf) to keep tabs on what I am writing next.

About the Author

Bestselling author KC Luck writes action adventure, contemporary romance, and lesbian fiction. Writing is her passion, and nothing energizes her more than creating new characters facing trials and tribulations in a complex plot. Whether it is apocalypse, horror, or a little naughty, with every story, KC tries to add her own unique twist. She has written fourteen books (which include *The Darkness Trilogy* and *What the Heart Sees*) and multiple short stories across many genres. KC is active in the LGBTQ+ community and is the founder of the collective iReadIndies.

To receive updates on KC Luck's books, please consider subscribing to her mailing list (http://eepurl.com/dx_iEf). Also, KC Luck is always thrilled to hear from her readers (kc.luck.author@gmail.com)

To follow KC Luck, you can find her at: www.kc-luck.com

Thank You!

Enjoy this book?
You can make a big difference

Honest reviews of my books help bring them to the attention of other readers. If you've enjoyed this story, I would be incredibly grateful if you could spend a couple minutes leaving a review (it can be as short as you like) on the book's Amazon and Goodreads pages.

Also By Kc Luck

Rescue Her Heart

Save Her Heart

Welcome to Ruby's

Back to Ruby's

Darkness Falls

Darkness Remains

Darkness United

Wind Dancer

The Lesbian Billionaires Club

The Lesbian Billionaires Seduction

The Lesbian Billionaires Last Hope

Venandi

What the Heart Sees

Everybody Needs a Hero

iReadIndies

iReadIndies

This author is part of iReadIndies, a collective of self-published independent authors of sapphic literature. Please visit our website at iReadIndies.com for more information and to find links to the books published by our authors.

Printed in Great Britain
by Amazon